THE RIGHT THING

The
Right Thing

Margie Keck Smith

Palmetto Publishing Group
Charleston, SC

The Right Thing
Copyright © 2020 by Margie Keck Smith

All rights reserved

This is a work of fiction. Names, characters, businesses, places, events, locales, and incidents are either the products of the author's imagination or used in a ficti-tious manner. Any resemblance to actual persons, living or dead, or actual events is purely coincidental.

First Edition

Printed in the United States

ISBN-13: 978-1-64111-852-1
ISBN-10: 1-64111-852-0

Dedication

This book is dedicated to my sister, Barbara Kimball, who has been with me through thick and thin, laughs and tears, with the patience I've never had.

Acknowledgments

THANKS TO THE WOMEN WHO told me their stories: Barbara Kimball, Lynn Czaban, Jean Place, and Norine Jones. Also a thanks to the members of the Lewis County Writers Guild for making me a better writer and to my husband, Larry Smith, for listening to me talk for five years about this book. And I can't forget to thank my walking friend, Gail Panush, for all the times she said, "You should write a book," and Phil Foster for telling me I should join a writers' critique group and Bonnie Keller for pre-reading this book and making helpful corrections and suggestions.

Table of Contents

There is no greater agony than bearing an untold story inside you.

—Maya Angelou

Prologue: 2013

ROBERTA JO FINALLY TOOK A moment to look around the roomful of people. Many of the chapters of her life were somehow making a show in this one room on this one day, the day of her mother's memorial service. *Maybe I need to sit down and take a big breath.* But instead of sitting down, she moved around the room to make sure that the right people got introduced to each other and to see that everyone helped themselves to appetizers, punch, and wine.

Roberta could see her sister and best friend, Kibby Jane, talking to the daughter of one of their mother's friends who was too frail to attend the memorial today. Roberta also spotted her son, David. He was brave to come to his grandmother's memorial since he knew so few people, and he had only met Helen once. Roberta wanted David to meet everyone but kept getting distracted.

Oh my God. Roberta spotted David's father, Peter, who had just met David yesterday. She watched Peter make his way over to her brother-in-law, Richard, greeting him as if they were long-lost friends.

Roberta rushed over to her sister. "Kibby, do you see Peter over talking to your husband? What the hell is he doing here? Mother never liked him forty years ago, and he always knew it. Why would he come to her memorial? I didn't think I would ever have to see him again once I introduced him to his son yesterday."

"Okay, Roberta, this saga keeps going on and on. I think you need to sit and write the whole story. Bring all the secrets out into the open."

Roberta stared down at her sister. "You know, I think you're right."

Part One
Helen: 1934

When love beckons to you, follow him,
Though his ways are hard and steep.
And when his wings enfold you yield to him,
Though the sword hidden among his pinions may wound you.
And when he speaks to you believe in him,
Though his voice may shatter your dreams as the north wind lays
waste the garden.

—Kahlil Gibran, *The Prophet*

CHAPTER 1

SEVENTEEN-YEAR-OLD HELEN SCHMITT STROLLED DOWN the main street of downtown Oliver, her hometown. She looked around at the closed-up storefronts; the dirty, broken sidewalks; the hot, dusty streets, as if she had never see them before. Perspiration dripped down her face (and other body parts) from the intense August heat. In the distance she saw heat waves shimmering up from the pavement. *God, I hate this place right now. Get me out of here.*

Two or three blocks made up the small downtown that her mother had said was once lively, well before the Great Depression that still lingered on today in 1934. She saw that maybe some of the buildings could have been interesting at one time but were now just old, dirty, and crumbling. The town had never really made it, however; no one of importance or fame had ever lived here. Helen had secret thoughts that maybe that could be her role.

Helen knew there was a lot of world out there to experience, and she was oh-so-ready to be a part of that world. She took in a breath of air so big it might have been her last, letting it out as a sigh. The thought of going out into the world sometimes made breathing difficult.

She worked at bringing up some good memories of Oliver and her life there as she continued her slow walk down the dusty sidewalk, trying not to trip on the cracks formed by uneven, broken concrete slabs. She peeked in the window of the old Rexall drugstore to see if the soda fountain and counter were still there. No. She could see that the inside was empty of all but the shelves. At one time, she had drooled over all the things she and her friends couldn't afford, like fingernail polish and lipstick.

With her nose pressed against the filthy window, Helen had a vision of herself and her best friend, Florence, just thirteen years old at the time, sitting in one of the booths, sharing a banana split. Even with the hot dusty air swirling around her, Helen could taste the three kinds of ice cream—chocolate, vanilla, and strawberry—nestled between two slices of banana and slathered with just as many sweet sauces. Her mouth watered at the thought.

Her mind's eye could see the two girls giggling over the three boys sitting on red-vinyl-covered stools up at the counter. Florence was whispering, "Oh my gosh, Helen, he's so cute! Do you think he'll ever even look my way. I think I'd die if he did."

Helen could hear herself responding back, "Oh come on, Florence. Heavens to Betsy, you're talking about Frank. I live next door to the creep. He and my brother used to catch grasshoppers and terrorize them until they died. You can't seriously think he's cute. Let's get out of here and do something fun."

Across the cracked street, Helen noticed the sign for Pierces Shoe Store. Dried-up grass was growing up along the foundation, so tall she wouldn't be able to see in the window even if it hadn't been boarded up. Helen remembered being so excited to go in the store with her mother to buy new shoes when she outgrew her old ones.

The store had always smelled of new leather and Mr. Jacob's spearmint chewing gum. He would make you sit down to have your feet measured. Helen could still see Mr. Jacob's skin, as cracked as the old shoes she had outgrown. "Now, honey, you know we have to measure your feet. How else would we know what size you need to try on?" Her mother was always in a foul mood because Helen's feet were growing too fast, and shoes were expensive.

Continuing down the sidewalk, the sweat now dripping down her legs and wicking into her socks, she saw the next empty store,

JCPenney. Every September, when they could afford it, Helen's mother would treat her to a new dress for school at this sad-looking store. She vividly remembered a red dress that came from there, the one with big white buttons all the way down the front. The fabric seams had been so stiff that they rubbed her skin raw in places. But it was the prettiest dress she had ever owned, so she had never told anybody how painful it was after a few hours of wearing it.

Helen cringed when she realized that the only stores still open were the Duck Inn Café, the tiny corner grocery, and Dices Hardware. The Duck Inn was there only because the locals had to have a place to go for a cup of coffee and piece of pie and maybe a sandwich. They also had to have Dices to be able to buy nails, screws, and everything else needed to keep things together and running. The busiest place in town was the grocery store, mostly because the post office was inside.

Helen was sure that none of these three stores had changed their looks in the last four decades. Somehow they managed to stay open, despite the bad times of the last five years, with people losing their jobs, their income, and even moving away.

Helen continued into the next block, when what was left of the old Fox Movie Theatre caught her eye. It had closed down just a year ago, having been a popular gathering place whenever money was available. Until recently, the movies had been silent with a player piano that played soft, sentimental music for the love scenes and loud, stirring music for the fights. Back then, a big pot-bellied stove was located on one side of the theater. The owner or janitor brought in coal for the stove but didn't pay any attention to what was on the screen. The black coal might have been shoved into the stove in the middle of a violent fight, or Clark Gable and Jean Harlow might have been gazing into each other's eyes. She would never forget the smell of coal dust that permeated the air as the stove was filled.

Helen sat down on an old bench, mindful of the splinters, to continue with her reminiscing. Still thinking of the movie theater, she recalled that the janitor had his personal seat halfway down the room, next to the wall where he sometimes laid his head to have a nap, leaving a greasy stain. The roof in the center of the movie theater leaked when it was raining, so that area had to be avoided during rainy conditions. A person's age was most important in selecting a seat, with the youngest moviegoers toward the front and teenagers at the back to be able to hold hands with their boyfriends and girlfriends.

Helen's mind floated back to present day when she saw her mother waving to her from across the street in front of the grocery store. She smiled, thinking her mother was the prettiest woman in town, tall and stately with long gray hair braided and rolled up in a bun at the top of her head. She had a sparkle in her eyes that made everyone want to be her friend.

"Hey, Helen," her mother shouted from across the street. "You ready to head home, or are you going to sit there and daydream all day? You can ride with me unless you think you're too good now to ride in the same car with your ole ma."

Helen stood up and crossed the cracked street to her mother, who was still talking. "Off to college in a few days. I can't believe it. My baby girl."

"You know I'll never be too good for you, Mom. In fact, to hear you tell it, I'll never be good enough. I know I'll never be the cook you are or the athlete you are. I just have to get out of here and find my own goodness. Whatever that is. Wahoo! I can't wait."

Helen went home with her mother and into her bedroom to work on her packing. She could hear a Duke Ellington tune on the big family radio in the living room. She knew it would only be minutes before her mother would change to another station looking for a big band, most likely Glenn Miller.

Helen was proud that she had, against all odds, been able to scrape up enough money to go to the big state university almost two hundred miles away in Seattle. Her mother's head appeared in the door of her room, as if she had read Helen's mind. "Do you know how proud your father and I are that our daughter was the salutatorian of her class at graduation and the only girl in her class to go to college? Amazing that for two years you have worked after school, saving every penny of what you earned."

"Well, you two have taught me that a person has to work hard to get what they want, and you know how bad I want to make a swell life for myself. It feels like a dream that it's all finally going to happen."

"And to think your boss at the newspaper office found you a job at a boarding house at the university. He must think you're somethin'."

Her mother popped back out, racing to get the delicious-smelling dinner out of the oven. She yelled back to Helen, "Would you mind finding something different on the radio? The news is coming on in about five minutes. FDR is supposed to be making some big announcement today. And I wanna hear about the first prisoners that are being sent to that new Alcatraz penitentiary."

Helen's father was a tall, charismatic, good-looking man who, like the town of Oliver, had never quite made it. Despite his lack of success, however, everyone loved her dad. He was a lot of fun and had many innovative ideas wherever he worked. But he had pretty much taken to drinking after a series of failures in farming and ranching, now working for others. He wouldn't be able to help her financially to get through college, but he had been supportive in accompanying her to the bank to apply for a small loan to help get her through to the end.

Helen's mother was just as much fun as her husband. One year for Christmas, the couple had their picture taken dressed in each other's clothing, her dad in her mother's sunbonnet and housedress and she in his coveralls, boots, and hat. Both of them wearing that typical somber, portrait look on their faces. That photograph was still displayed in the homes of all their friends and family.

Her mother was on a women's basketball team that, regardless of bad times, never missed a week's practice. They played hard but often lost points due to evil cases of the giggles. Her mom had been the third-born daughter, raised on a cattle ranch, and was expected to be one of the ranch hands where she was needed. She had become as much of a tomboy as a lady could be in her day. Helen hoped she would become as strong a woman as her mom was.

At dinner that night, Helen found herself staring at her younger brother, James, trying to decide if she would miss him. He was an exceptionally tall and slender teenager, an athlete who had inherited his dad's track skills as well as his charismatic ways. Somehow Helen had none of the family's athletic genes, but she could turn on the charm when she wanted to and could have just as much fun. Helen decided that she might miss James a little, certainly more than she would miss the town.

Since Helen was feeling so nostalgic that day, she went back to her room after dinner and took a good look at herself in the mirror. She saw a fairly good-looking young woman, not particularly tall for her family but tall for a woman. Helen had always disliked her height for fear people would notice her. She preferred being unnoticed, lost in a crowd.

She decided that she liked her new bobbed haircut. Turning her head from side to side in the mirror, she saw that the new cut showed off her brown-green eyes and strong jawline that added years of maturity to her image. *Not bad for a seventeen-year-old, I'd say. I give myself a B-plus. Maybe that skinny, awkward girl who reads books all the time instead of playing basketball or running track has finally grown into herself.*

A few days later, Helen was standing ready to board the train to set off across the state. Her last day in Oliver that early September was as hot and dusty as ever, so hot and dry she found it difficult to breathe. Her dad was at work, her brother in school, so her proud mother stood alone to give Helen a hug, to wave goodbye and wish her good luck.

Helen's hands trembled with excitement, a mixture of good and bad anxiety whirling around inside her head. She had never been on a train, and she had no idea how to be a college student, live in a dormitory, or work as a hasher (whatever that was). Helen had never been any farther than sixty miles in any direction from Oliver and only once to the neighboring state of Idaho. The good-anxiety part was the knowledge that this was day one of her dream.

The cocky conductor standing outside the train door helped her up the steps and into the train and told her she was assigned to seat 17B. "Hey, Missy, first time on the train? You must be off to visit relatives."

Helen managed to smile back as she climbed the stairs. Holding her head high, she announced, "No, I'm off to start college at the University of Washington."

"Jumpin' Jehoshaphat!" replied Mr. Cocky. "A bona fide college student. Ain't you somethin'? I guess you won't be back this way anytime soon."

If you only knew.

Helen sat down in 17B just in time to give her teary-eyed mother a final wave through the window. As the train took off, she looked around at the few other passengers, happy to see that no one occupied the seat beside her. She could catch her breath and collect her thoughts. *Oh yes, I can do this!*

Seven hours later, the same conductor came looking for Helen to make sure she didn't miss her stop. "Good luck to you, Missy. We'll be making your Seattle stop in about thirty minutes. Now, you study hard and stay away from those college boys. You don't want to have to come back home 'cause things didn't go right." He could have saved the lecture. Helen knew the boys would not be a distraction for her. Getting hooked up with a boyfriend was the least of her ambitions.

The conductor also needn't have been concerned that Helen would miss her stop. She had hardly closed her eyes the whole trip, wanting to see everything on the other side of the train window. She had never seen so many buildings and cars and people in one place, warehouses and small factories everywhere, more and more sets of train tracks as they got closer to Seattle.

"Don't take any wooden nickels," muttered the conductor as Helen Schmitt stepped down onto the concrete and looked around the huge depot platform.

Trees everywhere! Look at how green it is here, even in September. This is definitely not dusty Oliver. Thirty or more people were either standing in groups on the platform or hurriedly rushing to wherever they were going. She had never been anywhere so beautiful or seen people so busy. Her feet, however, were frozen to the concrete. *What do I do now?*

She saw her three pieces of luggage placed on the platform. She couldn't carry them all. Helen shivered, despite the heat from the sun reflecting off the sidewalk.

The conductor was still standing beside the train watching her. Now Mr. Helpful, he said, "If you need a ride to the college, leave your bags right there; ask the guy behind the counter inside to call for a taxi. The college is only a few blocks away, but you need help getting your bags there. Don't let the taxi driver charge you over fifty cents though."

Helen thanked him for the suggestions and managed to put one foot in front of the other to walk into the depot, reluctantly leaving her bags sitting on the platform. The man inside behind the counter smiled, giving her the much-needed confidence that maybe she didn't look like she had just stepped off the farm (which, of course, she had). Anyway, he wasn't laughing at her; that was good.

"Any chance you could call a taxi for me? I have to get my bags to the university."

"You bet, young lady. I'd be glad to do that. In fact, there's an empty taxi out there right now. I'll signal him for you if you want to go over and stand by your bags. He'll come and load them up for you."

The next two weeks were a blur. Every evening, Helen would write to her mother, even if she wrote just a few sentences. She wrote about the many new people she met every day and about how the campus was so big and beautiful. She wrote that she was constantly lost and frequently had to ask other students the way to her classes or back to her dorm.

Eventually, however, Helen learned her way around. She loved walking from building to building, amazed at how grand they were, set among huge old trees and surrounded by grass, shrubs, and flowers. The city of Seattle was another ball game. Initially, she pretended the city wasn't even there, never venturing off campus on her own the whole first year.

Helen learned very quickly what a "hasher" does. She basically cleaned up after everyone in the dining room of the boardinghouse. She tried to be as good a hasher as possible and managed to keep her job, even after dropping and breaking a tray of cups one day and accidentally dumping the macaroni and cheese into the chili on another day.

Most people were friendly and helpful. A few of the girls teased her by pulling on her apron and trying to trip her. She used her sense of humor to turn the tables, casually remarking, "Well, I certainly had a good trip there. Too bad you couldn't have gone with me." The girls usually ended up laughing with her.

Helen had dormitory mates who were much like her, coming from small towns, lacking any worldliness and sophistication. They leaned on each other, becoming lifelong friends. All was so big and new, sometimes too difficult to be entirely pleasant.

She missed sharing everything with her mother, who would have loved hearing detailed reports of her classes, her new friends, and her job at the boardinghouse. The nights she cried herself to sleep became less and less frequent, however, and eventually school and work kept her too busy to write even short letters home. Her mother continued to write Helen long letters, though, and she savored each one, reading them over and over again. Did she miss Oliver? Not really.

Helen was keen to major in a field she could sink her teeth into. Half way through the first semester, while majoring in general liberal arts, she had a conversation with a career counselor. He suggested nursing or teaching, the two areas that were common for women to study in the 1930s. "I'm afraid I've never been the science type nor the caregiving type. I need to major in something that will give me a career when I graduate, but nursing is definitely not it."

"What do you think you're best at? Or what has always interested you?"

"I guess math has always been easy for me, and I like it. I also like history, though, especially when people tell me their own histories or when it's made to seem real."

"You know, I think a major in accounting would be a good fit. It would certainly give you a career. Lots of opportunities there. You also might want to take the required classes to become a high school math or history teacher to give you a little more insurance for employment."

So Helen went for a double major. She enjoyed her accounting classes immensely…the education classes, not so much. By the end of the first year, she found the homework in her accounting classes took up too much time. All the calculating had to be done by hand; adding machines were not available for student use. Something had to go, and she couldn't quit her hasher job because it gave her the money she needed. So she dropped the accounting entirely and again, at the advice of her counselor, changed her major to sociology, a new field of study needing new employees. Government welfare offices were opening up all over the country because of the Depression. Helen couldn't wait for her second year to begin, excited about this new area of study and the classes she would take.

Helen's college experience was not all work and no play but involved laughter and having fun, mostly with her women dormitory mates. One Friday afternoon, Helen sat at the desk in her room, clothes and books strung about the floor and bed. She knew she should be studying, but the jazz music playing on her roommate's radio was distracting her. She kept wanting to get up and dance to the music. Ginger from the room across the hall bounced into her room. "Hey, Helen, I have a date with Frederick tonight. You remember him, right?" Not giving Helen a chance to respond, she continued, "He has a friend who wants to go along but needs a date. How about it?"

"Oh, that sounds like a swell idea. I'd love to get out of this dormitory for a few hours. I hope your Frederick's friend is an okay fella. You know I'm pretty picky about my dates."

Ginger smiled. "Well, Fred isn't always a barrel of laughs, but he's a ticket out for the night. If you go with us, you and I will have a good time regardless. We always do."

"Maybe we'll get a chance to do a little boogie-woogie. I'd love that."

"Fantastic. Wear your new duds, the dress with the great shoulder pads your mother just made for you; it has a swell square collar."

A few hours later, the two young men picked them up, and they drove to a bar to have drinks. The evening dragged on, the girls sneaking looks at each other because they were not having any fun. Finally Helen said, "Come on, Ginger. Go with me to the restroom."

When they got to the girls' room, Ginger said, "Can you believe these guys? All they can talk about are sports scores and brag about their expensive clothes. How can we get them to take us back to the dorm?"

"They could at least ask us to dance or tell a joke or *anything*! Maybe I could pretend I started my period or something equally embarrassing so they'd be glad to get rid of us."

Ginger giggled at the idea. "Oh, I'd be too embarrassed."

They went back to their table with no real plan in mind. To make matters worse, Frederick said as they sat down again, "Why don't you ladies go to Tacoma and spend the night with us?" Helen was insulted and saw that Ginger was feeling the same way. They didn't need a trip to the bathroom to talk about it.

But instead of showing her disgust, Helen replied with a slight smile on her face that only Ginger could detect, "Swell, but we'll have to go back to the dorm and check out for an overnight." Ginger nodded her head in agreement although unsure what Helen had in mind. The boys looked elated, looking like they had hit the jackpot.

Back at the dorm, Helen said to the boys, "We'll check out and meet you at the back door." Instead the girls checked in, went up to their rooms, and went to bed.

An hour later, Helen was sound asleep when the ceiling light went on in her room. In the doorway stood the housemother. "There are two young men outside the back door. The police caught them hanging around. They're saying they're your friends and are waiting for you. Do you know anything about this?"

"As a matter of fact, I do." Helen grinned. "I wouldn't call them friends, but Ginger and I did tell them to meet us at the back door so we could ditch them. They thought they were going to take us to spend the night with them in Tacoma. It was the only way we could think of to get back to the dorm and get rid of them. Maybe it was a dirty trick, but they had insulted us, and we didn't like their intentions."

The house mother smiled and agreed, "Don't that beat all. You girls are a hoot and, might I add, very smart! I think I can get the police to scare them a little, and they'll be on their way. Good night."

—⚉—

In 1938, Helen graduated in good standing, despite the lingering Depression; despite her small town, sheltered background; and despite being a woman. She was ready to tackle the world just as she had tackled a large campus and a big city.

Her mother was the only one able to come for her graduation. By this time, her parents had moved from Oliver, Washington, to California so her dad could find work. Her brother had graduated from high school and moved to nearby Rockford to work for the railroad.

Helen had to start work right away; she needed the money and had a small loan to pay off. Her family was still struggling financially, so she couldn't lean on them in any way. Many teaching positions were available, and she soon accepted a job teaching in a town just east of

Seattle. She wasn't thrilled about being a teacher, but at least it was a start at making her own way.

The day after accepting the teaching job, she was running around campus, preparing to leave Seattle. Hurrying from one errand to another, she ran into an old friend from Oliver whom she hadn't seen for two years. "Hey, Jim, where have you been? I thought I would see you around here a lot but haven't for a long time."

"I had to go back to Oliver for a year and help my dad. He wasn't well, and I was needed on the farm. But now I'm back and ready to hit the books again. How about you? You must be close to graduating."

"As a matter of fact, I did graduate, and, best of all, I got a job. Can you believe it? Me, little ole Helen Schmitt from little ole Oliver, a graduate of the University of Washington and now among the employed. I'm off to make my way in this world. I'm going to be teaching in North Bend at the high school."

"Congratulations! But I thought you were majoring in sociology. Why a high school teacher?"

Helen shrugged her shoulders. "Well, a girl's gotta do what a girl's gotta do."

Jim was silent for a moment and then looked wide eyed at Helen. "You know, my mom just wrote me that they have an opening in a new welfare office in Rowle County, right in Oliver. They're looking for a social worker."

"You've got to be kidding! A welfare office back home in Oliver, our old stomping grounds. I'm so glad I don't have to go back there."

"Well, give it some thought. It might be a way to get your foot in the door on your career as a social worker."

"Hey, there's no way I'm going back there. Thanks for the thought though. I gotta go. Good luck to you, Jim. Study hard; you'll get there."

The rest of the day, Helen couldn't stop thinking about Jim's suggestion. Teaching high school kids was not what she had hoped to be doing the next year. The social work job might be too good an opportunity to pass up. She called the new office in her old county and inquired about the position. "We have interviewed only two people, and neither one is really qualified," reported the person answering the phone. "Tell me your qualifications."

Helen tried to sound professional. "I just graduated from the University of Washington with a bachelor's degree in social work. In addition, I grew up in Oliver, and so I know almost everyone that lives there. I certainly know what the needs are."

"Well, Miss Schmitt, you fit the bill perfectly. However, since it's a government job, we have to follow the hiring rules. You have to interview with the county commissioners before we can hire you. And, unfortunately, we have to hire someone in the next two days."

Helen had no time to take the train, so she did what she said she would never do. She called her only relative in Seattle for help. She called her dreaded old, grouchy uncle Harley, explained her predicament, and asked if there was any way he could drive her to Oliver the next day.

"Well, well. I knew your going to college here in Seattle would one day cost me something. I've been waiting for this phone call to do you some kind of favor. You say you have to be there tomorrow?" growled Uncle Harley.

"I'm so sorry about the short notice, but I just graduated last week, and I found out about the job just today. I only have three days before I'll lose my chance. I'm really stuck, or I wouldn't have called."

"You say you actually graduated?" said Uncle Harley.

"Yes I did," Helen said, unable to hide the pride in her voice, "and this job in Oliver would make me a true social worker working for the government."

Uncle Harley took a few seconds to digest the news; suddenly his attitude changed. "I'll pick you up at seven a.m. sharp. Tell me where, and don't make me wait for you, young lady."

Helen made it in time to Oliver on time, was offered the job, and turned down the teaching position. She had managed to get all her possessions in Harley's car for the trip to Oliver for the interview, so she was able to move right into a boardinghouse.

The night after she had accepted the job, she took a walk down-town, stopping in her tracks on the dusty old sidewalk. *What have I done? I've worked so hard to get away from this dirty, tired town, and I've just circled right back here.* She looked around just as she had the weeks be-fore she left for college. The town had changed very little in the four years since she had lived there with her parents. *Oh, well, I guess I have to start somewhere.*

—ɯ—

Helen's next big challenge was to learn to drive. She had driven a tractor occasionally as a kid to help her dad, but she had never driv-en a real car. She turned to her brother, James, who lived in nearby Rockford. For his job on the railroad, he was often gone for days at a time. Fortunately, he was in Oliver when she accepted the job.

"You want me to *what*? The only women drivers I have been with were terrible at it. They want to talk the whole time instead of con-centrating on the task at hand. As I remember, you're not the most mechanical person in the world anyway. Do you know what it takes to drive a car?"

"Give me a break, James. I'm not promising I'll be good at it, but it's something I have to do. The job requires that I be able to drive myself around the county to see clients. I have to admit, I told a little white lie when I told them at the interview that I already knew how to drive. Come on. If I can go away for four years and get a college degree, I can learn to drive."

So James took her out in the middle of an empty wheat field and told her to get behind the wheel of his car, a 1932 Ford, and "drive."

"You have to give me a little instruction, you know! Jiminy Crickets, James. Help me here."

"Well, that pedal there is the gas, and that's what makes it go. The pedal to the left and in the middle is the brake, and that makes it stop. Got it?"

"Okay, what about the third pedal? What could it possibly be for?"

Helen looked at her brother and became even more nervous. He had a smirk on his face that meant trouble. "That pedal is the problem, believe me. That pedal is what separates the men from the women."

"We may be separated here, but you have to help me out. What does it do?"

James sighed. "That third pedal lets you change gears."

"What do you mean *change gears*? What's a gear?"

"Changing gears are what's going to let you go faster or help you to slow down."

"What are you talking about? You just said there's a go pedal and a stop pedal. What do I need to change gears for?"

"The only way to learn is to do. Start up the car using the key, but be sure you step on that third pedal first. By the way, it's called a clutch."

So James let her learn the clutch by doing, but before Helen got the hang of it, they laughed so hard, they had to stop and take breaks so they could breathe. She quickly realized why they had gone to an empty field for the lesson: there were no trees or buildings to run into. They did, however, suffer some whiplash from all her trials at starting and stopping.

Two or three hours later, she was ready for a real farm road. Smooth driving took a few more lessons, but at least she could make her way down any road required of her on the job. James even helped her find an affordable car to buy. In fact, he lent her the money.

Helen had a salary of $75 a month with an extra $25 per month for using her own car, a pretty good living for a woman in 1938. Helen figured that after a couple of years, she would be able to pay off a PEO (Philanthropic Educational Organization, a national organization, whose mission has been to promote educational opportunities for women since 1869) loan and the small amount she owed at the bank. She would have to buckle down, be the best social worker she could be for a few years, and then look for another job in some fantastically exciting area like New York City or even San Francisco.

It didn't take long for her to decide she was going to like being a social worker. Her clients showed her appreciation and respect. She was a local person who had gone to college and returned to help others less fortunate. She sat in their homes and listened to their stories. She found funds for the most destitute when she could and gave suggestions on how they could help themselves. Her clients always felt better after an interview with her; someone cared and was on their side. She liked that she was making a difference in their lives. In a small way, Helen had become an important person.

CHAPTER 2

HELEN'S NEW PROFESSIONAL LIFE WAS in Oliver but her social life took place in Rockford, ten miles away. The people living in Rockford were generally more her age, and the town was twice the size of Oliver. It worked better for her anyway to have friends who did not live where she worked. They loved their music and to dance. Frank Sinatra and Duke Ellington were big in the late 1930s. The Lindy Hop was popular, as well as the slow waltz. The best place to go dancing was at a hall five miles out of town and by the lake. The building was a barnlike structure without the high loftiness of a barn; it was more like a big, empty box with a covered porch wrapped around three sides.

She and her friends danced to live local bands, some better than others. They weren't picky; they danced to it all. Even though big orchestra-type bands and jazz bands were popular at the time, those bands didn't make it out to the rural lake dances. Traveling country-western bands made up of three or four musicians were the most common.

The bands performed on a stage at one end of the cavernous dance hall. A few tables where the dancers could buy a soda or sip a glass of water were at the opposite end. Chairs lined the two sides of the room, leaving an enormous dance floor. The smell of sweat and cigarette smoke permeated the room, no matter what time of the evening. The more people there were, the more fun it was, and the less chance the smell would even be noticed.

Going to dances was a good way for the gals to meet guys, but they were not shy about dancing with each other. They preferred that to being a wallflower and sitting in a chair along the wall all night.

Alcohol was legal again, following Prohibition, but wasn't sold at the lake. Instead, the men consumed it from flasks outside on the porches that wrapped around the hall. The participants got rowdy from time to time, always on the porch or in the parking lot where beer was consumed. The youth usually had short drunken fights, but some of the old codgers could have serious confrontations that included knives and the occasional gun. Women were warned to stay inside.

Helen had been a tall, skinny, awkward kid growing up and still felt she was feet taller than all the boys. As she matured, however, her height had become an advantage, as her long, well-shaped legs were admired by many. She had a grace that was difficult to miss. Her natural posture was head held high, making strong eye contact while showing great interest in her conversational partner. She had obvious intelligence and strong character. She was not unlike a giraffe who, at first glance, is a wonder only because of its height and boney structure. But as it walks across the field, an easy grace is evident. Helen had many close friends who knew her to have a keen sense of humor and to be ready to have a good time.

Besides going to the dances and the occasional movie, Helen and her best friend, Florence, spent a lot of their time at Florence's house in the company of her many aunts, uncles, and cousins. The family had fun together sitting around the table, talking and laughing. Florence's Aunt Phyl was frequently there at the table.

On one of those family gatherings, Phyl cornered Helen and Florence. "I just had an idea. How would you gals like to spend a week at my house, helping with some heavy household chores and spend some time with my two youngest? The four of you would really hit it off, and I could sure use the help after you get off work."

So on Saturday night of that week and after the kids were in bed, the three of them sat having a cup of coffee. The big radio in the corner of the living room was tuned to the news. The three women discussed the events as they were reported, the biggest topic being Orson Wells, and how everyone was shocked with what he would sometimes come up with on his regular program.

Phyl suddenly changed the subject and said, "Would you girls like to go to the dance at the lake with my son, Andrew, and one of his friends? They like to dance and have a good time like you gals. After all, it is Saturday night. Andrew is my favorite, and he has been working way too hard, just like you, Helen. You guys are a great match."

The two girls looked at each other. It didn't take long for Helen to speak up. "Why not? As long as you think these guys will treat us well, Aunt Phyl."

"They better, or they'll have to answer to me. I'll hang them out to dry if they don't do right by you."

Florence nodded her head. "You're right, Aunt Phyl. Cousin Andrew is a great match for Helen. I'm surprised they haven't met before." So Phyllis put them in her car and drove them to the Elks Club, where she knew Andrew was playing cards with his friends, as he did most Saturday nights.

Phyl knocked on the club door until finally a young man answered. "Well I'll be a monkey's uncle. Lookie who we have here. What do you good-lookin' ladies want?"

The gentleman leaned up against the door frame, eyeing the three of them up and down. A waft of air thick with a combination of cigarette smoke and decades-old beer came from behind him. Loud male laughter could be heard in the background.

Phyl wasn't put off by the young man's attitude. She stood up straight to all four feet, ten inches of height. "Go find Andrew Kindle for us. Tell him his mother is looking for him, and he's in trouble."

"Yes, ma'am!" The young man turned around and hollered, "Hey, Andrew, you better get here quick!"

Minutes later, Andrew showed up at the door looking skeptical and then surprised when he saw his mother. "Aw, Mom. What do you want? We're in the middle of a card game."

Phyl didn't hesitate a moment. "How would you like to grab a friend and take these two lovely ladies to the dance at the lake? You're guaranteed a good time."

Andrew looked at the two women behind his mom, recognizing and appearing pleased to see his cousin Florence. His eyes lit up when he noted the third in the party of three, indicating that he wouldn't mind taking those long legs for a whirl around the dance floor. "Sure, Mom. Give me a minute to talk to my buddies. I was losing this hand anyway."

Ten minutes later, the two young couples were off to the dance at the lake in Andrew's old jalopy. As they bounced around on the country roads, Helen had her doubts about Florence's cousin Andrew. Her experience had been that what people think is a great match, seldom turn out that way. She thought he was very cute, however. He had the bluest eyes she had ever seen. She was glad she had worn her straight skirt that showed off her long legs. Fortunately, she had also worn her only pair of dress shoes with a bit of a heel, so she didn't have to go dancing in her saddle shoes.

As it turned out, Andrew was a whole lot of fun, just as Phyl had said. He was shorter than she would have liked, but he made up for it by being a fantastically smooth dancer, especially for the slow dances. Best of all, he had a laugh that was infectious and attracted the attention of all those around him. His whole face and body went into motion when he laughed.

The couple danced to exhaustion and forgot all about Florence and her date. Helen was smitten as they talked quietly on the ride back home. She noted he could hold his own in a conversation. Helen hoped she would hear from him again.

—〰—

However, three weeks went by before Helen heard from Andrew again. By then, she was so wrapped up in her work that she had almost forgotten about him. Andrew had also been hard at work, and Helen might never have heard from him again except that a group of his friends planned an all-day trip to the mountains. "Come on, Andrew, you've got to do something other than work once in a while. Give that long-legged gal a call. You said you had a grand time with her at the lake."

"But that was so long ago. She might not even remember who I am. I should have called her a long time ago. I certainly have been thinking about her."

"Fiddlesticks! You'll never know unless you give it a try."

"Well, the boss did tell me I should take a day and get away."

Helen eagerly accepted his invitation, and off they went. Andrew's friends turned out to be great fun. The eight of them, four couples, fit into two cars. They drove out of town to a picnic ground, where they walked on a little trail that followed a stream, chatting and laughing the whole way.

Back at the cars, they spread out a couple of blankets on the grass under a big tree and ate what the guys had put together for a picnic. The luncheon fare was a strange mixture of crackers, numerous kinds of bread, leftover meats, a bit of cheese, and bits of leftover cakes and cookies, whatever they had been able to find in their parents' cupboards and fridges. Someone brought enough beer so that everyone had a bottle.

Nobody went hungry, but one of the girls said, "Next time, the girls will be in charge of the food. My idea of a picnic is cold fried chicken, potato salad, deviled eggs, biscuits, lemonade, and a big cake. And I mean the whole cake."

Andrew laughed. "No argument there."

After that, they dated frequently, many evenings sitting with Andrew's family around their round oak dining room table, the little room full to the brim with furniture and people. Two china cabinets piled with odds and ends of china cups and saucers somehow also occupied the space. Andrew's two brothers would occasionally drop in alone or with their girlfriends. They would spend hours talking and laughing, getting into friendly disagreements, sometimes calling someone they knew who could settle an argument.

Doc Kindle, Andrew's dad, a veterinarian, was a bit gruff when he had too much to drink but could be fun with his dry wit. Will Rogers, his idol, was often quoted: "Even if you're on the right track, you'll get run over if you just sit there" or "Never miss a chance to shut up." Phyl, also great fun, would come up with comments that would send everyone into howls of laughter. One of her favorites was "Come back when you can't stay so long."

Helen fit right into the noise and camaraderie. She realized she had fallen into something that was becoming the best thing to happen to her since graduation from university, second only to her adored job.

One day as Helen and Florence drove downtown to look for gloves to go with Florence's new shoes, Helen expressed her concerns about her new beau. "He has never been keen on school, you know. It took him almost two extra years to graduate from high school. Shop and sports were more important than serious classes. That's so different from how I felt about school."

The two women sat in the car not quite ready to hit the pavement. Florence laid down her argument. "Yes, but he's smart in so many other ways. His skills are taking things apart, cleaning them up, repairing them, and putting them back together again. I know he's only a car mechanic at a gas station right now, but he takes it very seriously. He told my dad that he sees the job as a ticket to something else later."

"I guess you're right. Liking and do well in school isn't everything. Many people make it big without even graduating from high school."

"Did you know that Andrew was the president of his senior class and president of the alumni the first year out of high school?"

Helen turned her head in surprise. "Gee whillikers! I didn't know that."

"Yeah, that says a lot about the guy, don't you think?"

"He certainly doesn't brag about stuff. But at the same time, he has confidence in everything he does. He's good at math and likes to think through problems and come up with solutions."

"That's for sure. You got a problem? Tell Andrew Kindle. He'll come up with something good."

—∿—

Andrew had his own concerns. Over coffee at his mother's kitchen table one morning, he got up the nerve to talk about Helen. "She's so smart and well educated, Mom. She has graduated from college, for Pete's sake. And she has an amazing job, especially for a woman. She works so hard, working late in the night sometimes to make sure everything is just right."

"And you don't work hard and late? Both of you work hard. You just do different things."

"But she seems to know exactly what she wants, where she's going. I barely made it through high school, and who knows what I'll end up doing with my life?"

"Yeah, she sure does know what she wants, doesn't she? You don't see many women who are so driven when it comes to their jobs."

Andrew went into the kitchen for the coffee pot to fill their cups. "I don't think dating a grease monkey from Rockford is one of Helen's dreams."

"Do you know what her dreams are?"

"She told me her big dream is to go to a big city and have a completely different life from the one she has had here in small-town Washington. She can do that with the education she has. What can be worse than having a girlfriend who's smarter than you?"

Phyl stood up from the table and put her hands on her hips. "Forget this 'smarter than you' stuff, Andrew. You're one of the smartest guys out there. You sure got your brothers beat. You and Helen just use your smarts in different ways. You can talk just as fast and hard if it's important to you. I certainly have heard you do that. And you have such a wonderful talent for making other people feel good."

"But my gosh, Mom, she's even taller than me!"

Phyl sat down again, but leaned into the table and her son next to her. "She is not taller than you. The two of you are about the same height."

Andrew hung his head. "But the guy is supposed to be taller. The woman is supposed to look up to her man."

"You can get over that. Give her reasons to look up to you in respect."

"I do think she likes me for the fun we have. Maybe we need to have a special evening, just the two of us. We're usually around so many other people that we don't get to talk much about ourselves, our dreams and goals. Besides a quiet, romantic evening with Helen sounds swell."

Phyl leaned back again in her chair. "Now you're talkin', Andy. You go and turn on your charm. I've seen you do that enough times."

"Thanks, Mom. You're the best."

—〰—

Andrew picked up Helen for their "special" dinner and drove to the Rockford Hotel restaurant for dinner and drinks. They sat at a corner table and talked nonstop for hours. Andrew told her something that he had never told anyone. "I want to someday own my own business. I'd like to be my own boss and develop my own ideas on the way things should be run."

After drinks, Andrew got the nerve to tell Helen how easy she was to talk to. "So many of the women I know only talk about their clothes or their hair, or they just giggle a lot. You're different, Helen, a good different."

"I'm interested in what you have to say, that's all. You have some great ideas." To his surprise, she added, "You know, you're a good listener too."

Andrew said, flashing his ever-charming smile, "My mother has always said that, but then she is my biggest fan."

They found that night, while downing thick steaks, that they had something else in common. They had both seen their fathers' drinking habits negatively affect their lives and the lives of those around them. "I like to drink as much as the next guy, but I don't want to ever drink so much that it ruins my efforts and my relationships," said Andrew.

"I agree. I need to feel in control of myself and my life. Do you think a person can enjoy drink but still be in control of their lives?"

"I don't know if others can, but I know I can. I'm determined to make something of myself in this world. I won't let alcohol ruin that for me. With that in mind, how about a cup of coffee before hitting the road?"

—⚉—

So Andrew and Helen continued to be a couple and continued to work hard at their respective jobs. Andrew was soon the manager and main mechanic at work. He worked long, hard hours, not always knowing when his work day would end. Within six months, Andrew was making enough money that he felt he could ask Helen to be his wife.

On Christmas Eve, 1939, after everyone else at the Kindle house, where he was still living, had gone to bed, Andrew gathered the nerve to pop the question. Helen didn't quite know what to think when she saw sweat starting to bead on his upper lip. She was about to ask him if he was feeling all right when he said, "Helen, I know this is kind of sudden, but would you marry me?" He pulled out a modest but lovely diamond engagement ring from his pants pocket and handed it to her.

Helen was dumbfounded! She felt her own palms becoming damp, her heart beating too quickly in her chest. She had the urge to giggle and fought it hard, knowing a giggle would not be at all appropriate. She could see the sweat now forming on Andrew's forehead and knew he was still nervous. She couldn't laugh at him. *I must be in one of those old silent movies. This couldn't possibly be real.*

Helen had never really given marriage much thought. In fact, she remembered saying to Florence and another friend one evening when several of them were sitting around a table at a bar and having a few drinks, "I don't think I'll ever marry. Marriage looks too hard and a perfect way to ruin a good relationship."

On the other hand, she was thinking of the good times they had together. He was so much fun and was always doing things to make her and their friends laugh. Their backgrounds and morals were similar, and they were almost exactly the same age. He treated her well, and he treated his mother well, which she figured said a lot about him and his relationship with women. And, of course, he was so doggone handsome. Was that a bad characteristic? It dawned on Helen, for the first time, that she was in love with this Andrew Kindle.

Somehow, that Christmas Eve, she managed to keep her mouth shut about her past feelings and comments about marriage. *I must have learned something from Will Rogers and Doc Kindle about keeping my mouth shut.* Most importantly, she managed to keep her giggles in check. Instead she surprised herself, looked deep into his blue eyes, and said, "Yes, Andrew, I want to marry you."

—◊◊◊—

Helen couldn't wait to tell Florence. "We're going to be related, dear girl."

"I knew it! I just knew you guys were going to get it together and get married. I couldn't be more happy, cousin."

Andrew and Helen set goals to make enough money to be able to buy their own house and later for Andrew to buy a business. Those goals had to be well on their way before they got married. Helen also needed to finish paying off her loans. They decided to wait until June. Helen buried her dreams of New York City, Miami, and San Francisco; somehow, they weren't as important any more.

Romance was new for Helen. She had only kissed a few guys in her life, and those kisses were not much more than a peck on the cheek.

Her mother and her father had always laid down the law about how "good girls" behaved. Good girls did not make out in dark corners or in cars. Realistically, most girls did do some petting, but they didn't tell anyone for fear of developing a bad reputation. She and Andrew were no exception, but they both worked at not putting themselves in a position where they would get carried away.

Helen's friends gave her a wedding shower, as did the PEO, which had lent her money for college. At that time, it was the custom to have a shivaree for the groom, so Andrew's friends tied him to a lamppost on Main Street while people in cars drove by slowly, yelling, honking horns, banging on pans, and laughing at him. One of his friends picked up Helen so that she could see it all. Afterward, he drove her around for a long time, telling her horrid stories of what else they were going to do to Andrew. None were true. After they untied him from the lamppost, they sat on the side of a dirt road, drank beer, and told each other lies.

—ɯ—

Two events happened in those months that the couple was continuing to get to know each other and working toward their wedding plans. The first event affected everyone in the country, not just Helen and Andrew. For a few years, there had been a war going on in much of Europe, and it looked certain that the United States would be joining that war. Andrew was the right age to be called to fight.

Being an automobile mechanic wouldn't keep Andrew out of the armed services, but fortunately, it kept him in his country. He picked up Helen from work as he always did on a Friday night. "There's good news, Helen."

"Do tell. I've always liked good news."

"I have the opportunity to go for training in airplane mechanics. The army will train me so that when I do join, I'll probably be stationed somewhere in the United States to work on planes. You know what that means, don't you?"

"Yes. It means I don't have to send you off to fight in this awful war, right?"

"You bet, but even better, or at least just as good, there's no reason we can't go ahead with our plans. You should be able to join me wherever I'm sent. Our plans will be safe. Can you believe it?"

By this time, they were in the tiny living room of her apartment. Helen collapsed in the one of her two pieces of furniture. "Holy moly! What a great piece of news, Andrew. And a huge relief!"

To celebrate, they made plans to return to the hotel of their earlier special date. "We've been so good to save our money; we haven't splurged once since we got engaged. We deserve a splurge with a good meal and a real cocktail. Put on your red dress, Helen, babe. We're goin' out on the town."

So they did splurge; they sat holding hands across the same hotel corner table, her dark-brown eyes and his light-blue eyes unable to look anywhere else in the room. The hotel had a phonograph playing all the latest Dinah Shore, Frank Sinatra, and Bing Crosby love songs. For all they knew, they were the only ones in the hotel dining room as they talked about their plans for marriage, a house, and a business.

Because they let down the reserve in their wallets that evening, they, unfortunately, also let down the reserve in their physical attraction for each other. The second of the two big events occurred that evening. This time, only Helen and Andrew were affected.

Women in the forties had new freedoms that were not possible for them before the war. Later, women worked at jobs that gave them the ability to support themselves and live on their own. They did not have the same sexual freedom that men had, however. Society was heavy-handed when it came to women having sex without marriage. A girl was either a virgin or a whore—nothing in between. Birth control was not something to take; it was something to do.

Helen and Andrew knew the rules, but their love for each other and their commitment to marriage got the best of them. They left the hotel, drove down the first dark dirt road they could find, and held each other, every last reserve floating out the open window of Andrew's old car.

Neither one regretted their actions the next day; they had made a pledge to each other. Nor did they give much thought as to any possible consequence.

———ᴡᴡ———

Six weeks later, however, Helen knew she was pregnant. Too late, she had regrets about what she and Andrew had done that night. She felt she could not face the world. A social worker was supposed to know better and do better. She wanted to dig a hole and bury herself in it, never to be able to dig her way out.

Eventually Helen told her best friend, Florence. They sat in Helen's car on their way for wedding dress shopping. "I need to talk to you about something, Flo."

"Sounds serious. Out with it."

"You know I've prepared myself for the fact that Andrew needs to live in this area to make a living and that life as a young, professional woman in San Francisco is probably never going to happen for me."

"I know what you have given up, and I respect you for that. What has changed? What's going on?"

"I can't start out my marriage with a baby, Florence." Helen was not surprised at the shocked look on Florence's face. "That's right...I'm pregnant, and I can't have a baby while my husband is off God knows where. I don't even particularly like babies. I don't know if I ever want to have children at all."

Florence sat without speaking for a while. She let Helen babble on until finally blurting out, "Oh my gosh, Helen, I have been so excited that the two of you were getting married. But, pregnant, now! I can't believe my ears."

"Yeah, I know. Only bad girls get pregnant before they get married, right?"

"But you're so smart; how did you let this happen? You're the smartest woman I know, the first and only social worker in the county. You've been my idol."

Helen's face stung as if Florence had slapped her. She made herself turn to look directly at her best friend. "Can you ever forgive me?"

"Of course I can. I'm just in shock, is all." Both sat without talking for a few minutes. "Helen, you're also the strongest woman I know. You're going to be okay. You have your mother-in-law to help you. Your parents don't live near, but you'll have their loving support. And I'll be around when I'm not at work. Maybe you could live with Aunt Phyl when Andrew has to go."

"Oh my, that would be the worst. I haven't told you, but Aunt Phyl may have been okay with my dating her son, but since we're now at war with the Germans, her attitude toward me has changed. She doesn't like the idea of her favorite baby boy marrying a woman of German heritage, a woman with a German last name. Can you imagine what she'll think of this German woman shaming herself by having sex before marriage? She'll have her opinion of me confirmed. No, I can't count on your Phyl's support in any way."

People walking by were beginning to stare at them sitting so long in their parked car. "No, I didn't know Phyl felt so strongly about Germans. Heavens to Betsy, she introduced you to her son."

"And my own mother is no help whatsoever. She told me years ago that if I ever got pregnant before marriage, to never even think about coming home to her. If I got myself pregnant, I would have to live with it."

"I'm so sorry, Helen. You are in a bind, aren't you?"

"I don't know what I'm going to do. But, Florence, promise me you won't tell anyone what I've told you. It has to be our secret. I haven't even told Andrew yet. What if he doesn't want to marry me now? I'm so ashamed. I feel so dirty. Please promise, no one must know, ever!"

"Of course, your secret is safe with me."

"Thanks. I think we better give up this idea of shopping. We'll do it another day. If Andrew still wants to marry me, that is."

Andrew had told Helen before that he was crazy about kids, so she figured he would want them some day. But they had never talked about it. She waited that evening until they were in his car on one of their many drives in the country. The evening air was warm, the sky lit by millions of stars. She did not ease him into the subject, but blurted out, "Andrew, I'm pregnant. I made a bad mistake."

Andrew didn't say a word until he had a chance to pull the car over along the side of the road. He turned to her, grabbed both her hands in his own, and looked into her large brown eyes. "For God's sake, Helen. You didn't make a mistake; we did it together."

They sat in silence for a few minutes, Helen's shoulders dropping with relief, thinking maybe she wasn't alone with this problem and allowing Andrew a chance to grasp the idea that they had made a baby. He was the first to speak. "Both of us so determined to do everything right and be in control of our lives, and we turn around and blow it. I could get called anytime. I can't go off across the country and leave you to have a baby on your own. No matter what, I'm with you a hundred percent."

From that moment on, Helen knew for sure she had found the right guy to be her husband. "We can't have this baby, Andrew. Your mother will never speak to me again when she figures it out. And believe me, she'll figure it out, just like everyone else in this county will figure it out. I'll be labeled a whore or a slut. They'll all be grinning ear to ear. 'So much for Miss Fancy Pants, Off to College. She's no better than the rest of us.'"

"Are you sure people will react that way?"

"Oh, I don't know for sure, I guess. But I can't do it, Andrew. Nice girls don't get pregnant before they get married. Besides, what kind of credibility will I have with my clients at work? Not only that, but our child will be labeled illegitimate or worse yet, bastard. Children conceived before the parents are married are considered inferior."

"I guess I never thought of it like that."

"Just last week, I was talking to a client who told me about a newly married woman in her neighborhood. She and her new husband came home from a trip with an adopted newborn baby. Everyone knew the woman had actually given birth to the baby before they got married. They had made up the adoption story. All those lies! I couldn't stand doing all that, lying just to make sure people didn't think I was a loose woman."

Andrew put his hand gently over Helen's mouth to stop her nervous babbling. "You are not a loose woman. You're a gal who fell in love with me and chose to show me your love. We made a mistake, that's all. We were stupid, and we got caught. We'll figure it out."

Helen's mind was still spinning. "You know, Andrew, there's another thing. Single women have professional careers now, but mothers don't. In fact, even married women lose their jobs when their bosses find out they're pregnant. I would certainly lose my job if word got out that I was pregnant before we got married."

"There has to be something we can do to make it work. I'm not leaving you to deal with it on your own, and I don't want you to lose the job you love and worked so hard to get."

"I guess we'll have to figure it out, but I can only think of one option right now. Let's sit on it for a while before we do anything. Thank you, Andrew, for being here for me."

Andrew circled Helen with his arms and pulled her close. "I'm here for *us*. We're in this together."

—⟪⟫—

Helen, as a social worker, listened daily to people's problems. The previous week she had heard a client's story that stuck in her head like a magnet to metal. Mrs. McMillan, with tears in her eyes, had told her how she had sneaked away to Spokane to rid herself of an unwanted pregnancy. "I went to a real doctor. I knew it was illegal, but my own doctor told me it was safe. I knew it was what I had to do. I already have six children, and my husband just lost his job. We rely on relatives just to eat. I can't think for a minute that my decision was wrong, even though my husband would kill me if he knew."

So the day after her talk with Andrew, Helen made up an excuse for another visit to see Mrs. McMillan. "I have another client who finds herself in the same position that you were in." Helen could feel her heart pounding in her throat as she lied. "Could you give me the name of the doctor you went to so that I might share it with this client?"

"Oh, Miss Schmitt, I can't do that. Abortion is not only illegal, but I have to tell you, I haven't had a good night's sleep since I made that trip. Tell your client that it isn't worth it. I think of that baby every moment of the day and night. Some days I can't get out of bed for thinking of the baby that never was. I'm a slave to my guilt!" The woman was sobbing by this time.

Helen took a big breath in an attempt to maintain her professional composure. "I'm so sorry that you're suffering. I'll tell her how you feel now, but if you could give me the information, she can decide for herself." Mrs. McMillan hesitantly handed over the information, and Helen left her house with the name and phone number of a doctor in Spokane.

That night, she shared with Andrew what she had learned. They sat in her little apartment, sipping coffee and talking about what looked like their only option. Andrew said, "I get it that Mrs. McMillan is so full of regret now, but remember, she didn't tell her husband before or after she had the abortion. You've been her only support, and that's not enough. But you have me. We're making the decision together, and I'll support you all the way."

"I think you're right. I can do this with you by my side. It'll make all the difference. Shall I call and make an appointment?"

"Yes, I think you better."

—⁂—

Helen called the doctor (she hoped he was a real doctor) the next day. After explaining her predicament, she made an appointment for the following weekend, a Saturday, in the late afternoon so Andrew could be with her.

As it turned out, Andrew at the last minute, couldn't take the time off. Helen couldn't put off the appointment and was forced to drive by herself to Spokane, fifty miles away. She might have asked Florence to go with her, but she had decided not to tell Florence anything about an abortion. Flo's disapproval of the pregnancy had been strong; an abortion would have sent her over the moon. Helen knew no one else to ask.

Helen was not that concerned, however; this appointment was only to meet the doctor and discuss the procedure. Andrew would be with her when she returned for the actual abortion. Besides she had made up her mind that going to this doctor was what she needed to do, and nothing would hold her back now.

Helen drove without event to Spokane and located the doctor's small clinic. She walked cautiously into the waiting area, looked around, and saw that everything was clean and tidy, smelling of antiseptic like every other doctor's office she had ever been in. A nurse dressed in a white uniform, sturdy white shoes, and a starched nurse's cap pinned to her graying hair greeted her and called her back to the office using her formal name. "Miss Schmitt, did anyone come with you?"

"No, I'm afraid my husband wasn't able to get off work today." The nurse's raised eyebrows told her the story was not entirely believed.

When the doctor entered the office, he, too, maintained a professional manner. He was soft-spoken and had a kind face, his breath smelling pleasantly of peppermint. He was short and stocky and looked like somebody's grandfather. Helen answered his questions, telling him how far along she was in her pregnancy and that she was in excellent health. He looked directly at her as he explained the details of the procedure. His voice was almost hypnotic, lulling her and reassuring her that she was doing the right thing.

After a quick examination, the doctor said, "I think because you drove so far today, Miss Schmitt, it would be best if we perform the procedure right away. You can stay afterward and rest for as long as you need to. Driving home should not be a problem. You appear to be very strong, physically and mentally. The nurse and I have the time to do that today, and you won't have to make the long drive again next weekend."

Helen was surprised but felt relieved that it would all be over in just hours. She wished with all her heart Andrew were there, but the two professionals were so kind, respectful and supportive, she was ready to go ahead with their plan.

The nurse was present throughout the procedure. She held Helen's hand in her warm hand during the entire time, except when the doctor needed her help.

Despite all this kindness and reassurance, and despite her resolve to do what had to be done, there was never any doubt in Helen's mind that she was alone among strangers. Andrew was not there; her parents were not there at a time that she desperately needed them. Her parents would be so ashamed and embarrassed if they knew what she was doing. *How did Mrs. McMillan get through this?*

Helen didn't mind the pain that the doctor had to inflict on her. In fact, she welcomed the pain as though she deserved it. If the doctor gave her anesthetic, she was not aware of it. She had been a promiscuous woman, and she had to be punished. The pain was her penance. She closed her eyes and forced herself to see Andrew's face and hear his wonderful laugh.

Helen lay on a comfortable cot for a few hours when it was all over. The nurse and the doctor checked in on her every fifteen or twenty minutes. The nurse eventually handed her a piece of paper that was a kind of invoice, a charge at the bottom of fifty dollars.

Helen had not come prepared; her purse contained only a few dollars. When she realized that the doctor was expecting to be paid right then before she left, she didn't know what to say. "I'm so sorry; I should have been better prepared. I feel so stupid."

Helen and Andrew had never considered that the doctor would have a set fee for this service, although they had discussed that they wanted to give him something for his time and efforts. The doctor had entered the room. Helen lightly grabbed his arm. "Can I return in a few days and give you the money then?"

He turned and looked directly at her. "I think that would be okay. You have an honest face, and you say that you are a professional person yourself." The nurse looked at the doctor in surprise but did not say anything.

They sent her home when she was feeling strong enough to drive the fifty miles. The nurse gave her aspirin to take for as long as she needed it and ordered her to stay off her feet for a few days.

Andrew held her for hours that evening listening to the story of her day, both glad it was over. "Promise me, Andrew, that you will never tell anyone about the abortion. It is important to me that you make this promise."

"Of course, I promise. Rest assured of that."

Helen felt able to go back to work on Monday, business as usual. She was weak and tired but told everyone that she might have a cold. The aspirin helped with the dull cramping. The following weekend, she and Andrew drove back to Spokane and paid the doctor the fifty dollars owed him, a big dent in their savings.

—✺—

At home alone in the evenings, Helen sometimes felt empty, a hunger that would not go away. When she thought of eating to satisfy the hunger, she was nauseous. The feeling returned, off and on, for months. Sometimes she just got into bed, pulled the covers over her head, and willed herself to sleep, regardless of the time of day.

She told Florence that she had had a miscarriage. Florence was probably just happy that the whole issue was resolved and that Andrew and Helen could continue with their plans.

The bouts of hunger and depression came less and less often as time went on. Andrew was there for her, at times making her talk about it. Months later, she found out at work that Mrs. McMillan had been admitted to the hospital because of a mental breakdown. Their children had to be put into foster homes, hopefully on a temporary basis. Helen never told Andrew.

And then as the years went by, Helen and Andrew talked about the abortion less and less, never talking about the actual unborn child. They were sure they had done the right thing.

CHAPTER 3

HELEN AND ANDREW WERE MARRIED in June as planned. A pastor friend performed the informal affair at his house. They didn't want to spend any money, nor did they want to give their two alcoholic fathers a chance to celebrate a little too much. Helen's friend and Andrew's cousin, Florence, and three other friends stood up with them. They all went to lunch together afterward and took a drive into the hills, jammed into one car, laughing the whole way.

When the newlyweds got to their new apartment in Rockford, they found that Helen's mother had arranged from California to have flowers and a full fridge waiting for them as her way of saying she wished them well. Andrew's mother, Aunt Phyl, kept her distance, although they suspected she had something to do with surprise offerings of odds and ends of furnishings left outside their door.

A month after the wedding Andrew came home from work. "Let's go on a honeymoon! Our money goals are doing well, and we deserve it."

Helen was now driving extra miles for her job in Oliver and welcomed a diversion. "Great idea. I bet Uncle John would lend us his cabin in the mountains for a week. We can stock it with food, put our feet up, and have some fun, just the two of us." The next day Helen started making arrangements for the cabin and to get off work.

A couple of days later, however, four of their friends decided to go to Wyoming to Cheyenne Frontier Days and asked Helen and Andrew to go along. Well, they couldn't pass up that kind of fun. They accepted the invitation and cancelled the week in the mountains.

Cheyenne Frontier Days turned out to be a blast. They ate a good deal of steak, drank a lot of beer with more than a few whiskey shots, and danced their legs off. Andrew entertained the whole barroom one night with his rendition of a German polka. Rumor had it that Helen and her girlfriends hopped up on a table and did a dance of their own. The newlyweds bragged and laughed for years about their honeymoon for six.

Andrew and Helen enjoyed living together and spending more time in each other's company. Their lives, otherwise, went on much the same as before the wedding. They continued to work long hours, each liking what they did and spending time with friends and family. Andrew had loved to play cards before but gave up his time at the Elks Club. He loved to put on little shows and create scenes with whatever was there and whenever he had an audience, dancing with the ironing board or posing as if he were in a professional photo shoot, pants tucked into new boots. Helen laughed the loudest at what her husband came up with.

Andrew found ways to make the couple's relationship richer. They took long drives in the country, parked, and talked out any problems or concerns. Occasionally they went to a quiet nightclub, had a few drinks, and, again, talked.

Somehow, Andrew didn't get called to go into the army like they had been told would happen once he had his airplane mechanic training. But he often returned to the hangars just outside of Rockford, where he received his training, doing what he could with the equipment he had learned to use. Helen wanted to see more of her husband, but she couldn't have both: a husband who worked from nine to five and a husband who enjoyed the work he did.

In November, after five months of marriage, and nine months after the abortion, Helen found she was again pregnant. Abortion this time around was never considered or discussed; now they were married. Helen still considered herself unprepared for parenthood but knew having the baby was their only option.

Helen soon quit her job. Being relieved of the drive every day from Rockford was freeing. Besides, married women were expected to stay home and be good housewives, keeping things clean, including the children.

After a couple of months of being home all day, she was restless, however. She read a lot, organized the house, reorganized the house, and tried to enjoy cooking. In July of 1941, Kibby Jane was born into the Kindle family. Once the baby came, being a housewife gave her more of a sense of purpose, and she settled into the job. If she felt regret dropping her career, she did not voice it to anyone, nor did she let it interfere with her marriage and feelings for Andrew.

Helen's friend Florence got married soon after Kibby Jane was born. She and her husband lived in town for a while before he was to be off across the country for the army. Flo frequently went to see Helen, helping her with baby chores. They sat and listen to Sarah Vaughan and Tommy Dorsey on the radio as they folded diapers and baby clothes. When Tommy sang "I'll Never Smile Again," they danced with each other, holding Kibby Jane between them. "So how is motherhood, Helen? Is it getting any easier?"

"I guess you could say it's easier." Helen smiled. "As it turns out, your aunt Phyl has been wonderful. It's amazing what a grandchild can do to a woman and her relationship with her daughter-in-law."

"That's good news. I guess it's okay for her to have part-German grandbabies."

"Yeah, I guess so. Phyl is the one who has taught me the best way to fold diapers, how long to let the baby cry, and all that stuff that I certainly didn't know before. I can't say we're best of friends, but we've found we can work together. Frankly, I don't know how I could manage without her. In fact, it looks like we may be moving into a little house a few blocks from them."

"Swell. Do you think then that Phyl would babysit so we could go shopping, maybe have lunch out once in a while?" Bing Crosby was now belting out "I'll Be Seeing You." The gals swayed to the music in the kitchen as they started dinner.

"That would be wonderful. I bet she'd go for it. I'll have to be careful not to overdo it, though. I don't want to ruin what we've got now."

Helen didn't share with Florence that day that spending more than three days alone with the baby created a darkness that sometimes closed in on her. When the baby cried relentlessly, she couldn't pull herself out of bed or off the couch, as she knew she should. She'd pull a blanket or pillow over her head and curl up in a ball, hoping the crying would go away.

Then she would think of Andrew and how disappointed he would be if anything bad happened to Kibby Jane. He was depending on her to be the mother as well as the wife. So Helen would drag herself out of the stupor and to the little creature in the crib leaking at both ends. Once the diaper was changed, the bottle warmed up, and the baby held tightly in her arms, she was ready to continue with her day.

Actually, she was more than ready. She loved Kibby Jane with all her heart. She didn't know how she could let herself lie so long in that bed. She would see that woman, herself, who went off to college on her own for those four long, hard years. She saw the woman, her mother, who went out in her dad's clothing and helped shovel manure in the barn and climbed up on a horse to move cattle. She knew she had the strength somewhere inside, and she could pull it together. *After all, babies aren't babies forever.*

When Andrew was home, he was 100 percent present for his wife. He changed diapers (a rare thing in the 1940s), fed the baby, and held her for as long as was necessary for Helen to do other chores that needed to be done.

He talked to Helen as he would a friend. "You would not believe the customer I had today. He came in to tell me he had run out of gas about two miles from the station and then expected me to drop everything, fill a can with gas, and walk it to his car. I was the only one there, and I couldn't just leave while he sat in a chair, smoked his cigarettes, and listened to the radio."

"He had a lot of nerve. What did you do?"

"I told him, 'Not for all the tea in China. Fill your own darn can, and walk it back to your car.'"

"Good for you."

"Yeah, but guess what?" Andrew leaned over Kibby Jane's basket. "He took off with my gas can and never brought it back."

"What a knucklehead. Okay, Kibby is asleep. Get out the cribbage board; it's game time."

—⁓—

On one of the girls' outings, walking to a nearby café to have coffee, Florence made a confession that came as a complete surprise to Helen. "We've been trying to have a baby, and I've thought I was pregnant three times now, only to be disappointed. I feel like I'm trying to join this very prestigious club, and I just can't fit in. I'm never quite good enough and get voted out every time."

"I'm sorry, Florence. I had no idea. I don't know what to say."

"You don't have to say anything. It's just good to talk about it. I feel so inadequate. Harold and I both do. We feel like we have committed some crime. We want to have a baby so bad, but it just isn't happening."

"That's heartbreaking. Do people actually say mean things to you?"

"You better believe it. Harold is being made to feel he's not manly enough. Friends make comments that insinuate he's doing something wrong in bed. Gee whillikers, he hasn't done anything wrong." By this time the two women were sitting in the café, whispering so people wouldn't overhear. Helen ordered coffee for both of them.

"Have you been to a doctor to find out what the problem is? Maybe there's something that can be done."

Flo blushed. "Yes, I have, but even my doctor seems embarrassed talking on the subject. He told me it may be some kind of hormonal imbalance or ovarian insufficiency, he called it."

"What can you do?"

"He said we should keep trying because it'll be harder and harder as I get older. I guess woman's eggs become abnormal as they age. But he also told me that the largest cause of infertility is the male's problems."

"So has Harold gone to see him?"

"No, I can't get him to go. I didn't dare tell him that the doctor said there was good chance that he was the cause. He already feels like a failure."

"Yikes, that's terrible."

"One of Harold's friends told him that he just needed to relax and enjoy sex. He said to quit trying so hard. He even told him he might try different ways or positions. Poor Harold's masculinity is being assaulted through all this. But men want to marry a woman who can give him children, right? I don't seem to be able to do that."

"My gosh. Neither one of you have done anything to be ashamed of."

"You'd be surprised how insensitive people can be."

Helen signaled to the waiter that they wanted a coffee refill. When she turned back to Florence, Helen saw that she was near tears. Helen reached out, patted her shoulder and handed her a Kleenex.

Florence sat for a while deep in thought and then suddenly sat bolt upright, her eyes wide and wild like a cat's. "You know, Helen, the worst thing is every time I thought I was pregnant, I saw in my head the face of my baby. I was sure it was real. But it wasn't real. I made it all up. I was never pregnant at all."

Helen decided the course of the conversation needed a new direction. "Do you and Harold ever talk about another way of becoming parents? You don't have to give birth, you know. You could adopt.

And besides that, there are other ways to use parenting skills. You could volunteer to work with children who are less fortunate and need adults in their lives."

The waiter finally arrived to refill their cups. The two women waited until he was far enough away to return to their conversation.

"We've talked about adopting. I think that's a viable option. Since he's in the service and we'll be moving around, it doesn't make sense to look into it right now. But I think we will soon. We need to move on to a new dream. Maybe moving away from all these friends who are having babies will help." Flo leaned back into her chair and sighed.

"Yes, I was thinking that too. Here you've been so helpful to me with my difficulties adjusting to motherhood, and you're dying to be a mother yourself. I've been selfish and inconsiderate."

"You had no idea what I was going through. I guess that's why I wanted to tell you now. I knew you'd understand; you're such a good listener. Don't beat yourself up. I've enjoyed helping you out in your time of need."

—⁂—

Helen eventually made new friends who had babies and friends whose husbands were gone to war. She found she was not the only one who felt stuck in an unexpected, difficult situation. Helping them deal with their needs sustained her like meat and potatoes as she chewed on their problems instead of dwelling on her own.

As the war continued and war needs changed, it finally became evident that Andrew would be drafted. He was told that enlisting in the air force division of the army would be to his advantage. So he did just that, in May of 1945. By then, Helen was again pregnant and didn't go with him. She gave birth to a second daughter, Roberta Jo, after he left. She had helpful support from friends and his family.

Helen and the babies soon joined Andrew in Texas, where he was stationed. But just a few months later, he was transferred to a base in

Mississippi. So Helen moved back to Rockford and into the same little rental house just blocks from Aunt Phyl and Doc Kindle's house.

—⋙—

One day, Phyl went to the little Kindle house and pounded on the door. She had been calling for two days, but Helen never picked up the phone. After five minutes of knocking, the curtain over the door window parted, and Helen's face appeared. She slowly opened the door to her mother-in-law.

Phyl saw a seriously disheveled Helen still in a nightgown, stains all down the front. Her hair looked to have not been combed for days, and darkness circled her hollow-looking eyes. The children didn't look any better. Kibby Jane, over four years old by then, was running around in her underwear. She had mushed-up crackers in her hand with as much cracker in her hair. Kibby Jane was ecstatic to see her grandma at the door, grabbing her legs, jumping up and down, yelling, "Grandma, Grandma."

Phyl was relieved to see that the baby, Roberta Jo, had a dry diaper, although that was all she had on. It looked like the blanket in the crib had not been changed for a long time. She was sleeping in a laundry basket instead of the crib, a good thing because the basket was cleaner than the crib. Clothes, toys, baby bottles, and food were everywhere.

The house smelled of the unpleasant side of baby care, not the sweet, just-shampooed-hair smell that mothers around the world swoon over. This was the smell of baby urine, baby feces, and rancid milk. The air appeared to not have been replenished for days.

Phyl's first instinct was to first hug and hold the children and then to start cleaning up. Fortunately, Helen's mother-in-law was smarter and more sensitive than that. Instead she calmly said, "Hello, Helen. How are you? You don't look so good. Come sit on the couch with me."

The two women cleared an area on the couch and sat down. Helen's chin rested on her chest, eyes unable to make contact. Her shoulders sagged as severely as the corners of her mouth. She tried to brush off the stains on her nightgown. Phyl noticed that her daughter-in-law did not smell any better than the room.

Eventually, Helen turned her head to look at her mother-in-law. Phyl saw what looked like signs of relief mixed with signs of shame on Helen's face. She was glad she had decided to be kind.

Phyl kept her voice calm. "Being a mother isn't easy, is it, Helen? I didn't have seven children with a man who worked long days and usually came home drunk and mean, without experiencing what you're experiencing. Talk to me, sweetie. Tell me what's been happening."

A flood of words came from Helen's mouth following Phyl's expressions of sympathy and understanding. She confessed to Phyl that she wanted to spend all her time in bed. "After I feed the children, it's all I can do to sit on the couch with them and stare out the window. I read books if Kibby insists, and I do make sure they're fed. But that's about all I can manage."

"I can see that," Phyl tried to sound positive.

"I'm not a proper mother to my children. I'm not cut out of that cloth. The only reason I have been able to get through the last five years is Andrew. He has been the glue that holds me together. Without Andrew, I couldn't do any of it; with him gone, I barely manage."

Once the flow of words stopped and the tears slowed, Phyl stood up as tall as she could, all four feet, ten inches of her. "Well, Helen, I suggest you do what I always did when I was feeling this way. You grasp your suffering by the neck, you throw it to the floor as hard as you can, and you grind it under the heel of your shoe!" Phyl demonstrated, standing among the clutter on the living room floor.

Then she pulled Helen up off the couch. They stomped, Phyl in her size-four shoes and Helen in her size-eight slippers, grunting and groaning for five minutes or more. Finally they plopped down on the couch again, exhausted.

"Damn, that felt good!" Helen spouted. Phyl smiled.

While Helen went into the bathroom to shower and clean herself up, Phyl found phone numbers. She picked up the phone and asked the operator to hook her up with Helen's friends and local relatives. She got them all to sign up for a few hours of every day to come and help Helen with chores and to be her companion. Aunt Phyl encouraged them to talk to her about anything and not to worry about saying the wrong thing. She said they needed to talk about anything that came to mind, and they needed to give Helen a chance to talk.

After all the phone calls Phyl and Helen tackled the children and the mess. They sang and danced and recited every nursery rhyme they could think of as they worked. Then Phyl put everyone, including Helen, to bed in clean sheets.

Friends and family came to the little Kindle family's rescue as requested. One friend finally convinced Helen to go to her family doctor, who wrote a letter to the army on her behalf. Andrew was honorably discharged and came home early to Helen and his babies.

—m—

Through the years that followed Andrew's homecoming, the couple continued to be best friends and lovers. They enjoyed each other's company, and their marriage gained strength as they learned the power of communication.

Helen's worst enemy was overthinking what needed to be done or overreacting to a situation. "She makes me so mad, Andrew. Doesn't Aunt Gwen know I'm doing the best I can? She's critical of every little thing I do and every little thing the girls do."

The couple was on one of their drives in the country, what they called "talk time." The kids had fallen asleep in the back seat. Andrew said, "I think Aunt Gwen likes putting her nose where it doesn't belong. She was a lousy parent to her own kids. She would like to think you're worse than she was."

Helen slid down in the car seat. "I guess yelling and then hanging up on her was not the best thing to do."

"Well, it did probably make her even madder. Just give it some time. She'll probably forget all about it."

"Then what do I do? Let her rake us over the coals again next time I see her?"

"Yes, and then let it go. Ignore her criticism, and change the subject. Maybe she'll stop doing it if she doesn't get a rise out of you."

"Okay, I'll give it a try. Thanks again, ole wise one."

Andrew had gotten a job repairing and managing a portion of an amusement company that owned jukeboxes, pinball machines, and pool tables. His boss had assured him that it might be possible to buy that division in the future. They were both excited about the possibility. He worked late hours, but Helen would wait up for him. When he finally came home, she would fix him a meal or a snack. He would eat, and they would talk. The kids were usually already in bed. She always listened to his reasoning, frequently following his suggestions to her problems.

To her friends and relatives, Helen appeared to rule the roost. They didn't know that she talked almost everything over with Andrew before she ruled. Because he was gone so much of the time, she had to do the follow-up, however, and many times, that was where she got in trouble. She had to backtrack and patch things up with her friends and her children. Andrew would quietly convince her that she had been too heavy-handed or not heavy-handed enough.

—⁂—

As Helen grew to be a mature woman, she would continue to experience dark days. She learned to go to her doctor for help when that happened. She also learned that being a stay-at-home mother was not enough for her. She did not feel fulfilled being just a mother and completing household chores. Andrew understood her needs and encouraged her to take on volunteer work.

Helen did have two more pregnancies that never went to term. She always wondered if that first baby might have been the son she was unable to give Andrew. He would have been such a wonderful father to a son. *Did we do the right thing?*

Helen continued to communicate by mail with her friend Florence, who never had gotten pregnant as they had hoped. Harold had never talked to his doctor, but they had recently adopted a baby girl whose mother had been unable to raise a child on her own. She wrote that as much as she learned to love this precious baby, maybe they should have looked harder for answers to their questions. She, too, wondered if they had done the right thing.

Part Two
Kibby Jane: 1960

Love as a power can go anywhere. It isn't sentimental. It doesn't have to be pretty, yet it doesn't deny pain.

—Sharon Salzberg

CHAPTER 4

KIBBY JANE DANCED AROUND HER kid sister, who wasn't really listening, "Can you believe it? Tomorrow I'm out of here. This hick town of Rockford says goodbye to this nineteen-year-old!" Kibby Jane didn't care that Roberta Jo wasn't even pretending to be listening. The excitement heading off to Seattle University had her filled to the brim. *Too rad.*

Kibby Jane and Roberta Jo occupied the Kindle living room, taking advantage of the fact that their mother was out of the house and they could listen to their own 45's on the big console stereo. Kibby tapped her foot to Ritchie Valens and "La Bamba," her favorite. She knew that soon Roberta Jo would be switching to Ray Charles, probably "What'd I Say," not her favorite.

While Kibby Jane listened to the music she flipped through the pages of her junior college annual. She realized her social life this year had been the best ever. But now she was done with having to tell her mother where she was going and when she planned to be home again.

Still restless and wanting to make plans for her last night in town, Kibby Jane went to the phone in the hall and closed the door. She picked up the receiver, and the operator said her usual: "Number please."

Kibby Jane replied, "Six, six, nine please," and waited. There was no answer, so she hung up and went back into the living room and picked up the brochure photos of the campus dormitory where she would be living. Her dorm area was going to be a little like an apartment, with six girls together in a pod. Three would share each of the two bunk rooms, while all six used the common area to cook, eat, and hang out. *It's all sooo groovy.*

Roberta Jo finally looked up from her book, stuck out her tongue, and crossed her eyes as only a fifteen-year-old can. "What are you so antsy about? I'm trying to read here, and you keep muttering at me."

"I'm just excited, that's all."

"Yeah, lucky you. No more Mother driving you crazy. She's such a control freak. Don't leave me here with her by myself. Please, please."

Kibby Jane shrugged. She couldn't say it to Roberta Jo because her little sister would refuse to listen, but she thought their mother had been super in many ways: listening to problems without judgment, helping figure out solutions, not just telling them what to do. Helen didn't insist on knowing everything she and her friends did. And she would never forget that her mother had made her the coolest poodle skirt in town, pink with big brown poodles! *As happy as I am to get away, I've had a mother my friends envy.*

"You'll be just fine, Roberta. Let her win and have her way sometimes. Don't pick fights over every little thing. Then, when there's something you really want to win, you can go after it. She's good at compromising, really."

"Easy for you to say. You're getting out of here."

"And don't forget Daddy. Get him on your side; then you've got it made. Besides, Mother's so busy with all her volunteer work, she sometimes forgets we exist."

"Yeah, Daddy's the greatest, although he's a workaholic and not home much. I bet you'll miss him, huh?"

"That's for sure. He's always fun and almost never gets angry. When he's here, we have a righteous time, don't we? Mother loosens up too, when he's around."

"I'm still ticked at you that you're leaving me behind." Roberta Jo went back to her book, leaving Kibby Jane to her JC memories and college dreams.

———◊◊◊———

When Kibby Jane and Roberta Jo were small children, Helen had talked to them about the birds and bees. She had them draw pictures of babies growing in women's tummies. She would draw the birth canal and show how the fetus would make its way through it and out their vagina. The girls were given a clear vision and understanding of how babies entered the world. Kibby Jane knew this was much more information than most of her friends got.

But somehow, Helen never quite got to how the fetus got into tummies in the first place. They had been on their own in understanding how a woman got pregnant. Kibby Jane had learned the man's role from her good friend Nancy. When the girls were about eleven years old, they sat on the rock fence beside their school. The subject went from puppies to how babies were made. Kibby said, "Yeah, well, how are they made? That's the mystery."

Nancy proudly blurted, "Well, I know how I was made. My daddy put his penis in my mother's vagina, and that made an egg grow inside my mother. That egg grew bigger and bigger and became me!"

"Are you kidding me? Your father put his penis in your mom's vagina? Yuck! No way Daddy's going to do that to my mother. She wouldn't let that happen."

"Well, that's the way it works."

"Why do you say that?" Kibby Jane jumped up from the wall and placed her hands on her hips. "I'm never going to talk to you again!" She spun around and ran all the way home without looking back at her baffled friend.

At home, she began to remember and think about the fetus lessons she had gotten when she was a little girl. *Maybe Nancy was right. But I'm not going to say anything to Mother. I might get in trouble for talking about it.*

Roberta Jo was four years younger than Kibby Jane, so their lives growing up hadn't intersected much, but they got along okay.

Kibby Jane had fond memories of going to piano lessons with her mother and sister. Helen would drive them out on a country road to where the piano teacher lived. Usually they had to go in their daddy's old, beat-up pickup that smelled of hot oil and dirt. The paint was badly peeling on the fenders and hood, and the homemade wooden stock racks in the back were splintered and broken in places. To start the thing, Helen had to wrap two wires together, push the button, and say a prayer.

On one trip, Roberta Jo had said, "I don't want to go in this ugly old thing. I'm embarrassed to be seen in it. Can't we go in the car?"

Kibby Jane remembered Helen's eyebrows shooting up. "I didn't raise my daughters to think they were better than anyone else. I guess we'll always go in the pickup from now on, even when your father needs it."

She had looked at her sister in disgust. "You are such a princess, Roberta! Now look what you've done."

Kibby Jane had thought it was kind of fun going to piano lessons in the old truck. It had no radio, so they would sing the whole way there and back, bumping along on the dirt road. The exhaust system was so loud, they had to sing at the top of their lungs to be able to hear themselves. The most popular songs were the old ones Helen had taught them, songs like "Ain't She Sweet," "Walkin' My Baby Back Home," "On the Sunny Side of the Street," and "Five Foot Two, Eyes of Blue."

The last few years, prankster events had been common in the Kindle house. Kibby Jane remembered one evening when Roberta had a friend for a sleepover while Kibby was out on a date with their history student teacher. The two younger girls made a big sign reading, "Come on, go ahead and kiss her!" They hung it on the front porch for them to find when he brought her home.

The girls fell asleep before the couple got home, so they missed the reaction to the sign. They would have been disappointed to know that

Kibby Jane and her date weren't embarrassed but had a good laugh. The girls' student teacher took the sign home to show his roommates. Kibby said nothing the next morning and knew they wouldn't dare ask him about it at school.

On another occasion, Roberta Jo and her girlfriend hid all of Kibby Jane's bras in containers in the freezer. They replaced the bras with a note that led her on a scavenger hunt around the house. Kibby Jane was not impressed and, this time, complained to her mother. A lot of good that did; she heard Helen having a good laugh about it with Andrew when he got home. Andrew had said, "I'm happy that our two daughters are having fun playing pranks on each other despite the difference in their ages. Usually they seem to pretty much ignore each other."

Kibby Jane for sure would never forget her disastrous effort at trying to get even with her little sister and friends. For Roberta Jo's fourteenth birthday, a slumber party was planned. The six friends, including Roberta, were to sleep on the carport roof attached to the house.

Kibby Jane and a junior college friend offered to take the girls to the drive-in outdoor movie theatre and then home again to the roof. They took Andrew's new pickup so all six could ride in the back and then watch the movie in the chairs outside the concession stand. As they were getting ready to leave the drive-in, Kibby Jane's friend, Gail, said to the birthday party girls, "I wonder if you gals could help me out with something I need to do for my biology class."

"Depends, but yeah, we're pretty much open for anything," Roberta Jo said.

"Righteous! This'll be perfect. I need to find some ground squirrels. They have to be caught alive, but they only come out of their holes in the dark at night," explained Gail. Kibby Jane had known that Gail was describing snipe hunting, which was not true hunting but a prank to make fools out of the hunters and to eventually leave them stranded. She was hoping Roberta Jo and her friends had never heard of the prank. If they had, it might not work as planned. They called it "ground squirrel hunting" to ward off suspicion.

"Okay, here's how it works," Gail continued. "We're going to drive out of town a ways until we find a nice, big, flat ditch. Then I'll give each of you a gunny sack. I know it's dark, but we have a couple of flashlights you can use. You guys will go find holes in the ditch and hold your gunny sacks over the holes. If you talk very softly as you do this and maybe even sing softly, the ground squirrels will be curious, run out of their holes and into your sack. Just be ready to close up the gunny sack when they get in there. Understand? Kibby and I'll be waiting in the truck for when you bring the squirrels back." Kibby Jo had to keep tucking her chin into her chest to keep from laughing. Gail was really playing it up. Kibby Jo didn't know how she could keep a straight face with all those details.

"Far out!" was the eager response from one of the birthday party girls. "Maybe I'll sing a Paul Anka song like 'Head on My Shoulders.' I'm sure the ground squirrels would like that one."

They drove a few miles out of town until they found a flat ditch that Gail thought was just right. The night was pitch black, and a warm breeze permeated the air, a perfect summer evening despite the lateness of the hour. The girls, still discussing what song they were going to sing, climbed out of the back of the truck. They grabbed flashlights and gunny sacks and started looking for holes. They had to step over large clumps of grass and watch for the occasional cactus and sharp yucca grass. The task was such a great adventure; they didn't seem to mind the soft dirt that worked its way to their toes around their sandal straps.

If it hadn't have been so dark out, Kibby Jane might have noticed that her sister, Roberta Jo, and friend Ellen were getting suspicious. They looked at each other with frowns on their faces. Roberta Jo whispered, "Hey, Ellen, are you thinking the same thing I am?"

"Yes, this whole thing is starting to sound a lot like snipe hunting," Ellen whispered back. "I've never been snipe hunting, but from what I've heard, this is it."

Kibby Jane and Gail had their own whispering going on. "Listen to those girls giggling and singing softly from their positions in the ditch. I'm going to pee my pants, Gail; they looked so ridiculous! They actually fell for it."

After about twenty minutes, Gail nervously waved her hand to signal to Kibby Jane that it was time to get out of there. Kibby snorted and started up the pickup, slowly pulling away. Then she turned on the headlights and hit the gas pedal. Gravel flew as they sped down the dirt road. They hollered, "Eehaw" and "Woohoo," heads thrown back in laughter.

—m—

Days later, Roberta Jo told her side of the rest of the sniper story. The family of four sat at the kitchen table after dinner. It went like this:

"We looked up to see Kibby taking off in the pickup, leaving us in the ditch. My friend Jeanette yelled, 'What the heck? Where are they going?' She sounded truly scared. Ellen told them they had been sniped. Four of the gals had never heard of snipe hunting, so Ellen had to explain what was happening. Jessie was also getting very nervous. It was late and very dark. She said she was worried they wouldn't get back to town.

"Meantime, I was forming a plan in my head. I told them not to panic. You know, Kibby and Gail picked the wrong place and the wrong girls to try that trick. Ellen and I have ridden our horses all around that part of the country a million times."

Andrew had leaned back in his kitchen chair, a wide grin on his face, before turning to agree with Roberta Jo. "I guess they did pick wrong. You're right about that."

"The others were relieved to hear that I knew what to do. I told them that when we saw the pickup coming back, we would hide in the ditch so that they couldn't see us. I had no doubts that they would be coming back to get us. I knew you would have their hides if they didn't."

Andrew's smile went wider as he nodded his head in agreement.

"So about fifteen minutes later, we saw the headlights coming toward us. We hit the ditch, lying on our bellies as flat as we could when the pickup went by. Five minutes later, it went past us again, this time much slower. On the third drive-by, we heard Kibby and Gail calling our names, this time sounding very worried. The fourth time, the calls were more like pleas. I swear I even heard some sobbing. When I gave the okay, we all popped up out of the ditch, laughing and shouting, 'We got ya!'

"Kibby and Gail were not laughing. They said they had been scared out of their minds. We laughed again when we apologized for not getting the ground squirrels."

Andrew and Helen were laughing themselves at this point. "Now let's hear your side of the story, Kibby Jane."

—◊◊—

Kibby's rendition of what happened that night went like this:

"Roberta was exaggerating big-time. When the girls were in the ditch, Gail and I just drove down the road to look for a better place. The girls panicked. That's all. We went probably twenty feet down the road and came back. No big deal."

Kibby Jane saw Roberta Jo's mouth hanging open in awe at the simplicity of her sister's side of the story. She looked at her parents and saw they looked skeptical. Andrew and Helen didn't say anything about the discrepancies between the two stories. Kibby quickly got up and went to her room so no questions would be asked.

Kibby Jane remembered, though, that the fun had not been over that evening. After Roberta and her five friends had gotten settled in on the carport rooftop, Kibby and Gail watched them crawl over the fence around the football field next door. By this time it was really late. In fact, morning was approaching, but a half moon now lit up the night so that flashlights were not necessary.

The two older gals watched the six as they chatted and giggled, walking across the long field to the bleachers on the other side. They grabbed rocks they found on the ground and climbed the stairs to the top. Kibby was shocked to see them throwing rocks at the big overhead lights, obviously trying to break them. Fortunately, none of the girls could throw very well, so the lights stayed intact. Kibby decided they needed to be scared a little. Maybe revenge was somewhat on her mind as well.

The birthday party became spread out as they walked back home, getting tired and ready for their sleeping bags on the roof. But before they got back to the fence, Kibby Jane and Gail ran down the side street with bedsheets draped and flowing over their heads. They enhanced the ghostly effect by making a series of weird and eerie noises.

"Look, you guys. What're those things? Let's get out of here!" could be heard from the street.

The six young girls began running fast, bunching up at the fence as they all tried to go over at the same time. Fingers got stepped on in the chain links. Much yelping resulted. By the time they all managed to get back over the fence, the ghostly figures had disappeared. They climbed onto the carport roof, some of the girls begging to move inside. Roberta Jo talked them into crawling into their sleeping bags to finally get some sleep. "Okay, Gail, we got the last laugh."

Kibby Jane's mind came back to the present, back to where she was going the next day. She went to the phone to try her friend again. "Hey, Janie, how about going out tonight and buzz the drag for a few hours for the last time before I head out of here. Maybe we could go up to the Skillet and have a beer. My packing is done. Wanna go?"

"Sounds like a good plan, Kibby, but you gotta quit rubbing it in. I have to stay here in this bad-news town for another year. I guess I can handle a little celebration though. I get off work at seven o'clock, and then I'm ready. Hey, maybe we can do one more Chinese tag for old time's sake. Remember last time we played?"

Kibby smiled and sat down on the floor beside the telephone table. "Do I ever remember. When we stopped at the stop light and got out to run around the car, Linda tripped and went flat on her face in the street."

"Yeah, and remember, no one knew she hadn't gotten back into the car. We left her there, blood dripping from her knees. We drove around the block to pick her up once we realized what had happened."

"Man, it was a miracle we got back to her because we were laughing so hard. We might never have discovered she wasn't in the car. Good thing only her pride was hurt, just scraped-up knees."

"Hey, wait till you see the new pedal pushers I bought yesterday. They're the most beautiful orange. I'll wear them tonight. Are you picking me up?"

"Sure, I'm sure Mother will let me have the car on my last night." Kibby Jane hung up the phone. *There's never anything to do in this hick town but drive up and down the main streets, flashing headlights at our friends doing the same thing. Or we sit at drive-in restaurants sipping on a Coke for as long as we can get away with it. Then there's bowling and going to a movie that changes only once a week. Seattle has to have a lot more to do than this.*

Kibby Jane had decided to major in social work. Yeah, sure, that had been her mother's major, but a hundred years ago. Besides, she was going to Seattle University, not University of Washington like her mother did.

That night, her last in Rockford, Kibby Jane sat behind the wheel of her parents' car and started thinking of her mother. It was one thing trying to convince her little sister that Helen was okay and another thing to accept all that she did. "She can be so unpredictable. You never know with her if you're going to get in trouble of not."

"What do you mean? You have a great mother, the best!"

"For example, last month my parents went out of town for a few days and left Roberta and me on our own. I had asked a few friends over to just sit around and talk. Well, the word got out that my parents were gone, and twenty to thirty friends showed up, many with booze in hand."

"Oh yeah, I was there. What a party."

Kibby Jane paused to beep and wave at a passing carload of boys. "Well, the next morning the house was a disaster. Even Roberta was furious when she saw it. We found the silverware drawer completely pushed in and dropped down behind! A big gouge had been made in the kitchen wall. I even found mother's jewelry box dumped out onto the floor…under her bed!"

"Yeah, I heard you were calling friends to come help clean up."

"That's why Roberta was so mad. She had to help me 'cause she figured we would both be in trouble. We created a miracle in the cleanup, but when Mother and Daddy got home, the first thing they saw was a couple of beer cans under the car in the carport. They didn't have to wonder a minute about what had gone on while they were away. Of course they knew."

"Did you get grounded for life?"

"That was what was so weird. For some reason, Roberta got the brunt of the interrogation from our parents. She tried not to rat on me, but she couldn't lie. Lying is not what you do in our family, believe me."

"You mean Roberta got in trouble and you didn't?"

"That's right; Roberta didn't get grounded or anything, but she got the interrogation. All I got was a short lecture. Roberta is still mad that I didn't get in trouble. Mother always seems to be on Roberta's case, as if she were the only one doing something she shouldn't. If Mother only knew the things I've done the last few years. I'm not as innocent as she thinks."

Kibby Jane and Roberta Jo, had shared a room until two years ago when their parents developed part of the basement so Kibby could have her own space. "Space" was just about all you could call her new room. To get to it, you had to walk through the mudroom, down the narrow, steep stairs, down the narrow hallway that housed both the freezer and a corner, make-do shower. At the end of that hallway was the door to her little room that had just enough space for an oversize twin bed, a dresser, and a desk. But Kibby Jane loved having privacy from her parents and her little sister.

Kibby Jane had recently broken up with the love of her life. She suspected that she had not been good enough for his parents and that they were behind the breakup. After all, the Kindles lived in a small house on the "wrong" side of town from all the popular kids. She was still pretty messed up about the breakup. He was going to University of Washington to become a big shot lawyer; she was glad they wouldn't be at the same college.

Kibby had never been the cheerleader or football-queen type, but she had many good girlfriends and was well liked by all. She was known for her sense of humor and ability to be a good friend. She could be described as *cute* with the personality to match. She had managed to inherit her mother's dark-brown eyes and dark hair but had gotten stuck with her dad's short legs. Her sister got the long legs, curly hair, and blue eyes.

Kibby Jane was sometimes resentful of her sister. Roberta Jo seemed to let her personality fly whenever she wanted, while Kibby felt she was always holding back, afraid someone might think less of her. She wanted more than anything for everyone to like her. Kibby had had polio in her back when she was twelve years old; the pain left her feeling she was not always in control of her own body. Maybe that was why she was unable to fly like her sister, Roberta.

As it turned out, Andrew alone drove Kibby Jane to begin college. At the last minute, Helen decided to go to California to help her mother, leaving just the two of them to make the drive and the move into her dorm. Having her dad to herself for a couple of days was a treat. Kibby and her dad had a special relationship because of Andrew's frequent visits to the hospital when she had polio. He had always made her laugh, and she would forget the pain for a few minutes. The bond from those visits had lasted through her teen years.

Besides, Kibby Jane thought, if Helen had been with them, she would have orchestrated the whole moving-in thing, telling her and her new roommates what to do, how to arrange their rooms, and how to organize their closets. Poo, she might have even given her roommates lectures on staying away from the boys because they needed to concentrate on school.

I have heard that lecture enough times. I don't know how Mother and Daddy ever had any babies. Mother must have gotten pregnant by artificial insemination. What a prude and control freak my unpredictable mother is.

Kibby Jane liked her new roommates a lot, despite the too-frequent dinners of tuna fish casserole and Jell-o salad. She loved Seattle University as well, especially her social work courses. She dated a number of guys, never getting serious about any of them. Going out with groups of friends, laughing, and having a few drinks was what she most liked to do. She hated it when she drank too much. That didn't always stop her, however.

Kibby eventually decided she had to grow up; her grades were suffering from too much partying. She had dropped the Jane from her name because it sounded more grown up. Most important, she opted for the rule that she could party, but only if it didn't interfere with her school work. *Is this my mother's voice making its way into my head?*

"What a waste my mother's education was," Kibby told one of her roommates, as they sat around their pod one evening. "All this hard work and, don't forget, all the money being spent, but then you only work a few years? Then...you have two babies, and it's too late to have a career. I don't understand how she gave up her dreams so easily. Today she's a social worker, all right. She sits and has coffee with her friends, listening to their problems for hours on end. That's not my idea of a job or a career."

"Yes, but your mother's superbusy with all kinds of stuff," argued Kibby's roommate Carol, who had just joined in on the conversation. "Can I get anyone a Coke or something?"

Both girls nodded their heads. "Coke, please." Kibby continued, "Yeah, my mother does volunteer hours and hours teaching swimming and running all kinds of programs at the pool. Without my mother, probably nobody in Rockford would know how to swim. She's also deeply involved in the Girl Scouts, training leaders. But then she makes no money doing all that. No wonder we could never afford to move into a bigger house."

Carol brought in three bottles of Coke and sat down on the lumpy couch. "Didn't your dad complain about her being so busy doing stuff away from home? My dad would have had a fit."

"Never. In fact, I think he's proud of her and her accomplishments. She gets her name and face in the little local paper at least twice a year. I guess I'm proud of her, too, but I'm sure not going to lead the same life. Mother has hammered into us that we need to go to school to get out into the world. She didn't do it, but I'm doin' it."

Drinking too much at times was not the only thing that distracted Kibby's from studying. Her roommates and other friends were constantly asking for her time and attention. "Kibby, what am I going to do about Freddie?" Becky came to her one day. "Don't tell the other girls, but he wants me to go all the way with him, but I just don't want that. We make out for hours, and then he thinks I want it, but I don't. I want to wait for that very special guy."

The next day Carol would be at her door. "Kibby, help me get my parents off my back. They want to know absolutely everything I do every day. When are they going to let go of me? I have too much to do to talk to them every day on the phone. They'd come visit every other weekend if I let them. What do I say to them to get them to back off without hurting their feelings?"

Kibby didn't always know that to say to these gals, but she learned in one of her classes she should listen with all her attention but not offer advice. She found her friends usually came up with their own solutions when she did this. "Sounds like Freddie's pressuring you too much, and you're thinking that he isn't *the one*?" or "Your parents are needy, aren't they? They love you so much, but you are twenty years old now. You both need your own lives."

Kibby's second year of college soon turned into her third year. She came up with more rules: no going out in the evening except Friday and Saturday nights, getting home those nights by as close to midnight as possible, only two alcoholic drinks a weekend night, and no alcohol at any other time. The self-regulated rules began to pay off, and her grades improved.

—◊◊◊—

Probably the most traumatic event in Kibby's life during those college years was her involvement in a roommate's tragedy. Callie May was from Texas and from a family of much more wealth than the rest of them, but they all enjoyed her vibrant personality and her quirky sense of humor. She was openly promiscuous but the first to make fun of herself. "I bet the guy I marry will thank me for having all this sexual expertise. I'll be able to teach him a thing of two, and he'll love it. Y'all want some pointers?" Callie said with a wink of her eye. Her Texas accent added to her charm.

Kibby and Carol were the only ones home one Saturday night as they prepared for upcoming semifinals. They had been in bed thirty minutes when they got a call from the campus police. Kibby answered the phone. "This is the campus police. Is this the residence of Callie May Johnson?"

"Yes it is. Is there a problem? Where's Callie?"

"We're here at the campus health clinic with her. We're calling to make sure you're there before we bring her home. She's okay, but we don't want her to be alone at this time."

"What do you mean? What's happened?" Carol's eyes grew big staring at Kibby, trying to figure out to whom she was talking.

The campus policeman answered, "Callie has asked us to not disclose that information. She wants to talk to you herself."

"Both Carol and I are here. We're her roommates. Please do bring her home." Kibby hung up, unable to explain to Carol why the campus police were bringing Callie home.

The two roommates only had to wait ten minutes before the two campus police walked Callie down the hall and into their pod. She was a mess. Both her blouse and skirt were dirty and torn. Her usually immaculate hair was matted, dirt mashed into the wads of hair.

Callie's face was hardly recognizable. One eye was swollen shut and starting to show black-and-blue bruising. Her lip on the same side was sporting a butterfly bandage over some stitches. Her face had been cleaned up, but no amount of cleaning could hide the look of fear and shame in her one eye and the fact that she had been crying. She didn't look directly at her roommates but hung her head down, eye darting from side to side.

"Oh my God, Callie. Come in here, and lay down on the couch. Tell us what's happened to you. Can we get you anything?"

The police quickly left, seeing that Callie May was safely in her roommates' hands. They told her they would be back to talk to her again the next day. When Callie saw the sympathetic looks on her friends' faces, she began to cry again. Carol went to get her a glass of water, and Kibby sat with her on the couch, head in her lap.

Carol pulled up her chair close to the couch. "Callie, take a big breath. You're going to have to start at the beginning and tell us everything. Something awful has happened to you tonight, and you have to spill it all to us, every detail."

The words were not yet able to come out of Callie's mouth, so Kibby started talking in hopes of getting Callie to begin to tell what horrendous thing had happened. "When you left here, you were off to have beer with some friends of yours. You were all excited because your friends had said they wanted to introduce you to someone they thought you would like."

After a few sips of water and a few minutes to recover from her crying spell, Callie began to talk. "Yes, I was looking forward to meeting this guy. His name is Jason. We all went to my friends' fraternity house, where there was a small party going on. Jason and I sat on the stairs talking and getting to know each other. I was my usual chatty, flirty, Texas self, no more than usual. I'm sure, however, that I gave him the impression of being a loose, 'bad' girl. I guess I usually do, and I did have on my lowest-cut blouse."

Callie took in a few short breaths and sobbed, "But I always talk and act that way! That's who I am. I'm not really a bad, bad girl."

"Of course you're not. But were you drinking a lot?"

"I had a couple of drinks that Jason fixed for me. They tasted pretty strong, but I thought I could handle it. Come to think of it, I hadn't eaten since a light breakfast. You know, I've been trying to drop a little weight."

"Okay, what happened next?"

"We got up and danced. They played a bunch of Buddy Holly tunes, and you know how I love his stuff. I was feeling pretty sexy, and he was a very good dancer. After four or five dances, we ended up going outside to cool off and get some fresh air. We walked down the sidewalk about a block, and the next thing I knew I was on the ground, smashed into some bushes. Jason was ripping at my clothes, trying to get my skirt off.

"I fought like hell, and he didn't like that. I guess that's when he smashed my face. I don't remember anything else. But I don't really want to remember anything else. I know he raped me though. I'm hurt where I shouldn't." At this point Callie curled her whole body up into a tight ball, her knees almost to her chin.

"It was awful. I may be a flirt and a little loose talking, but I didn't deserve that. I'm not a whore! Am I? Do y'all think I'm a whore?"

"Of course not!" both girls exclaimed at the same time.

Callie began to sob again. Carol and Kibby let her cry for a while, her body loosening up some as Kibby rubbed her back and shoulders. After a few minutes of being quiet, she began talking again, mostly about how ugly Jason got. She couldn't forget the look of hate and then the look of glee on his face. "It was like turning a page in a book back and forth. One minute he was hate and the next, glee, and then back to hate again."

Kibby was horrified for her friend. The girls didn't know what to do to console her, so they just let her talk, and eventually helped her the best they could to take a long shower and wash her hair. Her face was such a mess, they were afraid to touch anywhere on her head. They put clean sheets on her bed, and she climbed in. The clinic had given her some tranquilizers, so she soon fell fast asleep.

Kibby and Carol also got into their beds but had a harder time falling asleep. They were worried about their roommate and friend. Callie was usually so confident and self-assured; it wasn't like her to be ashamed of her actions.

The next day, the campus police returned. They questioned Callie again, hoping she could tell them more than she had the night before. The police, however, were the ones with more information. By then, they had talked to Callie's friends who had introduced her to Jason. With what they had to offer and with some investigation, they found out that Jason had a very dark past. He had raped before when he was younger, but had gotten off with some counseling and a short time in a home for juvenile offenders. He had also been in trouble for breaking and entering and shoplifting.

Callie's friends had known he had been in a little trouble but were not aware of how severe it had been. A few days later, they came to see her and offered to help however they could. They, of course, were upset that they had put Callie in such a bad position.

Kibby found that was not the end of her roommate's story. Callie was unable to go back to her classes. She continued to blame herself for leading Jason on. Her roommates could not convince her that he was the wrongdoer, not her.

Callie May's parents said they wanted her to come home. They were not concerned enough for her welfare, however, to come see if she was okay. She refused to go home. So Callie was allowed to stay in the dorm until the end of the term, despite the fact that she was not attending any classes. She received limited counseling on campus. Everyone was hopeful that she would get her feet back on the ground and return to classes by the beginning of the next term.

Then things got even worse. Six weeks later, Callie told Kibby that she was pregnant. She was devastated. By then, Jason had been found and was being held in the campus jail. Callie was going to have to testify against him in court.

"I don't even want to look at him again, let alone spend time in a courtroom with him." Callie had continued to have nightmares of his changing face. She called it the look of the devil. The thought of carrying his child in her body was more than she could bear. "What can I do? I can't have the devil's baby. I want to throw up to think of what is inside of me."

Kibby and the other roommate took turns being in the pod with her, making sure she was never alone. Eventually Callie appeared more and more stable. She purchased a TV and watched it for hours, playing solitaire at the same time. She rarely left the pod.

One Friday night the roommates all agreed that she was ready to be left alone, so they left her for the first time. Kibby, however, started to worry after a few hours, so she dashed home. She found Callie laying facedown on her bed with the TV blaring. A half empty bottle of prescription tranquilizers was lying open on the bedside table. Kibby could not rouse her. She called the health clinic, and they sent the ambulance. Callie May was fortunately okay, saved by Kibby's premonition of disaster.

However, Callie was still pregnant with what she thought was a monster. She spent five nights in the clinic on suicide watch and with daily counseling. The nurses told Libby that they found small knife cuts all over her abdomen. None of them were life threatening or seemed to have bled much. Kibby thought they told the story of the hate for what was going on in her growing uterus.

While Callie May was in the clinic, Kibby, Carol and her other stunned friends talked daily that something had to be done. Going back to Texas with her family was not an option; there was not enough support there. Her mother had quit calling, as Callie frequently refused to talk to her.

Kibby made an appointment with the counselor whom she knew Callie had continued to see since the very beginning of the whole mess. "We're so worried about Callie. The way her other friends and I see it, she can't continue to carry this baby in her body. We think she'll continue to try to get rid of it by doing away with her own life. As Callie's counselor, is there anything you can do?"

"Thank you for coming to me. Callie is lucky to have such caring friends. I'm also worried about her and her future. Leave it with me for now, and I'll see what I can do."

"Thank you so much," Kibby said. "I appreciate what you're doing here, but please, call me for whatever reason. I don't want to just dump this in your lap, but we don't know what else we can do."

"What you should do is exactly what you've been doing. Be the best friend you can be to Callie. Listen to her, be there for her, and support her in any way you think of. You have been wonderful. Keep on being wonderful. Call me if you need to, and of course, I'll call if I think of anything else you can do as friends." Kibby left feeling much better but still nervous and worried for her friend.

Callie May ended up staying in the clinic for ten days. When she came home, the roommates had a little welcome home party for her, complete with balloons and ice cream. The last few days had been encouraging. She was smiling some and seemed happy to see all of them. She was watching some TV and eating regular meals.

After a few weeks of being home again, Kibby and the other roommates knew for sure that Callie was no longer pregnant. They didn't hear from the counselor, but they were pretty sure what she had arranged. Callie was definitely not the chatty, licentious person that she had been before, but she was mentally stable, having some joy in her day-to-day living. She enrolled in classes for the next term.

Callie was Kibby's roommate for another year. It turned out to be an interesting time for all, as Jason was brought to trial. Kibby attended as much of the trial as she had the time for, and they all had to testify in court regarding Callie's general behavior, especially regarding men and sex. Her language and the way she dressed were on public display. For much of the trial, Kibby felt like Callie was being charged and accused of committing a crime instead of being the *victim* of a crime.

One night during the trial, Carol and Kibby were taking a break from their studies when Carol said, "Callie seems to have become a scapegoat for newfound sexual freedom of women in the 1960s. Don't you agree?"

"Yes, I do. We even talked about it in my social behaviors class last week."

"You did? What was said?"

Kibby explained, "The professor said that women were now feeling more and more free to talk about sex and have sex. But society, men and women both, don't know what to think of that freedom. Men specifically feel threatened by less control over their sexual relationships. They don't know what their role is anymore and sometimes act out to try and gain control."

"Did he say anything about Callie's trial?

"Yes. He said that Jason's lawyer has tried to blame Callie for his violent attack on her, trying to show that she brought it on by the way she talked, behaved, and dressed. The lawyer has tried to make it look like Jason couldn't help himself because he was a male. The women of the 1960s, more or less, made him rape her. Can you believe it?"

"That's just not true. Jason is responsible for his actions. Just because Callie is free to dress and act provocatively doesn't mean he shouldn't get control of his sexual feelings."

"Callie came on to Jason but did not invite him to throw her into the bushes, rape her, and beat on her head. Men and society in general are going to have to accept that women have new freedoms and learn to deal with their impulses."

News reporters badgered the roommates, wanting personal interviews, but the girls were coached to not talk to anyone until the trial was over. Callie was surprisingly strong throughout, but then, she had a great cheerleading team behind her. Jason was eventually found guilty and given a jail sentence.

Kibby was relieved when it was all over but also relieved that Callie May's pregnancy was never publicly revealed. She felt confident that Callie May had done the right thing.

CHAPTER 5

"HURRY UP, KIBBY. WE HAVE to be in the parking lot at seven thirty or they'll leave without us," shouted Carol.

"Come on, Carol, I didn't want to go out tonight in the first place. I know you're anxious to meet some new guys, but frankly, I'm tired of these college boys who just want to party and try to get in our pants. Can't I just stay home? I need to study anyway. You can let them get in your pants. Besides, if I stay home, I can watch the *Dick Van Dyke Show* for a study break. You wouldn't want me to miss that, would you?"

"Are you kidding me? It's Saturday night. You've been studying all day, and you have all day tomorrow."

"Yeah, but semifinals are next week, and I still have a project to finish up." Kibby really didn't want to stay home; she wanted to not be sorry tomorrow that she'd stayed up too late. She was also aware that she had gained another few pounds and wasn't happy about it. Kibby somehow linked weight gain to ugliness, believing that only slim women were worth looking at. *Who would want to talk to me anyway?*

"I think you'll like these guys," Carol said, as if she had read Kibby's mind. "They're friends of Jake's and are almost all serious engineering majors. They aren't the usual party frat animals. Please! We can talk Jake into bringing us home if we aren't having a good time and the others want to stay."

Still reluctant, Kibby said, "Okay. Give me a minute to change clothes. Hopefully I can find something to fit into."

They got to Jake's house after 8:00 p.m., and the party was in full swing. Carol was right; this party looked different. Girls and guys were standing and sitting around the little apartment in small groups talking. There didn't appear to be much booze being consumed, as only a few people had beers in their hands. She liked that.

Carol took off to talk to Jake, so Kibby circled around, eavesdropping on various conversations. She settled on joining a group of four who were discussing their statistics class. Statistics had been the class she most dreaded since starting college. She had heard too many students complaining about how grueling it was.

A dark-haired guy with a brush cut was saying, "You would not believe this professor. He actually makes the class passable and maybe even interesting. There's a quiz at the end of every week. But he spends the whole week preparing you for it. By Thursday, if you have kept up with the homework, you feel superprepared. Then that's it; your final grade is based on all those weekly quizzes. Would you believe there's no final exam?"

The conversation changed as another student joined them, but Kibby wanted to hear more about this particular professor. She went over and tapped the crew-cut guy on the shoulder. He was kind of cute in a studious way. "Hi, I'm Kibby. I don't think we've met, but my roommate is a friend of Jake's. I'd really like to know more about your statistics professor's name. Is that class as great as it sounds?"

"Hi, my name is Richard, and, yes, it's the only way to do statistics. This guy actually makes sense of it all. The key is to keep up with all the work on a daily basis, and if there's something you're not getting, he's open to helping you out either in class or one to one in his office."

"Far out. I'm liking the sound of this guy."

"I'm an engineering student, but of all my classes, it's the one I had been dreading the most."

"Me too. Math has never been my thing, and I'm scared to death of failing this one class. I know a few students who have had to take it twice to get a passing grade. I'm just not willing to do that. I can't afford to flunk anything."

Richard and Kibby sat down on a couch and talked for a long time. He was indeed a serious student. She found out that he wanted to graduate as quickly as possible. In fact, he was already working part-time for an engineering firm in the city. They were expecting him to graduate and immediately be a full-time employee.

The two exchanged phone numbers and talked about going for coffee sometime. Kibby was impressed. On the way home, she told Carol of her conversation with Richard. "Coffee, not a peek in your pants. Can you believe it? Thanks, Carol, for the invite tonight. I had a good time and met someone I hope to see again."

"Hey, I think I see a spark in your eye for this guy."

"Yeah. Well, Richard is attractive enough, but I wish he were taller. Best of all, I didn't overdo the booze tonight and will be able to study tomorrow. I only had one beer all evening. My only regret: I missed Dick Van Dyke."

The next day Kibby put in a full day studying. About 4:00 p.m., she got called to the phone in their pod. "Hi, Kibby, are you game for that coffee tonight after dinner?"

At first she was puzzled, wondering who was on the other end of the phone. Then she remembered. *Oh my gosh, it's that cute crew-cut guy I met last night. He meant it that he wanted to see me again.*

"Hi, Richard. Your timing is perfect. I've been hard at the books all day and ready for a break."

"Me too. Want to meet me at the student union?"

"Super. How does seven o'clock sound?"

"Perfect."

She hurried to tell Carol of her phone call. "Well, to heck with my extra few pounds. He met me with them on, and he still wants to spend time with me. They must not be all that bad."

"Of course not. You go and have a great time." Carol rolled her eyes at her roommate. "Kibby, get over this weight thing. You look great. You're not Miss Slim Jim, but you're not one bit overweight.

I think it's your mother's paranoia talking. She's so scared of being overweight herself that she has made you the same way. We love you just the way you are!"

Kibby and Richard instantly hit it off and soon became a couple. Kibby felt she could just be herself with him. Most of their dates were going to the library, studying, and then finding a place to drink coffee and talk.

They frequented a few neighborhood coffeehouses where the atmospheres were dark and smoky. The regulars were mostly beatniks, bearded guys and long-haired gals wearing long, flowing clothing. They sat on pillows on the floor; people read poems, played guitars, or beat bongo drums, the music always interesting. Kibby, Richard, and their friends were a striking contrast with their khaki pants and worn-out sweaters but were as welcome at the coffeehouses as anyone else.

Although Kibby thought Richard was cute, she wasn't physically attracted to him at first. He was shy and self-conscious, never making a move on her. They did hold hands walking about campus, and he occasionally put his arm around her. He gave her quick pecks on the cheeks or lips when they said goodbye. Kibby liked it that way.

—⁂—

Right before Kibby was to go home for Christmas vacation, Richard did really kiss her. Not just a peck on the lips this time, but a kiss that went down in history.

They were sitting on the steps in front of the library, both avoiding the discussion of not seeing each other for a couple of weeks, both reluctant to go to their respective housing. The temperature was close to freezing and way too cold to be sitting outside for any length of time. A light drizzle had started. Kibby thought her hands and nose were going to freeze.

Eventually Richard reached over, touched her cold cheek, and drew her near by pressing lightly on the back of the neck. Kibby suddenly lost all concern for the weather. She felt warm from the top of her head to the bottom of her booted feet. Richard took his time with that kiss, making sure it would stay with her over the long holiday.

Indeed, that one kiss was the kiss that lasted a lifetime for both of them. Kibby went home to her family in Rockford with nothing else on her mind but that kiss. She wasn't unfamiliar with kissing; she wasn't even a virgin. She and her first love had cast away her virginity in the backseat of his parents' car years ago. Kibby couldn't be sure, but she didn't think Richard would forget her, either, while he went home to Oregon for Christmas.

When Kibby and Richard got back to Seattle, they were both ready for a second kiss. A few dates later, the second kiss was developing into a whole lot more.

Richard had some help realizing that condoms would soon be needed. A friend had told him before the Christmas break that he better kiss Kibby so she would not forget about him while they were apart. That same friend sat him down again and said, "So, Richard, you and Kibby seem to have gotten the kissing thing down pat. Have you stopped to think that maybe you better have some condoms on hand in case you two get bored with just kissing?"

"I guess you're right. I never thought of that. The last thing I need is to get her pregnant. Graduation has to happen before I can think of anything serious with her. Thanks, buddy."

So Richard went to a drugstore. Blushing to his fingertips, he made his way to the back pharmacy counter. His friend had told him condoms had to be directly purchased from the pharmacist; they couldn't be bought at the front counter. He poked around, faking an interest in cold remedies and headaches for at least ten minutes. Out of the corner of his eye, he watched the ancient pharmacist behind the high counter, trying to decide if the man was going to be a nice guy or an old ogre. He couldn't make up his mind one way or another, so he stepped right up to the old guy. *Why do they have to make this so hard?*

"Excuse me, I'm wondering if I could purchase a pack of condoms?"

The gray-haired, wrinkled-skinned pharmacist looked out over his reading glasses and gave Richard the evil eye. "You don't look old enough to know how to use condoms, young man. Are you buying these for your dad?" Richard detected a sarcastic smile behind the ancient one's eyes.

"No, they aren't for my dad. I happen to be a junior at Seattle U."

"Okay, then, do you know how to use them?" said the pharmacist, turned ogre.

By this time, Richard had just about had it with the old man's attitude. Condoms were legal, and he didn't have to be interrogated to buy them. "I guess I'll find out soon enough. Do you want to sell them to me or not?"

He got out of there with the condoms in hand, but he wasn't sure he would ever repeat the experience. If he could have afforded it, he would have bought a lifetime supply so he wouldn't have to ever do it again.

—m—

Carol and Kibby were enjoying a beer they had sneaked into their pod while listening to an Everly Brothers' marathon on the radio. All the roommates were thrilled that Kibby had found a boyfriend and had accepted him into their circle of friends.

Carol turned to Kibby and said, "You guys are made for each other, you know that? In fact, I can see way into the future: Richard, a handsome, famous, and rich designing engineer for a very prestigious firm, makes partner in five years. Kibby Jane, his gorgeous wife, a well-renowned social worker, completes the writing of her first textbook at the young age of thirty-five. The two of them live in a huge home designed by Richard's own firm. They begin a family only after their careers are well on their way. Of course, money is never an issue for this handsome, brilliant couple."

"You are too funny, Carol."

"Man, I wish I could find my Prince Charming now. Hey, I helped you find yours; where's mine?"

—⁓⁓—

As it happened, Kibby's parents, Helen and Andrew, were in Seattle in early February and were able to meet Richard. They had come to the city to make purchases for Andrew's company, wanting to get there before the World's Fair opened in April. The city would then be a zoo all year. They liked Richard very much and were quick to let Kibby know it. "We like that he is such a serious student and that his future is a priority. He has great manners and seems to treat you with respect."

Helen liked that the couple's backgrounds were similar. Richard had grown up in a small community similar to Rockford. His parents did not have the money to help him through school, so he had to work in the summers, apply for scholarships, and, now, work part time.

On the drive home to Rockford from Seattle, the Kindles had much to talk about. They had seen the Space Needle in the last throes of its construction. How could they miss seeing it? The structure could be seen from almost everywhere in the city, an amazing sight.

But more exciting than the Space Needle was Kibby's beau. Helen said, "They both still have over a year to go before graduating. Anything could happen from now until then, but maybe there's a chance for a lasting future for these two."

"Now don't count your chickens before they hatch, Helen. You don't know at all what's going through their minds. They have their own dreams of careers and futures. You'd be furious if our parents would have planned out our future for us."

"You're right again, Andrew. Let's just go home and see if we can finish raising the wild one. That's who we need to keep an eye on, not Kibby Jane. She sowed a few wild oats, I know, but Roberta Jo has a whole hundred acres of them."

"Never fear; Roberta Jo is going to be able to take care of herself. She may look like a wild one, but she's like you. When she knows what she wants, believe me, she'll go for it. Don't you remember that Little Miss Oliver who went off to college, regardless of where she came from? Let's just hope Roberta Jo soon figures out what she wants."

—m—

It seems Richard forgot (or was too shy, or too broke) to buy more condoms once the couple went through the pack he had purchased from the ancient pharmacist. It was that simple a mistake. Like mother, like daughter...Kibby was very fertile.

When Kibby told Richard the news that her period was not happening, he gasped, just as she had gasped. They looked at each other, took a deep breath, and decided immediately they would get married.

"But can we afford it?" Richard was first to say. "We would both have to move out of our inexpensive living situations and somehow pay for an apartment of some kind."

"Somehow, we'll just do it. We have friends who have gotten married and are happy; we can too." Kibby spoke confidently, but failed to add, "But they don't have a baby to take care of."

Two days after making the decision, Kibby's second thoughts came bouncing to the surface. "I don't think I can have a baby and finish school too. And Richard has to keep going to school. He can't quit and go to work full time to support a family. He's so close to the end and has such a wonderful future as an engineer. What am I going to do?" she confided in Carol, as always.

"Well, as I see it, your other choice is to have an abortion. They're still illegal but possible. You hear of gals having them all the time; just ask Callie May. I'm sure we can find out where and how."

"You know, Carol, I think I'm going to have to tell my mother I'm pregnant. She's going to be madder than hell, but she'll help me figure out what to do. Oh God, I'm going to get that Helen *look of scorn*, I just know it."

Kibby went home for the weekend. She and Helen sat at the dining room table where all Kindle discussions, serious or humorous, took place. Kibby broke the news, explaining that she and Richard had agreed to get married, but Kibby, on her own, was having second thoughts.

As predicted, she got the *look of scorn* from her mother, along with a few choice words. Something like, "How could this be happening? I thought I taught you everything when you were little, and I've certainly given you many warnings since then?" After a few minutes of ranting, Helen backtracked, as was her way. "Okay, Kibby Jane, we've got a problem, we'll work it out. What do *you* want to do?"

"I'm scared. I'm only twenty years old. I'm not ready to take care of a baby! I want to do social work. I want to have my own apartment, take care of adults, and help with their problems, not change diapers and have my own problems. But I do love Richard. He's been so caring and sweet and responsible through this whole thing. I want to marry him so much, but not like this! We don't have any money. He has a little bit of an income but not enough to take care of three people. Where will be live? How do we even buy groceries?" Relieved that her mother had slipped into her helping mode, Kibby couldn't stop the flow of words.

"There are other options, you know? You could have an abortion, or you could give the baby up for adoption. I'll help you deal with either of those options if that's what you choose."

"They both sound dreadful."

"Your father and I would much rather you get married, of course. We like Richard a lot, you know. We would help you with money as much as we could, if that's what you decide to do."

Andrew had joined them at the table when he came into the house for lunch. Once Helen told him Kibby's news, he kept quiet, letting Helen lead the conversation. He nodded his head occasionally to let Kibby Jane know he agreed with what she was saying.

"There is third option. It's an option that I would have the most difficulty supporting. You could have the baby, keep it, and raise it on your own. Your chances of finishing college would be almost nil though. Being a single parent of an infant isn't an easy task. But, again it's your choice, and your father and I will help with what you decide. Isn't that right, Andrew?"

Andrew again nodded his head. "You bet."

The three sat back and were silent for a few minutes. Helen finally spoke up again. "You need to think this through overnight and talk to Richard on the phone. He needs to know you are having these second thoughts. We do need to act on any of the choices immediately. Promise me this: keep asking yourself, 'What do *I* want to do?'"

Helen had carefully avoided eye contact with Andrew throughout the whole conversation with Kibby Jane. She remembered only too well that they had had a similar discussion twenty-four years before about their own future.

Once they were alone and in bed, Andrew said to Helen, "Right now, Kibby Jane needs our help, not our emotions. We have to focus on her and leave out our own feelings. But maybe it's time we told the girls that you had that abortion before they were born and before we got married. I think it might help her to know that we understand her predicament."

Helen sat bolt upright in their bed. "No. You promised me, Andrew. You gave me your word that we would never tell anyone. Promise me again."

"Okay, Helen. I promise. I just wanted you to consider it. That's all. We won't tell her, if it is still that important to you."

Helen laid back in bed and put her arm around Andrew stroking his whiskery cheek. "Parenting doesn't get any easier once the kids are grown, does it? I hate being such a hard core mother to these girls. No wonder they get so angry with me. I want to be soft but I end up so rigid. What I want is to save them from some of the hardships we have had. But it's not working, is it?

Helen got no answer but felt better after talking it all out with Andrew. She still cried herself to sleep that night thinking of her abortion, the baby that she never knew, and that question that always came back: Did she do the right thing?

In the wee hours of the morning, Helen whispered to Andrew, "The last thing I want is for Kibby Jane to decide to have an abortion. I'm sure telling her that I had one isn't going to keep her from going that route. I know we are right not to tell her. I think it's going to be hard enough for her to show the world that she is pregnant and not married. It is 1962 and not 1940, and getting pregnant before you're married is more acceptable now. But most people still don't really approve."

"But we can't make the decision for our daughter. All we can do is support her in the decision that she makes for herself or that Richard and she make together. Thank goodness Richard appears to be such a responsible, smart young man."

"That's for sure. I know what I want them to do. Cross your fingers that they come to the same conclusion."

—ΩΩ—

When Kibby went down to her old room the night after telling her parents, she was fairly certain what her decision was going to be. She had ruled out the abortion because it just sounded too scary. Girls actually died from bad abortions. If it had been legal, she might have given it more thought, but it was too dark and dangerous.

She remembered her former roommate Callie May and her situation. Kibby knew she was nowhere close to that predicament. She was carrying Richard's baby in her belly; Callie had been carrying a devil in her belly. When she thought of a little Richard or Kibby growing inside of her, she was excited, wondering what that baby might be and look like.

Giving the baby up for adoption and raising a child on her own meant she would still have to go through with the pregnancy. She would probably have to drop out of school for a quarter in her last year, maybe never getting back to finish. A million secrets would have to be kept from friends and relatives. Besides, she loved Richard and really did want to marry him.

In the back of her mind, Kibby was thinking that being pregnant was like being seriously sick. She had had much of that in her youth, with polio and earlier, with rheumatic fever. She hadn't wanted those illnesses, either, but she had learned that you have to deal with what is handed to you.

But Kibby did what her mother suggested and called Richard and told him of her second thoughts and of her conversation with her parents. She heard Richard take a big breath. "I confess that I've had those second thoughts as well."

He was silent for a few seconds, and then said, "Before you say any more, forgive me for having to do this on the phone...but...Kibby Jane Kindle, will you marry me? I love you and want to spend the rest of my life with you. I've nothing to offer you at this point but my love and my future. I have no money, but I think we can make it. Just don't expect anytime soon that mansion and fame that Carol dreamed up for us."

Kibby smiled, sighed, and fell back onto her childhood bed.

—m—

"Okay, mother. Are you ready for what *I* want to do?" Kibby marched into the kitchen and gave her mother her most confident look.

Despite her restless night, Helen managed to look calm and collected. "Before you say anything, let me go get your father so we can discuss this together as a family."

Fortunately her little sister, Roberta Jo, had spent the night with a friend and wasn't in the house to be part of the drama, and the three had been able to talk freely. Sitting at the table again, sipping their freshly made coffee, Kibby said, "Richard actually proposed to me on the phone last night. He loves me and truly wants me to be his wife. He's ready to do whatever is necessary to make a marriage and to continue with his plans." Kibby looked directly into her mother's eyes and then into her daddy's eyes. "I've decided to marry him and have the baby. That's what I want to do."

Andrew let out a sigh of relief and spoke up first. "That's wonderful, Kibby Jane. Your mother and I hoped that'd be your decision. We're ready to help you however we can. We love you, and we think you're capable of doing whatever you have to do to ensure your future. I like Richard and look forward to having him as my son-in-law."

Helen took a few extra minutes to breathe before saying anything. For once, she let Andrew do the talking. Well, she let him do the talking for the first few minutes anyway, before she jumped right into the details.

"Well, I guess we've lots to do then, don't we? We need to plan a wedding as soon as possible. We can't have you walking down the aisle in a maternity dress. The relatives are going to be talking as it is. And promise me, Kibby Jane, don't go overboard eating. You just can't gain a bunch of weight. It'll only help to make you look pregnant."

Helen was all business. Kibby only assumed her father had also spoken for his wife and that she approved of the decision.

The small wedding took place a month later. A few of the local Kindle friends and relatives and a few of the bride's and groom's friends attended. Richard's parents were elderly and not well enough to travel for it. Kibby thought a great time was had by all at the reception following the church wedding at her parent's home.

They were young: twenty and twenty-one years old, but not the first couple to be so young and pregnant. The relatives didn't know for certain that Kibby was expecting, but she figured the quickly arranged wedding told the story. All Kibby could do was follow her mother's instructions to keep her mouth shut and let them talk behind her back. She was willing to live with it. She and Richard had as good a chance of making a good marriage at their age as anyone. They both thought they were doing the right thing.

CHAPTER 6

KIBBY AND RICHARD FOUND A small basement apartment located close to the firm where Richard worked. They chose the area because the rents were cheaper. It hadn't been easy to find anything in 1962, as Seattle was abuzz with the World's Fair soon to open.

The apartment had its own entrance, but they had to go through an unfinished part of the basement to get to it, walking by the water heater, a utility sink, shelves overflowing with storage boxes and the furnace, overhead pipes and wires everywhere. The living room and kitchen were of good size, but the bedroom and bathroom were tiny. The apartment did come furnished with odds and ends of obvious thrift store items. The floors were linoleum and cold in the winter. Every room had at least one small window placed high up on the wall. The low rent was the best part, and they were grateful for that. In fact, they loved their *cozy* little first home.

Kibby's and Richard's friends were all living in similar situations, the Bohemian life of the early sixties. They didn't have the money to go out, so a splurge was to buy a six-pack of beer and make it last three nights, sometimes three weeks. One beer was Kibby's personal pregnancy limit anyway. The price tag on food was the biggest concern.

Richard continued working part time. His bosses even gave him a bit of a raise when they heard he had gotten married and was expecting a baby. He kept his full schedule at school as well.

Kibby also kept her school schedule for the remainder of their junior year. She enjoyed cooking for the two of them and went beyond the tuna casserole recipe in no time at all, always keeping to a tight budget, lots of beans and rice. Through the summer, they both went to summer school to pick up a few extra courses so they could graduate as soon as possible. In the fall Kibby took only a few classes so she would be able to keep on studying when she had the baby in November.

One especially cold evening, Kibby snuggled up to Richard on their thin-cushioned couch. "Thank goodness for the monthly check Mother and Daddy send us every month. I don't think we could make it otherwise."

"Hey, did I tell you your dad said we could use their second car, the '53 Pontiac, for as long as we need it?"

"You're kidding…no, you didn't tell me. How did that come about?"

"We had a conversation about how we were going to manage the fall quarter with having so far a drive to the university while having one of us stay home with the baby. And he offered us the car."

"Fantastic. That'll really help."

"My dad said he could slip us some money once in a while too. Maybe we can save that for unexpected things that aren't written into the budget."

To Kibby, it all felt like a great adventure, out of her parents' and even roommates' clutches. She had loved her roommates and her interactions with them, but they had also been demanding of her time and attention. Having no set hours that they had to be home and being able to eat when and where and what they wanted was freeing.

In many ways the newlyweds were getting to know each other for the first time. Kibby soon found that Richard was more driven than ever. His other commitments, which included classes, studying, and his work at the firm had to come before his family and their social life. He frequently had to be away all day and into the evenings. As a result, she spent many evenings and large parts of weekends on her own in their sparse living quarters. Before the baby, it didn't matter because it gave her time to study and have alone time, which had always been important to her.

They had been given a little TV, which gave her a break from studying. Dick Van Dyck was still a favorite, but the nighttime soap opera *Peyton Place* quickly moved into first place. She was thrilled to have caught Marilyn Monroe's rendition of "Happy Birthday" to President Kennedy on their tiny TV sitting on its rolling trolley.

On occasion, Kibby felt socially uncomfortable that they were so young and expecting a baby. Comments like "Oh, my goodness, you're expecting? And didn't you say you've only been married a few months?" could not be avoided from time to time. Kibby imagined finger counting and light bulbs going off. She was so glad she wasn't living in Rockford, where their predicament would be the talk of the town. She figured her mother was getting raised eyebrows from the Rockford community.

Kibby was healthy and carried the baby easily. Her growing and moving belly brought back memories of previous loss of power over her own body, reminiscent of polio days. She was often hungry but allowed herself only small, healthy portions. She gained less than twenty-five pounds during the entire pregnancy, but she felt huge.

Kibby's mother still preached the importance of not becoming a fat girl. "How much did you weigh at your doctor's appointment this month?" was the usual question from her mother after each of her checkups, not "What did the doctor have to say? Is everything okay?" that Kibby hoped to hear.

November came quickly for the busy newlyweds. Unfortunately for the rumor mill, the labor pains came a month early. Coming late would have been much better for those counting the months on their fingers.

In the last month of her pregnancy, Kibby had dealt with a yeast infection that her doctor wanted to clear up before the baby's birth. The doc said the infection could affect the baby as it came through the birth canal. The remedy involved douching with a dark purple dye. Kibby had a surprise when, shortly after she inserted the dye, her water broke and it, too, was purple. Everything went purple: her legs were purple, her hands were purple, the bathroom floor was purple. Even the toilet water, after repeated flushings, was purple.

With his work and study schedule, Richard's absence from home when Kibby's water broke was assured. Thinking he had weeks before the birth, he was not on alert to keep in close contact, checking in regularly to see if she needed him. Kibby left messages at his workplace and with friends, but there was no finding him quickly.

So, after cleaning up the purple as best she could, Kibby dealt with the labor pains on her own. And…it just happened to be Halloween night. Neighborhood kids kept showing up at their outside door for trick-or-treating. Kibby was diligently running—well, sort of running, maybe waddling—up and down the stairs to deliver treats. Little did she know that the physical activity was speeding up the labor process.

Sometime, between dealing with purple and dealing with costumed trick-or-treaters, she called Carol. "Uh, Carol, what're you doing? Are you busy?"

"Not really. I'm grabbing some supper before I go out to study. What's up?"

"Well, it seems this baby is going to come early, and I can't find Richard." Kibby suddenly felt scared and more than a little desperate. Up until then, she had been too busy to worry about being alone at a time when she needed help. The tension was obvious in her voice.

"Oh, my gosh, Kibby. Do you need to get to the hospital now?"

"No, I don't think so. I'm sure I still have plenty of time. The contractions aren't that close together yet. But I just wondered if you could be near a phone so I could call you if I do need to get there and I haven't found Richard yet."

"Of course. I can just study here and wait by the phone. But do you want me to come over and keep you company? I can do that."

Kibby was tempted to say, "Yes, please come," but she knew Carol needed to study. "No, I don't think so. Richard might be here just any time. I'm not that desperate. But I sure wish the trick-or-treaters would stop coming so I wouldn't have to keep going up and down the stairs."

"Just turn off the lights, and they'll think you aren't home. You can sit in the dark or go back and lay down in your bedroom where you can turn on the light and they won't see it."

"Great idea. I'm going to do that right now. And don't worry, I'll be okay. Just wait by the phone."

Richard got home about a half hour later to find their apartment pitch black and Kibby lying on their bed, trying to get comfortable. "What is all the purple on the toilet and bathroom floor?"

Kibby tried to explain it all to him, but he only look puzzled. They waited around, counting the minutes between contractions until eight or nine o'clock, when they decided it was time to get to the hospital.

Kibby was relieved to have him with her but saw that he was exhausted. He kept falling asleep and wasn't all that much help as she tried to cope with the pain. She finally sent him home to get some sleep. The nurses didn't want Richard hanging around anyway.

Kibby had been warned that labor would be bad but was given no instruction on how to deal with it. The nurses taught her how to breathe and pant with the pain, a new procedure that they had themselves just learned. But Kibby was uncomfortable sitting, standing, and lying down. At one time, she walked down the hall to the hospital phone and called Carol, her mother, and few other friends just for something to do and for some company. Sitting on the hard stool to talk on the phone was not comfortable either, so she didn't talk long.

The night dragged on until about five o'clock in the morning. After one of seemingly a million examinations, the nurse told her she needed to go to the delivery room. "It's time."

Kibby's dark-brown eyes got darker. *Dealing with the pain is dreadful, but how am I ever going to get this baby out of my body?* She knew she had no choice. She was able to squeak out a request between contractions that were now almost constant. "Okay, but would you call my husband and tell him to get here? He'll want to be at the hospital when the baby comes."

"Sure, but after we get him on the phone, you'll need to get yourself in the delivery room. We'll come help you."

A few minutes later, the nurse returned. "We have tried a couple of times to reach your husband, but there's no answer."

Kibby was not alarmed and managed to tell the nurse between contractions, "Richard's a supersound sleeper. I'm sure he's there but not hearing the phone. Just call him again, and let it continue to ring. He'll get it eventually. I do it all the time to get him up. I really do want him here."

The nurse did as she had been told. When she got back to the labor room, she was surprised to see Kibby on the floor crawling toward the door. She scurried over to her bulging body, holding both shoulders to give some needed support. "Oh my, Kibby, dear. What're you doing on the floor?"

Kibby gasped, "The pains were…so bad I couldn't stand up. When I tried…I was afraid the baby…would just fall out. Oh my God…I can…feel him…coming out!" She didn't realize she had begun yelling between words and gasps of air.

Kibby could not be persuaded to stand up and walk. So the nurses let her crawl on hands and knees to the delivery room, supporting her as best they could. They hoped Richard wouldn't show up to find his screaming, disheveled pregnant wife crawling on the floor. She made it to the delivery room and was helped up onto the table just as her doctor arrived, ready to deliver the baby.

The delivery was quick and uneventful. Richard had arrived and was in the waiting room to receive the news that he had a son. He joined her in a room once she was settled there. A nurse brought their baby boy in an hour or so later. "Look, he has all his fingers and all his toes. He's perfect!"

Young, naive Kibby frowned at the nurse. "Well, of course. Why wouldn't he be perfect? Aren't all newborns perfect?"

Kibby and baby Bart stayed at the hospital for the customary three days. Richard continued with his studies and classes, going to see them as frequently as he could.

—ɯ—

Kibby was pleased that she only missed three days of school but also had two major tests that had to be made up later. All her assignments were, thankfully, up to date.

At Kibby's request, Helen traveled to Seattle as soon as she could, arriving home the same day Kibby and Bart did. Surprised to hear they were home so soon, she reported that she had stayed in the hospital for ten days for each of her babies. She stayed with the young family for two weeks in the little apartment. It was tight, but everyone did what they had to do, the inexperienced couple needing all the help they could get. Helen slept in the bed with Kibby; Richard slept on the couch, continuing his work and study schedule.

At the university, no one knew that Kibby had had a baby. She liked it that way. She was a student at school and a struggling new mother at home.

Breastfeeding did not come easy, probably because Kibby was nervous about doing it right. Helen told her that many premature babies have a weak sucking ability. Both mother and baby were frustrated.

Helen was supportive but was not always the best nurse. Having never experienced breastfeeding herself, she could only offer suggestions that made sense to her. Bottle feeding had been the thing to do when she'd had her girls. However, her recommendations regarding the best way to bathe the baby, or the best place for the baby to sleep, or how often to feed the baby were helpful.

In fact, it was Helen's idea that Kibby try sipping a beer before and during the feedings. By this time, Kibby's nipples were sore and even bleeding. She couldn't relax when there was so much pain involved. Bravo! The beer worked wonderfully. For weeks Kibby drank a beer every evening for the best nursing of the day.

By the time Helen left, a routine existed that Kibby and Richard could manage on their own. The young couple couldn't believe how much they loved their little boy and were completely committed to the task of parenthood.

—⚒—

After Helen left, reality set in for twenty-one-year-old Kibby. She was a mother, and she had the biggest responsibility for this little one. Richard did what he could but was so busy outside their home. She realized she had been unrealistic in her preparations. They didn't have enough diapers or baby clothes. She had to do the laundry every day without relief. Buying more was not an option on their budget. Having enough groceries on had was a problem. She couldn't just go out to buy something when they ran out, and she couldn't always reach Richard by phone to tell him to bring something home. Even the smallest task was difficult when this crying, spitting, peeing, and pooping baby needed her attention. Forget reading a book or cooking something interesting for dinner.

Once again Kibby felt like the "fat girl," her body out of control. She couldn't get into many of her regular clothes, especially pants and skirts. She had to go to school three or four days a week, so she couldn't just hang around in her nightgown or baggy pants all day. Helen had lent her a wraparound skirt, which turned out to be the one thing she could fit into. For the first three weeks, she had to wear that hand-me-down wraparound skirt every day to school. All she could vary was the top that fit over her still-bulging body.

"For goodness' sake, Richard. My mother's skirt! I don't want to be this fat person. To think Mother had been so happy to give me this god-awful thing. When I can finally get into my pants, we're going to burn this skirt. I'll never wear it again, and I'm not giving it back to her! I didn't like it when she wore it. I hate it now!"

Every week life got a little easier as Kibby became a more competent parent. In fact, one day she decided she had her act together enough that she could cook a special dinner and ask her ex-roommate over to join them. She had it all worked out until she realized that she needed a can of creamed soup. She would need the soup way before Richard or Carol could bring it to her.

She thought, *I can do this. I can pack up Bart, put him in the car, and drive to the store.* It took her thirty minutes to get him ready to put in the car, however. Winter weather required her to put on his little hand-me-down bunting suit. What with getting Bart ready and herself presentable, she was exhausted.

She got him to the car but wasn't sure where to put him. She eventually tucked him in a bundle of baby blankets in a cardboard box she found in the back seat. She drove the ten minutes to the store, only to realize she would have to take him into the store with her. *I can't leave him in the car!*

The parking lot was as icy as a frozen pond, and she was terrified she would slip and drop him while carrying him to the door. She made it, but then her arms were getting tired. She didn't know where to put him while she shopped (all this for one can of soup!) and waited in line at the checkout. She managed to lay him all bundled up in the bottom of a grocery cart, but by this time, he was howling because he was so hot. She halfway unbundled him, fanning him to try to cool him off.

In the meantime, all the housewives also standing around, waiting in line, were staring at her. She wanted to get in their faces and scream, *I'm doing the best I can! Don't tell me you haven't been in my position.*

One young woman finally offered to help, but by then, Kibby was angry. "I'm fine." Kibby finally got through the checkout again, having to bundle him up to make the return trip to the car.

The whole procedure was an hour and a half long—all for a frickin' can of soup. At home again, Kibby sat on the couch to feed Bart. She had a silent cry thinking about this being the rest of her life!

With Carol's help to make the salad when she got there, Kibby did manage to put the dinner together. When Richard arrived she told them the story of her trip to the store. They all had a giggle at her expense. It felt good to laugh.

The couple arranged their schedules to allow for minimum babysitting help. Consequently, Kibby spent even more time alone in their underground abode than she had before. She watched so much stupid stuff on TV, she thought her eyes were going square. She sat feeding and rocking Bart, silently crying some days. Learning to read and feed him at the same time was a revelation.

Carol came by frequently, sometimes to babysit for a few hours and sometimes to just keep Kibby company. On one such visit, Kibby confided in Carol for the first time. They had just put Bart to sleep in his laundry basket, and were sipping a beer. "I didn't go off to university to end up in this position. I went off to university to have a career and to get away from Rockford and see the world. What have I done? I could have had an abortion and been done with it. Richard and I could've continued to be a couple and then gotten married when it felt right. For Pete's sake, I could have gone off somewhere and just had the baby at one of those unwed mother places and given Bart up for adoption. I've done just what my mother did and what I swore I'd never do."

"What're you saying, Kibby? Think about it. You're talking about Bart, this precious little guy. You and Richard are crazy about him. I get it that it's hard now, but do you really think you could give him up to a stranger?"

Kibby sank back into her chair and hung her head down. "I guess not."

"And even worse, do you think you could have gone through with an abortion? And poo on not having a career. You can still do that. You're soon going to finish your degree, and you'll always have that. You can have the career later when Bart is older. You'll still be so young."

"You're right, of course. I love this little bundle of trouble. I feel connected to him like I have never been connected to anyone. I guess I wouldn't want it any other way. Thank you for listening to me and setting me straight." After Carol left, Kibby felt much better. However, that same regret came crept back into her head from time to time.

—⁓—

Kibby did graduate at the end of that summer. Richard graduated four months later and immediately started working full time at the firm. He didn't slow down his hours away, but Kibby had further adjusted to her time alone with Bart. Much to her delight, she had quickly lost her baby fat, and she was happy in her role as a young wife and mom.

The couple had many friends. None of them had babies, but they were all crazy about Bart, and they took him under their wings, welcoming him everywhere they went. Richard and Andrew bought a 1940s Willys Jeep together, allowing the young couple to go jeeping with their friends and a chance to have outings as a family.

The young couple became eligible for a mortgage on a little two-bedroom house in their same area. They furnished it with their own cheap secondhand furniture. It had a yard for their toddler to play in and even a washer and dryer for the never-ending diapers. Someone had to sit on the washer when it was spinning, or it would make its way across the kitchen floor. But Kibby learned to grab a book to entertain herself while she sat on it, and Bart thought it was great fun to sit on his mother's lap while it did its overzealous vibration. The couple could now afford a six-pack every Friday night and frequently drank the whole thing in just one night!

During this period, sisters Kibby and Roberta became good friends, more so than before. Roberta had followed her sister's lead and also dropped her middle name. She was going to college just a few miles away and would frequently come for the day or even just for dinner. Kibby had taken an interest in cooking and loved having an extra dinner guest, especially a guest who was glad to try her culinary experiments.

Occasionally, Kibby still thought of that career that she didn't have. Three and a half years after Bart's birth, they had another baby, a girl, Lisa Anne. The career went further back on the stove.

It just so happened that Roberta Jo went home for a weekend in Rockford right after Kibby told her of the pregnancy. Roberta was too excited to keep her mouth shut. "Guess what, Mother? Kibby and Richard just found out they're going to have another baby. Isn't that far out?"

Helen didn't look very excited about the news. In fact, she was frowning. *Uh oh, I shouldn't have said anything. Mother's not happy about this.*

Helen had that famous *look of scorn* on her face that both Kibby and Roberta had learned to avoid. She finally said, "I sure hope they know what they're doing. Can they afford to have another baby now?"

"Of course they can afford it. Richard has a great job. They're certainly living within their means, and Bart is almost three years old. They shouldn't wait too much longer to have another."

The scorn was still there, so Roberta added, "Aren't you happy for them?"

Helen adjusted her face to a little more pleasant look. "Yes, of course I'm happy for them. I just worry about them. It hasn't been easy."

"They're fine. I think it will be great to have a new niece or nephew running around."

Roberta never told Kibby how their mother reacted to the news. She couldn't understand how Helen could be so negative about a new grandchild. *Sometimes she can be so hateful, so critical. Why couldn't she be more agreeable? I never know if she will react this way or be supportive.*

Kibby knew all about those surprise reactions that could come from Helen. During the days of their early marriage, she and Richard had an argument over a purchase that she had made. Kibby thought she was doing a fantastic job keeping to their budget. She felt she deserved a splurge, so had spent ten dollars on an outfit she found on sale at the May Company. In retrospect, she knew she shouldn't have even gone into the store. But she and Carol had met for a lunch downtown and decided to do a little window shopping. A neighbor had taken Bart for a few hours. "It never hurts to have a little look around at what's new" was Kibby's mantra.

Well, Richard was not happy with the purchase. They argued, not for the first time, but maybe a little louder than usual. Richard ended up storming off early for work. Kibby continued to be upset that he was being so stingy. She called Helen.

"Mother, I need your help. Is this a good time to talk?"

"Sure, what can I do for you?"

"Richard and I had a huge argument that started last night. But he's still angry and being so stingy, I can't believe it." Kibby told her about the purchase and how he didn't understand her needs. "I'm so mad at him. I want to pack up Bart and come home. Are you and Daddy going to be there?"

Helen was not at all understanding. "Oh for goodness' sake, Kibby Jane. You know good and well that Richard's right. You should have asked him if it was okay to have a little splurge. You could have pointed out how you have been doing such a good job and that the outfit was a good buy."

"But, Mother, I did tell him all that, and he wouldn't listen. I thought you would understand and be supportive. He's gone so much of the time; surely I deserve something special once in a while."

"Yes, but you told him in the heat of the argument. You may deserve it, but you needed to discuss it before you bought it."

"Okay, but can I come home? I want him to know how mad I am."

"No, you can't come home. You need to work this out with him. Maybe you both need to compromise a little. Anyway, you both need to cool off and then have a discussion and not an argument. I'm not doing this to be mean, but to give you a lesson in how to work out problems in your marriage. Running away is never a good option."

Kibby sighed. "All right, Mother. I'm sure you're right…as usual. It does seem kind of silly now."

"Sit down and think about it for a while. I'm sure you'll see that coming here is not a solution."

"Okay, I'll talk to you later."

And of course, they did work it out. And Kibby did learn a lesson in making a marriage work.

—m—

Kibby Jane kept busy and productive. She joined the YWCA's wives' club. She took classes on childcare and parenting that were helpful and social. She taught regular swimming lessons and swimming for handicapped children at the Y.

After a few years she was asked to be in charge of one of the many Y clubs. It proved to be a great boost to her self-esteem, and she enjoyed the new responsibilities involved. She sat on the board of directors and was involved in managing many of the activities that were offered.

Kibby even became the treasurer of the organization, much to Richard's surprise. She had been avoiding math tasks since junior high. Years later, she would say that it took years for the Seattle Y to straighten out the books after she was treasurer. All was rewarding for her, however, and helped her to become an interesting woman.

Did Kibby and Richard do the right thing? They thought so.

Part Three
Roberta Jo: 1963

My mission in life is not merely to survive, but to thrive, and to do so with some passion, some compassion, some humor and some style.

—Maya Angelou

CHAPTER 7

"OKAY, PATTY, THE COAST IS clear. Mother's in bed, so we can get through the house and to the bedroom undetected." Roberta Jo and her cousin Patty had been out with friends and had a few beers. Patty was only seventeen and underage. Roberta Jo was eighteen and of legal age for beer, but her parents would not have approved of their drinking. Not only that, but they also would not have approved of who they were with that night.

Once they got safely into the basement bedroom, Roberta Jo whispered, "I don't know what Mother thinks goes on when we hang out with those guys. They're just good friends," She turned the radio down low to listen to The Beach Boys sing "Surfin' USA."

Patty and Roberta Jo had spent most of the summer together for the second year in a row—the first month at Patty's house in Colorado and the second month at Roberta Jo's in Washington. They had a blast at both places, hanging out with friends, driving around in cars, and drinking whenever they could get their hands on some booze—never drinking a lot, but enough to get a buzz on and have a good time.

Colorado was all about the cars. Some of the guys had cool cars that they got to drive once in a while, buzzing up and down the main streets. In Washington, their lives revolved around horses. Roberta Jo belonged to a horse drill team, performing at rodeos. Patty was an experienced rider, too, so she fit right in. At one rodeo, she and Patty had learned to chew and spit tobacco. Roberta Jo found she could outspit any of the gals; the boys were a little harder competition.

Last summer during the Kids' Rodeo Roberta Jo and Patty, were invited to be part of a wild-cow milking team. The captain forgot to ask if any of the town girls had ever milked a cow. So, the night of the rodeo, the young teens sauntered out into the arena, trying to look like they knew what they were doing. An audience of hundreds sat in the bleachers ready to be entertained, the smell of horse and cow droppings permeating the air, the day finally cooling off since the sun had gone down.

The chosen cow was turned loose into the arena with the rope around its neck dragging in the dirt. Each of the gals scurried and fought for a position as far down the end of the rope as they could get. Their cow was as docile as any dairy cow anywhere. She stopped cold and mooed, "Come and get it." But the empty milk bottle was again handled like a "hot potato".

The team captain finally approached the cow, and reached for one of the dangling pink spigots, making contact for just a second. The cow kicked out, and startled the captain so badly that she dashed back to her teammates, who were still desperately hanging on to the end of the rope. Finally time ran out, and the girls ran for the safety of the fence.

The audience had jumped to their feet, howling with laughter, yelling out advice to the town girls. Roberta Jo's dad would never be able to tell the story of this competition without getting tears in his eyes; he laughed so hard. Roberta Jo and Patty doubted they could ever tell the story to anyone.

The cousins were amazed how little supervision they had from their parents in both states those summers. They did tell a few little lies or at least were brief in explanations of their whereabouts. They stuck together, however, and somehow never got in trouble.

Usually Roberta Jo and her mother fought continually. She remembered one time when her father came in the back door, walked through the house, and went right out the front door when he heard

Helen yelling, "Now, get in here. All you have to do is take a pill three times a day."

Roberta Jo yelled back while rolling her eyes, "But those pills are huge, they taste awful and I burp them all day. I don't want to take them, and I won't."

Helen had picked up the bottle of pills and tossed them across the room at Roberta Jo, fortunately missing her or anything breakable. The two stopped in their tracks, surprised at Helen's violent action. Helen sat down in a chair, the wind out of her sails, while Roberta Jo marched to her room and slammed the door. She stayed there the rest of the day until her mother knocked on the door and went in. "I'm sorry. I shouldn't have gotten so mad."

"I still won't take the damn things."

"Watch your language, young lady. You are too lippy for your own good. I don't know what to do with you anymore."

Scenes like this took place over and over again. Roberta Jo didn't remember it being like that with Kibby when she was still home. Kibby had always just sucked up to their mother. Anyway, Patty's presence for the summers was a welcome relief from Helen's hovering. They pretty much ignored Helen and went about their business.

Roberta Jo didn't consider herself at all pretty and sometimes worried about it. She spent hours ratting her hair to make it as thick and smooth as possible, using enough hair spray to cover an airplane. She had inherited her father's light-blue eyes, which made a striking contrast to her dark-brown curly hair. If Helen thought her girls were attractive, she didn't share it with them. They were told what they did mattered, not what they looked like.

At one time Roberta Jo had enjoyed being a majorette for the high school marching band. But when she found she was not good at playing an instrument, she gave up band and lost her majorette position. Soon she dropped out of Pep Club and all other school clubs. None of them interested her, or if they did, she was afraid she wouldn't be good at the activities. She went to football games and sat wherever she wanted, ignoring her friends in band and Pep Club. She stayed away from attending most other games like basketball and wrestling. She liked it that way, being independent and her own person. Roberta Jo was eager to get out of Rockford—the sooner the better.

Another reason she wanted to leave town involved her on-again-off-again relationship with her boyfriend, Peter, her first love. In the beginning, at age fifteen, she and her good friend, Vicky, had started hanging out with him and his buddy. They spent most of the time in Peter's family barn, where the boys worked on old cars. The four of them had fun together with no boy-girl games.

Peter was different from the other boys. Just a year older than her, he didn't date or drink. He worked on cars...period. Roberta Jo thought he was gorgeous despite the grease behind his fingernails and sometimes even streaked across his face. He had sea-glass-green eyes that were captivating—if she could get him to look at her, that is. He wore his hair in a crew cut that was way too long. It was different, just as he was different. His shyness around girls was charming. She was smitten right from the beginning but didn't know how to win him over, so she didn't try.

One lazy Saturday afternoon, Roberta Jo found herself alone in the cool barn with Peter while the other two were on an errand. She roamed around, noting all the hanging spiderwebs and the smells of animals that had lived there at one time. An old dusty radio in the corner of the barn played the Everly Brothers, singing "All I Have to Do Is Dream." Somehow it was all very pleasant. She had worn her oldest pair of cutoff jean shorts and a baggy tank top and hadn't spent a lot of time on her hair before coming. It didn't matter. Peter, as usual, had his head stuck under the hood of his rusted-out 1940 Ford. She wondered why she hadn't gone to town with the others.

To pass the time, she began to flirt a bit with him, and much to her surprise, he played the game a little. Roberta Jo didn't push, and Peter got into the fun of playing what was new to him.

"Okay, smarty pants, if you don't like the color I want to paint my '40 Ford project, tell me, what you would paint it?"

"Oh, nothing but candy apple red, thank you very much. Why would you want it competition orange when you can have red? Orange, for Pete's sake, is just ugly. Candy apple red is boss."

Peter responded with a big grin on his face, "You are so wrong. According to the car magazines, competition orange is the color of the decade for restored cars."

Roberta Jo loved it and became more and more enamored by his charm and, of course, those green eyes. She liked that his crew-cut look was different from anybody else's.

Peter surprised her even more saying, "I'll tell you what. If you go with me to the movies next weekend, I'll change my mind and paint the '40 candy apple red."

Roberta Jo couldn't believe her ears. Was he asking her out on a date? "Well…yeah, I'd like that."

"One other condition. You can't tell the other two what we're doing. It'll be just you and me. What do you say?"

"You'd do that?" Roberta Jo sputtered. "No problem, you're on. Movies next weekend, our big secret."

Soon Roberta Jo and Peter were a couple, and in a few months, they were going steady. Roberta Jo said to Vicky, "I'm a little worried about this steady thing."

"Why? You're crazy about Peter."

"Yeah, but it means I can't date anyone else. I guess I shouldn't even flirt with anyone else. Oh well, it's worth it. Peter just takes my breath away. Right now I don't want to date anybody else."

Helen didn't like Peter right from the get-go. "He doesn't have any kind of future. Can't you see that?"

"No, I can't see that. He's seventeen years old, for Pete's sake. He doesn't have to have his whole future planned out."

"But he doesn't ever study. He just works on his cars all the time. You said he isn't planning on going to college but is going to work for his dad doing road construction. He'll probably live here in Rockford the rest of his life. Besides, I don't like what you turn into when he's around. You become a silly, distracted, irresponsible child."

How would you know? I never feel comfortable enough to have him around here. It's okay for him to be here with Daddy; they talk about cars a lot. They've even listened to a few football games together on the radio when you weren't here. I think Daddy likes Peter, and they could be friends. Why can't you like him? You're just so square."

"You watch your mouth, Roberta Jo. I don't know what you and Peter do with all your time, but I don't think it's all innocent. You be careful. You'll end up living the rest of your life in this town like a few other girls we know."

Roberta Jo sank back in her kitchen chair, having thoughts she couldn't say to her mother, knowing she wouldn't understand. *Not fair. I work very hard at not getting too carried away when we make out in the car. I'm proud of that. I love Peter, but going all the way is not what I want to do. Mother should give me some credit.*

"Yeah, well, just because Kibby got herself knocked up, doesn't mean I'll do the same. I'm a whole lot smarter than she was, even though you like her more than me."

"What? We love the two of you just the same. We always have."

Roberta did her eye roll again, knowing it made her mother mad when she did it. "You have a strange way of showing it."

Roberta retreated to her room, as she always did after a battle with her mother. She lay down on her bed and gave more thought to her mother's warnings. *I really do like kissing Peter; a little petting is exciting too.* Patty had told her that a girl could get pregnant if she let the guy lay down on top of her or if they rubbed up against each other. She knew that wasn't true but was scared what might happen if they went too far.

The steady thing with Peter went on for close to a year until Roberta got restless and interested in a few other guys. She wanted to party and to dance, to twist to Chuck Berry and Jerry Lee Lewis. She complained to her best friend, "Peter doesn't like hanging out with a crowd. Worst of all, he refuses to even try dancing, and sipping a little beer is definitely a no-no in his book."

The two would break up for a while, and Roberta would date someone else. She wanted more out of life than he could give her—the theme of their relationship. And now Roberta was going off to college in western Washington. Getting away from Peter was a good thing. She would miss him, but they needed to go their separate ways.

—∿—

So in September of 1963, Roberta was off to a university that neither her sister nor her mother had gone to, Western Washington University, north of Seattle. She wanted to get out of Rockford, but she wasn't ready for the city. Besides, she liked it that it was her own adventure and not her mother's or her sister's. She knew Helen wouldn't miss her all that much, and her father was probably ready to have some peace in the house too.

Helen and Andrew drove her to college and installed her in the dormitory. Roberta Jo's mother took control of the shared room, volunteering Roberta for the top bunk. The room was supposed to house two students, but three were assigned to the one room. Three sharing the space was going to be difficult, but Helen instructed the girls on how they could divide up the two closets and ten drawers. Roberta took deep breaths, trying not to roll her eyes, forcing herself not to yell at her control-freak mother. She noticed Andrew was holding his breath, eyes darting around the room, looking fearful that an argument would break out at any time.

Roberta Jo managed to keep her cool, and before long, the Kindles were gone on their way back to Rockford. Roberta was ecstatic. She had hours that had to be kept in the dormitory, but they were liberal and doable. At least she didn't have to put up with her mother waiting on the couch for her or telling her she needed to study.

One of her roommates became a good friend. They had water fights and played practical jokes and card games in the hall all hours of the night and day. The Beatles were huge, and posters of the band were plastered on every dorm room wall. They danced in their rooms and in the hallways playing 45 records on their portable record players. She and her roommate played "Stay," by Maurice Williams, at least five times after dinner every night.

Roberta Jo, now just Roberta, dated a mix of boys those first two years. She would see a guy for a few months and then move on. Somehow, she managed to keep from having sex with any of them. If they got too insistent, she refused to see them again. Some of her friends were more promiscuous, but she resisted.

By this time, the early to mid-1960s, the girls in Roberta's life were comfortable talking to each other about having sex but knew little about preventing pregnancy. The gal across the hall advised them to stand up right away after sex as a preventative measure. "Don't just lay there with gunk all over you. Get up and go to the bathroom as soon as you can."

Roberta's roommate offered another solution. "I douche as soon as I can. It's always worked for me, or at least, I haven't gotten pregnant. Anybody can borrow my douche bag if they want."

"You know there are birth control pills you can get from a doctor," offered another girl across the hall.

"Oh great! Who can afford that? And what if my parents get called for permission?"

Condoms? Girls didn't buy condoms, only the boys did that. They were what the gals giggled about and the guys put in their billfolds but seldom used.

Roberta asked, "What about diaphragms? I found one in my mother's dresser once. At the time, I had no idea what it was or what it was for. Anybody know how to get one?"

Everyone in the room shrugged their shoulders. "I don't think I would carry it around in my purse, even if I did have one."

Despite the freer conversations about sex and birth control, if a girl got pregnant when she wasn't married, society still considered her a loose woman. If she didn't get pregnant, she was considered smart.

—∿—

Studying? Well, Roberta tried. She almost never missed a class and diligently handed in assignments, but her grades weren't terrific. Helen had helped her figure out what to major in.

"You know I've always wanted to be a physical therapist," she told her mother one day while they were discussing her plans for college. "Remember Kibby's physical therapist when she had polio? I loved watching her work with Kibby and other patients. Besides, I have always liked science, and I think studying the human body would be cool."

The two had sat at the kitchen table looking through the WWU catalog. "But, Roberta Jo, Western Washington doesn't have a program."

"What a bummer. Wouldn't you know."

"But look here in the catalog—they have a program for speech therapy. It looks like there's a lot of science involved, anatomy and neurology. You would be in a field where you would be helping people with difficulties just like a physical therapist does. It looks just right for you."

So that's what Roberta did. The courses were hard, but she liked them. What she didn't like were the liberal arts requirements, such as history and literature. "What do these stupid courses have to do with being a speech therapist?"

—∿—

The summer after her freshman year, Roberta returned to Rockford, where she got a job as a swim instructor and lifeguard at the local pool. The job paid fairly well, a dollar an hour. The other pool employees were also college students her age. Much to her delight, the pool was the social hub for returning students. They all checked in a few times a week to chat and to see what was happening around town.

Roberta and Helen were able to ignore each other through the summer, and Roberta hooked back up steady with Peter. He had a ski boat, so her days off involved ski fun at the lake. Roberta's mother still didn't like Peter, her disapproval hanging in the air like some kind of disease when he was at the house. Peter's shyness made interaction difficult, but he always behaved politely around Helen.

In that summer of 1964, Roberta lost her virginity in the back seat of one of Peter's cars, an inevitable event. Peter had been much too shy to find his way to the drugstore pharmacist for rubbers. If he had gone to the drugstore for them, everyone would know his business. Besides getting pregnant was "something that happened to other kids." Roberta and Peter were beyond that, right?

———w———

Roberta went back to school for her sophomore year and stayed again in the dorm. She and Peter had decided they would date others, and they did, not seeing much of each other the whole school year. Peter was becoming much more worldly, dating other girls and doing some drinking and partying.

Roberta got a summer job at another pool in a Seattle suburb that following summer. This pool was not the social hub as the pool in Rockford had been, but she had great fun living in a little basement apartment with a roommate while not having to study.

She bought a car with a little loan from her dad; a gorgeous '57 Chevy convertible, very cool, kind of a butterscotch brown with a cream-colored top. The car had sat in a gas station across from the pool where she worked. She could see the car and its For Sale sign from her perch on the lifeguard chair. The car called to her. "Hey, Roberta, you want me! Come get me."

"Daddy, you would love this car. I know you would. I think it's a good price too. I had Richard look at it, and he thinks it's worth the money." Roberta knew better than to ask her mother for the money, but it didn't take much for Andrew to cave in to his daughter's pleas. After all, he was a car guy himself.

Roberta and her roommate bombed around in her new convertible, top down, radio blasting out the latest rock tunes. A couple of weekends, they drove to neighboring towns, sleeping in the car.

—⟫⟫—

At the end of her sophomore year, she had decided that the speech therapy program was too difficult. She hadn't been able to pull the grades she wanted and needed.

Kibby looked at her kid sister, eyebrows raised, "What? Secretarial training? What is that all about? You've never wanted to be a secretary. You aren't even a very good typist. Do you know shorthand? Are you sure about this?"

"Well, I can finish it in a year and a half, maybe sooner. If I stay in speech, I won't graduate for another two years. And there are rumors that I would probably have to get a master's degree eventually. That's just too long and hard." Helen and Andrew also voiced their disappointment in the decision, but Roberta didn't listen to any of it.

During Roberta's junior year and first year on her new study path, she and her friend Jan rented a university-approved basement suite. The doors between their bedrooms and little living/study room were nothing but plain white curtains. The one window in the whole suite was a very small window high up in Jan's room. Roberta's room had no window, and the water heater for the house was behind a portable partition beside her bed. She hung her clothes on a metal rod that hung by heavy string from the ceiling. The place smelled of mold, and the girls were forced to dress in layers to stay warm.

Despite the drabness and cold, they loved being totally on their own. The approved housing had no set time they had to be in at night, but they weren't allowed to have male visitors or any kind of party. Not a problem. Life was still good and exciting for Roberta. Maybe a little too good.

CHAPTER 8

ROBERTA AND PETER WERE IN separation mode all that summer and into the fall that Roberta returned to college for her junior year. At Christmas break, however, while Roberta was in Rockford, they reconnected and decided to try and make another go at a relationship. Peter was still a part of the life that she couldn't quite give up.

The winter weather and the 250 miles between them were obstacles, however. Travel over those miles could be treacherous with snowy or icy roads. If they were going to spend time together, they had to put in the extra effort. In late January, they decided to meet in the middle of the state for a weekend.

In the past, their intimacy had been limited to heavy petting in the front seat and moving to the real thing in the back seat. This meeting would be different; Roberta was nervous. That weekend, the weather was good to them. They met in a motel parking lot as planned, checked in, and drove to a nearby restaurant for a romantic dinner. Rebecca wore her favorite miniskirt, the hem a fashionable eight inches above the knee, with matching angora sweater. She knew she looked good, Peter's initial lingering gaze telling her that he thought so too. The restaurant was well decorated with low lighting and soft music, not the Beatles.

Roberta felt like Elizabeth Taylor in a romantic movie scene and soon forgot her nervousness, slipping easily into the role. But after dinner, driving back to the motel alone together, the nervousness returned. "This is weird. Are we really doing this?"

"Yes, I'd say we're really doing this."

"It's kind of exciting, though, don't you think? I feel like we're in a movie or something."

"Well, wait till you see what's in my suitcase."

Once they were in the room, Peter put his suitcase on the bed and opened it up. Inside was a full bottle of wine. He had even remembered to bring a corkscrew. Roberta watched with amazement as he opened the bottle and poured some into plastic cups. *Where did he learn to do that?*

"Oh, how romantic. I didn't know you drank wine."

"You'd be surprised what I have learned while you've been off to school."

Roberta's eyes opened wide as he handed her a glass. "I like this new you."

—⁓—

Well…maybe those girls had been right: "Birth control means getting up right away after sex and peeing as soon as possible." Roberta did not do that. And Peter had not packed condoms in his suitcase along beside the wine. They made love for the first time in a real bed and fell immediately to sleep. It had been an amazing, romantic weekend, but the price was about to be paid.

Roberta's next two periods did not happen, and she knew why. She confided in her roommate, Jan, as they sat in their drab little living room. "That weekend was so stupid. Not even a whole weekend, only one night. How could I be so juvenile? My gosh, I'm twenty years old, not fifteen. I should know better. What am I going to do?"

"Yes, you were pretty stupid. I guess you and Peter will be getting married. Do I get to be your bridesmaid?"

"Oh, shut up, Jan. You're being mean when I need a little support here. Where's my best friend? Think of all the times you thought you made a mistake having sex with a guy. I listened to your whining and wailing and offered my sympathy."

Jan looked long and hard at Roberta. "I'm sorry, Roberta. Come over here where I can give you a good hug. Let's have a cry together." Roberta went over to where Jan was sitting on the couch. They wrapped their arms around each other and had that cry.

Jan continued, "I was sure I would be the one to get pregnant. You've always been so good not to jump in bed with every guy you were crazy about. I've been the bad girl, not you." Jan blubbered, reaching for a box of Kleenex.

"Yeah, I thought you'd be the one too…about a hundred times."

"At least you're in love with Peter. It was probably only a matter of time before the two of you would get married anyway. You've been together off and on since I've known you."

"You think so? We've never talked about marriage. I've thought about it, I guess, but never brought it up. I guess he probably has thought about it too."

Jan blew her nose. "Tell me again what Peter said when you told him."

"He was as shocked as I was. You know Peter. He's not a man of many words. He said, of course we'd get married. He told me he loved me and he'd do the right thing. It wasn't very romantic, but I guess it was a proposal."

"I didn't think Peter was ever very romantic."

"I guess you're right. He isn't, but he's been trying lately." Roberta got up to make tea. "But me…married? That doesn't sound right. I guess that's what my sister did. She got pregnant when she was twenty and had Bart when she was twenty-one. I'm the very same age that she was. And Bart is great. I love that kid. Your sister had to get married, too, didn't she?"

"Yeah, she spit out three kids before she was twenty-four. She wasn't married yet when she was pregnant with the first one. They're doing okay, I guess. They don't have any money or anything. Suzie wanted to be a lawyer, but I guess that isn't going to happen anytime soon. Her husband works at Sears and hopes to be a manager of a Sears store someday. An exciting life, don't you think?"

"At least Kibby and her husband were both able to finish college, but they don't have much money. They're expecting another baby in the next few months. At least Richard has a great job with a super future. Doesn't anybody just get married because they want to anymore? I didn't want to have an instant family at my age. I wanted to have a life first…a career, my own money, gorgeous clothes, a new car, see a bit of the world, party some more. Surely there are other options. Why do I have to do what my sister did?"

"I guess you don't have to."

"I'm not sure Peter is crazy about getting married either. He's been going out, downing a few beers with the guys, and doing a lot of skiing. He makes pretty good money for a single guy and can afford to have a little fun and is having it. Playing with cars isn't everything anymore."

After talking her doubts over with Jan, Roberta called Peter again. "I'm having second thoughts, Peter. Are we really ready to be parents? Isn't life great right now just the way it is? I feel I've just gotten started. If we get married and have a baby, we've just stepped from one family tie to another family tie."

"I get what you're saying. But what else can we do? Would you consider an abortion?"

"Oh, I don't think so. What if Kibby had had an abortion? There wouldn't be a baby Bart. And besides, they're illegal. I can't do that. You wouldn't ask me to do that, would you?"

"No, I'd never ask you to have an abortion. I told you I'd marry you, and I will. I don't know what else we can do."

"I've got to go study. I'll call you in a few days. What a bummer of a mess."

Roberta didn't have a lot of time; she had to tell her parents. So she drove the 250 miles to Rockford the next Friday night without telling them or even Peter that she was coming.

The task ahead of her was going to be the hardest thing she had ever done. She knew her parents would help her, but she also dreaded the look, the I-knew-you-were-a-bad-girl look. *The look of scorn* Kibby called it. Now her parents had two bad girls.

The plan was to tell her mother as soon as she got home. Her father probably would still be working. They could tell him together when he got home.

Her plans did not work out as expected, however. Helen's car was not in the carport when she got there, but her father's truck was. *Oh my God, what do I do now? Where could Mother possibly be? I can't tell Daddy on my own. He'll take it so hard.*

Roberta drove around town for an hour. Finally she couldn't stand it any longer and drove into the carport. The front door was locked, so she rang the doorbell. Andrew opened the door and stared down at his daughter as if he were seeing a ghost. She stepping into the living room and blurted out between sobs, "I'm pregnant, Daddy...I'm so sorry."

Andrew took her into his arms without saying a word. He sat her down on the couch while they cried together for a long time. Roberta had never seen her father cry. He finally said, "It's going to be all right, Roberta Jo. We're going to get through this just fine. We love you and we will do whatever needs to be done...together."

"But you don't understand. I'm not like Kibby Jane. I don't know what to do. Peter says he'll marry me, and I know he loves me, but I don't think I can get married. I'm not ready. Besides Mother hates Peter."

"We're going to talk this over with your mother, and you know she always has good solutions. We'll help you make the decision. We'll be behind you a hundred percent."

"But aren't you terribly disappointed in me? Kibby got pregnant before she got married, and then I go and do the same thing. How could I be so stupid as to do the very same thing?"

Andrew took ahold of Roberta's shoulders and looked into her eyes. "No, I'm not one bit disappointed in you. In fact, I'm so proud that you had the courage to come and tell us. This can't be easy. And I'm proud that you want to do what is right for you. Never, ever think that you might disappoint me. Okay?"

"Okay, Daddy. Will you help me tell Mother? She is going to be bummed out and will probably come unglued."

"Of course I'll help you tell her. If she rants and raves, it'll be short-lived; it always is."

Helen got home about an hour after Roberta had arrived. *The look of scorn* was already on her face as she walked in. Surprisingly her words did not match the look. "Well, hi, Roberta Jo. What a surprise. We didn't expect you."

Roberta stood up but did not approach her mother. Her father stood up beside her. Roberta felt his arm around her shoulders. "Mother, I came home because I have something important to tell you. I already told Daddy...I'm pregnant." Her voice was louder and stronger this time. She had Andrew's support.

Helen stared at her youngest daughter, her body rigid, head held high, and chin tilted upward. Her eyes drilled into Roberta's eyes. She hung on to her purse as if someone was trying to take it from her. "Oh," was all she said for at least ten seconds.

Then, "Do you even know who the father is?" the anticipated *look of scorn* never leaving her face.

Roberta was not surprised by the look, but the comment was like a slap on her face. She couldn't say anything at first. She felt her father's arm tighten around her shoulders. Her body wilted, and she might have fallen to the floor if his arm hadn't been there. "Of course I know who the father is, and so do you."

"Don't tell me it's that Peter? I thought you were through with him a long time ago."

"Yes, it is Peter. Why are you being so mean? I know I've disappointed you, and I know I made a mistake. But right now, I need your help. Please. I guess I shouldn't have come home. I should have just called you and told you." Roberta Jo turned and collapsed, sobbing into her father's arms, the shame of her predicament returning, her confidence gone.

As usual, Helen made an about-face in her attitude. Soon she was calmly discussing the problem with the two of them as though she hadn't said in that one sentence, what Roberta would never forget the rest of her life.

"Well, I guess we need to plan another wedding and do it quickly before everyone starts talking. Spring break is coming up, and maybe we can do it then. Only problem is your sister's baby is due about then. That may be a problem."

Roberta felt relief that her mother's attitude had reversed. But she had more to say. She took a big breath. "That's just it, Mother. Peter says he'll marry me, but I'm thinking I don't want to do that. I'm not ready to be a wife and a mother. And I'm certainly not ready to spend the rest of my life in this town being those things. I'm twenty years old, and there's so much to do before I settle down to those roles. I'm not like you and Kibby. I can't do it."

Helen swallowed hard. "You need to think about this some more. Heaven knows, I need to think about this some more. Let's all go to bed, think on it, and talk more tomorrow."

Roberta didn't call Peter that night. He didn't know she was in town, but she felt she needed to know her own mind for sure before talking to him again. But the next morning, after a restless night, she still hadn't changed her mind. She was determined to stand by her decision.

The Kindles had a fitful night as well. Once they were alone, Andrew let Helen start the conversation. "Can you believe this? I feel like we're riding on a merry-go-round and can't get off. We go around and around, always getting back to the same old problem. And heaven forbid, this daughter, always the renegade, doesn't want to get married. I can't say as I blame her; Peter's no catch. When do we get off this ride?"

While Helen rambled on, Andrew was undecided about what Roberta should do.

Helen continued, "You know what's going to happen don't you? For now, she's going to decide not to get married. Then a few months down the line, she's going to change her mind and decide she can't live without the guy. Then what?"

"You got a point."

"Or she'll find that being pregnant is too hard. So, in the end, they'll be walking down the aisle eight and a half months pregnant. And you and I will listen to the tongues in this town wag. It'll end up being the worst four months of our lives, and Roberta will feel sorry for herself because she has a baby and a husband to raise. Peter's not going to leave this town. She'll be stuck here in Rockford for the rest of her life."

"We don't know that for sure. Peter could be a fine husband, provider, and father, especially with some support from us and his family."

"Maybe, but I think we need to talk her into getting married now and be done with it."

Andy could usually talk sense into his wife when she came up with what he thought was a bad idea, but this time he understood what she was saying. "Yes, maybe they should just bite the bullet. I think I agree with you. But how do we get her to see our reasoning?"

"I have an idea, but I need to think about it. We'll talk in the morning." The two finally rolled over to get a few hours' sleep.

The next morning, Roberta sat down at the dining table, hoping the coffee in her hand would help clear her muddled head. Her parents sat down with her, and told her they thought she should get married. What? All her life they had pushed her to go to college, make a future, get out of this town. Now they wanted her to get married at age twenty, have a baby, and probably live here forever. Her mother had never liked Peter, had probably never even had a real conversation with him. Now she wanted to be his mother-in-law?

Helen presented her plan. "I think you should call Peter today and arrange to talk to him. Discuss this with him again. He has said he'll marry you; he knows it's the right thing to do."

Andrew spoke up. "I think she's right. It's the best decision for you."

Roberta's resolve to stand strong with her decision weakened, and she agreed to call Peter. He sounded surprised to hear she was in town but picked her up as she requested.

She slid into the seat of his car and blurted out. "Okay, Peter, I need you to be straight with me. Would you believe that my mother thinks we should get married? Actually, even my father agrees that we should. I need to know your thoughts since we last talked about backing out of marriage."

Peter parked the car in an empty parking lot, took a big breath, and replied, "I haven't thought of anything else since this whole mess started. I agree that we're way too young to be having a baby. I'm liking my life right now, just like you said on the phone. You know I'd marry you today if that was what you wanted, but I guess it isn't my first choice either."

Roberta sighed and relaxed against the seat. "Okay, I guess I can go back and stand up to my parents. I'm glad we're on the same page."

"You won't have an abortion, so what else can you do?"

"I don't know what I'll do. I have no idea. I need to go home now and talk to them. Would you please take me home? I'll call you later."

"I love you, Roberta Jo. I'm so sorry all this is happening. I wanted us to work out as a couple, but we just aren't ready for marriage yet."

"I love you too. We blew it, didn't we?"

"I'm afraid we did."

Roberta went home to her parents with the news that she and Peter had decided not to get married. Helen didn't look happy with the news but took control, like always. "You know this is it. You can't change your mind down the line? You either get married in the next month or never. Getting married when you are eight or nine months pregnant is not an option. Do you understand that?"

"Okay, I get it, Mother. This was my idea, remember? I'm not going to change my mind."

Helen was not looking for a fight. She was calling the shots. Her shoulders were squared; her voice was clear. "This is what we're going to do. I'm going to find a place for you to go away and have this baby. It's going to be a big secret. You can't tell anyone that you're pregnant. And afterward, you can't tell anyone that you had a baby. You have to tell Peter that he can never look for you. And he can't tell anyone that you're going to have his baby. Anyone. The baby will be given up for adoption. It'll be very difficult. Do you understand?"

"Got it." Roberta was not up for a fight either. She knew her mother well enough to know that she was taking a strong stand, a stand that couldn't be broken. Roberta had made the decision, but Helen was in charge. For the first time in years, she did not argue with her mother about any of it.

—⁕—

Roberta's sister and her husband were the only ones, other than Jan, who were told the secret. Kibby made an appointment for Roberta to go to her Seattle doctor.

The nurse ushered Roberta into the exam room, told her to take off all her clothes and lie down on the table, and gave her a paper sheet to cover herself. The nurse, in her crisp white uniform and heavily supported white shoes, was all business. It seemed to Roberta that hours passed before she came back in and instructed her to put her feet in the stirrups. That meant her knees were up in the air and spread apart. Roberta blushed, sweat forming on her forehead and in her armpits.

A few minutes later the doctor came in, coldly introduced himself, and shook her hand as she lay in that outrageous position. He examined every part of her body, poking and prodding with his hands and who knows what else.

She wanted to cry but didn't. She closed her eyes as tight as she could, never looking directly at the doctor. She answered his questions with yes and no answers. If she had questions, she didn't ask them. The doctor told her that indeed, she was pregnant, and everything looked okay. She got out of the office and building as fast as she could.

Kibby had waited for her in the car with Bart. She took one look at her sister and said, "It was awful, wasn't it?"

Roberta could only nod.

"I'm so sorry. I wish I could have gone in with you." They drove home in silence. Kibby was the big sister that Roberta needed. Kibby's own pregnancy made conversations sometimes uncomfortable. Giving up the baby was an untouched topic. Roberta never knew if her sister approved of her decision, but she never felt Kibby judged her in any way.

Roberta was still in school, finishing out the spring term. Her roommate, Jan, stuck to her promise to keep the secret. Her other friends didn't understand why she didn't date, didn't see Peter, and didn't even party anymore.

She worried that she might start to look pregnant, so she didn't go out except to her classes. She studied and watched TV with the family who lived above their little apartment, waving goodbye to Jan as she went out in the evenings, not once hearing from Peter. She told everyone that she had a job lined up for the summer. Lying was a big part of her life now. She had to get used to it.

Roberta hoped she was doing the right thing.

CHAPTER 9

ROBERTA WAS INITIALLY TOLD THAT she would be going to a Catholic home for unwed mothers. Helen had found a place in Michigan to get her as far away from Peter as she could. Much to Roberta's horror, Kibby's doctor had suggested they look for a home operated by the Salvation Army. Her vision of the "Army" was one of women wearing dark uniforms complete with pioneer-type bonnets ringing bells and banging tambourines to beg for money. Roberta pleaded with her mother not to have to go to one of these dreadful homes. Before, Roberta would have put her foot down and refused to go, but now pleading was her method. News of the Catholic home was a relief.

Roberta was scheduled to leave right after the end of the school term. Helen said it had to look like she was rushing off to the summer job that she didn't really have. May seemed early, as the baby was not due until October; Roberta didn't argue.

Two weeks before she was to leave, Jan and Roberta were sitting down to TV dinners in their little apartment. They were listening to the latest Beatle's album, *Revolver*. Roberta especially liked the song "Eleanor Rigby." She could certainly identify with "all the lonely people" in the song.

The phone rang, and Jan got it since nobody ever called Roberta these days. Helen was on the line, so Jan handed it over. "Hello, Roberta Jo. I'm afraid I have some news you aren't going to like."

"Great, what's going on?"

"I got a call from the Catholic home. It seems they are overbooked, and they don't have room for you after all."

"Oh no...what now? Please, please don't tell me I have to join the 'Army.'"

"I have called everywhere, but there seems to be a shortage of places for unwed mothers right now. The only two homes with openings in the next month are a Catholic one right in Seattle and a Salvation Army place in Colorado. Seattle is no good. You might be seen there by any number of people. We can't take that chance."

"So the it's the 'Army'?"

"I'm afraid so. But it'll be okay. I'm sure of it. They sounded real nice on the phone."

"Easy for you to say, Mother. You don't have to live there." Roberta showed the phone her longest finger. "How could you do this to me? I told you this was the last thing I wanted to do. I've got to go study. Bye."

Roberta slammed down the phone, not waiting to hear any of the ugly details her mother might have planned to tell her. She turned to Jan, who had heard Roberta's end of the conversation and had seen the finger gesture. Her roomie didn't need to be told her mother's end.

"I can't do this, Jan. I'm bummed out," Roberta said as she plopped down on their sagging couch, dinner forgotten. "The Army! Doesn't that sound dreadful?"

"Yes, it does. Are you going to have to stand on a corner somewhere and beg for money?"

"Sounds like it. Can't you see me standing outside a store in my cute little maternity outfit with matching bonnet? Maybe they make a special maternity dress in Army uniform style. You know, black with the hem almost to my ankles and a collar that buttons right up to my chin."

"I'm so sorry. I guess you could still get married. It's not too late to do that."

"Are you kidding me? My mother would be furious. I have no decision-making power at this point. If I told her that I was getting married, I'd probably never see my parents again."

That night Roberta had a dream. She was outside a department store in a big city. Cars were buzzing by; horns were honking. The smell of pollution was overwhelming. She was standing by herself, watching people go in and out of the store. She had a huge bell in her hand, but it was so heavy she couldn't ring it. All she could do was try not to drop it. She looked down and saw that her belly was huge, and she was wearing a black jacket that was so tight around her bulging body, the buttons were ready to pop off.

She was reaching up with her other hand to feel whether there was a bonnet on her head when she saw Peter walking toward her. He was pointing and laughing at her. He came so close that she could see his beautiful green eyes, but he suddenly looked embarrassed and his eyes went very dark. He ducked into the store as fast as he could. A little old lady approached her and pressed a dollar bill in her hand, saying, "You are a bad, bad girl! You should be ashamed of yourself."

Roberta woke up in a cold sweat, unable to get back to sleep, not sure she wanted to go back to sleep.

———⁂———

The day before she was to leave for Colorado, Roberta drove with all her belongings to Kibby's house in Seattle. Richard had agreed to sell her beloved convertible so the money could go toward expenses at the home. Her parents met her there. She was flying to Colorado by herself and someone from "the Army" would pick her up at the airport.

Roberta had never flown before. In fact, she only knew one person who had ever flown in a commercial airplane. At one time she had dreamed of being an airline stewardess. It sounded so sophisticated. Never in her wildest dreams had she imagined her first flying experience would be such a bummer.

That evening, the family went out to a restaurant for a "gay farewell dinner." They talked about the weather, and they talked about things like crop failure. Roberta noticed no one talked about where she was going the next day, like it wasn't going to happen at all. She didn't participate in any of it. Three-year-old Bart had a grand time running around the restaurant, everyone busy trying to keep him out of trouble. Roberta wanted to hold him in her lap and never let go, but he wouldn't have it.

Kibby had had her baby by then, a little girl, Lisa Anne. She was adorable. Kibby and Richard seemed to be such happy parents. Whenever Kibby attended to Lisa, she glanced at Roberta. "Would you like to hold her?" Kibby finally asked.

Roberta's eyes met her sister's eyes. "Not right now. Maybe later."

"Okay, when you're ready." Kibby gave her a smile that told Roberta she understood. *How could Kibby understand when I don't even understand how I'm feeling about this baby thing?*

The whole evening was surreal. Everyone avoided looking at her or engaging her in conversation. She needed something from them, but she didn't know what. She was like a lone black cloud hovering over a picnic of people trying to have a good time despite the pounding rain.

Roberta tried but couldn't eat anything. The steamy restaurant smelled of overcooked fried food and garlic. Bart was squealing and running around and around the tables and chairs. Nausea soon bathed her in sweat.

She excused herself to go to the restroom but only made it halfway across the restaurant when a blackness clouded her vision. She slowly sank to the floor. Kibby and Helen rushed to her and helped her to the restroom, where she could sit down. By then Roberta was sobbing. She looked up at her mother and sister standing over her pressing wet paper towels to her forehead. "I'm so scared. Do either of you have any idea how scared I am? I have no idea where I'm going tomorrow or what my life is going to be like the next five months. And you guys are acting as if nothing at all is happening."

Kibby looked at her sister's wet, troubled face and bent down for a hug. "No, we do know what is happening tomorrow, but we don't know any more than you what your life is going to be like. We don't know what to do or what to say to you. I guess we're busy pretending it isn't happening and hoping it'll all just go away. We're scared too. I'm so sorry, Roberta."

Helen stared at her two embracing daughters. She dropped her arms to her sides, cast her eyes down, and said nothing. Roberta looked up at her mother and thought she looked out of place in the cramped restroom.

Roberta pleaded, "Please get me out of here. I just want to go to bed."

—m—

The next day Helen and Andrew took Roberta to the airport and put her on the plane. She experienced her first flight through a blur of tears. The stewardesses kept asking her what was wrong, eventually handing her a whole box of tissues. She couldn't look at them, so she didn't answer them. Her instructions had been to never discuss the big secret with anyone. She was officially a "bad" girl and had no choice but to live silently with her shame.

The stewardesses offered her something to drink and eat, but she refused it all. The smell of food in such tight quarters made her nauseous. Her first flight was nothing like what she had dreamed of. She could have been on a public bus for all the pleasure it gave her.

The plane finally landed, and Roberta followed the other passengers down the aisle and down the airplane stairs. She walked across the tarmac and entered the airport. A number of people were greeting each other with hugs and exclamations of joy. Weaving through the crowd, she saw a smiling airline employee walking up to her. "Are you Roberta Kindle?"

"Yes, I am."

"Great, I caught you in time." It flashed through Roberta's head that she was going to be told that being there was one big mistake and she could go back home. Fat chance.

"It seems the people who were to meet you aren't able to get here. Instead, you're supposed to take a taxi and go to the address written on this piece of paper. You're to tell the taxi driver that he will be paid when you get there." Roberta's heart sank. Her tears had run out, but she felt more alone than ever. Roberta had never taken a taxi either. A day of firsts.

Carrying her big suitcase she followed signs through the airport that led to the taxis. The smiling lady had told her how to collect her suitcase, but she was on her own finding a taxi. She went outside through a big glass door and saw a number of cabs waiting.

Roberta walked up to the third one in line, the driver standing outside his door. She picked him because he was older and looked like he could be someone's grandpa. He smiled at her and said, "I'm sorry, Miss, but you have to take the first taxi. We have to take our turns."

"Oh, I'm sorry. I didn't know." She shrank back as if she had been bitten by his words and hurried up to the first taxi in line.

This driver was young with greased-back hair. He looked her up and down like the frat boys at a party. "Hey there. Your bag looks pretty heavy. Let me put it in the trunk for you."

Roberta didn't know if she should get in the front seat or the back. *This greaser might think I'm being rude if I get in the back by myself.* She opened the front door and climbed in.

She was instantly sorry she hadn't gotten in the back, as the front smelled of sweat and yesterday's lunch. The dashboard hadn't been wiped off for years and was littered with papers. Too late; the driver was already in. She handed him the slip of paper with the address of the Salvation Army written on it. He looked at it for a minute or two and then looked back at her, again checking her out from head to toe. "Okay. I know where this is. Been there before. You don't look very pregnant."

Roberta froze. Her secret was out. He knew she was one of those "bad girls." She saw it in his eyes and heard it in his voice. He dropped the slip of paper on the seat between them. She grabbed it, stuffed it into her bag on her lap, and sat bolt upright, sliding as close to the door as she could.

"Yeah, I have a sister that got herself knocked up too. Mom and Dad didn't have the money to send her to where you're goin'. It's not the Ritz, but at least you're away from your parents. They were on her case the whole time she was pregnant. You goin' to give up your baby?"

The cabbie chatted as he eased away from the curb and entered traffic. Roberta stared straight ahead and didn't answer him. He asked her a bunch more questions, but she ignored him and said silent prayers that he would take her to the right address.

Eventually the taxi pulled up to a large old three-story brick building. It took up a whole block in an old neighborhood that was a mixture of nice-looking homes and others needing some work. The building looked a lot like the old nursing home her aunt Pearl had lived in for years. The large lawn had recently been mowed, but there was no other landscaping of trees or flowers. Wide concrete stairs lead up to a big double door. Roberta was relieved to see a small sign over the door that read "Salvation Army/Gibson Home." At least he had brought her to the right place.

Roberta turned to the greaser. "Wait here; someone will come out to pay you."

"Okay, but I'll get your bag and carry it up for you."

She had forgotten about her suitcase. She turned and looked him in the eye for the first time. "Thank you." He had been kind, but she didn't have the words to say anything more.

He looked back at her and softly said, "Good luck to you."

She got out of the taxi and slowly walked up the sidewalk through the grassy area and climbed the stairs. By the time she got to the door, three women were waiting for her. One paid the taxi driver. The other two stiffly shook her hand as if she were applying for a job. One of them said, "Welcome to your new home. Sorry we couldn't meet you at the airport. We were shorthanded here today. Besides it would have meant two taxi rides to be paid for. We have to watch our pennies, you know." Roberta tried to smile.

The speaker introduced herself as Miss Pinkerton. She was very short and very wide, wearing regular clothes. No uniform and, thank God, no tambourine. Her hair was mousy gray and in need of a trim. Her smile was genuine, however, and Roberta was grateful for that.

The second woman was Major T. With these introductions, Roberta realized for the first time that Salvation Army people had rankings. This major was petite, about one-tenth the size of Miss Pinkerton. She had short brown, very curly hair and buck teeth and was constantly blinking her eyes. And yes, she was wearing the uniform, minus the bonnet. No smile from Major T. Both women were of nondescript age; they just looked old to Roberta. Together, they looked like caricatures she had seen being drawn at the fair.

The third greeter was Major B. She was the most intelligent and "normal" looking of the three but was also the most stern looking. Roberta didn't think they were going to be friends anytime soon. Her posture was good enough for the military, her uniform tidy and perfectly tailored to her trim figure. Major B did not say much, but her roaming eyes made Roberta feel she was being sized up and judged. A smile was present but not genuine.

Miss Pinkerton continued, "Do you have any money on you? If you do, we must take it and put it away in safe keeping so it won't get stolen by any of the other girls. You can ask for it at any time."

Great. Roberta shuddered. *The other girls are going to be thieves and juvenile delinquents, and I'm soon to become one myself if I expect to fit in.*

Roberta followed Pinkerton through the old doors and into a wide hallway. The floor was wooden, worn smooth and shiny from years of use. Her suitcase had been placed just inside. One of the many doors off the hallway was slightly open. As they passed by, Roberta thought it looked like an office of some sort. She wondered what all the other doors went to. The hallway, dark and smelling like a hospital—a very old hospital, a mixture of disinfectant and mold—was not pleasant.

Miss Pinkerton pointed to the wooden double door at the end of the hall. "Go on in, Roberta. I'll introduce you to the other girls and your new roommate." The two majors disappeared without a word, taking her change purse with them. It contained all the money she had in the world. She hoped to see it again.

Roberta pushed on the door, expecting it to creak like an old door in a horror movie. It opened silently, however, to a large common room and several young girls in various stages of pregnancy. Roberta sighed in relief to see that this room was well lit by a bank of big windows on the far wall. Green trees with branches waving in the wind were visible beyond the windows. Four girls sat around a large table, painting pottery. Others were reading in soft, worn chairs or couches placed in corners. Two were working on a jigsaw puzzle at a small table. The radio in the corner quietly played a familiar Beach Boys song.

"Girls, if I could please have your attention. I want you to meet our newest friend, Roberta." The girls glanced up at her, checked her out, and continued with what they were doing. Not exactly a friendly greeting overall. One girl, however, smiled at her, got up from her puzzle, and walked over. "This is Andrea, she's going to be your roommate."

"Hi, Roberta. I've been so excited since they told me you were coming today. My old roommate had her baby three days ago, and I've missed her."

Pinkerton said, "Andrea, you girls go get Roberta's suitcase and take her back to your room. Maybe give her a tour of the areas, teach her the ropes."

Roberta was relieved to see that Andrea was about her own age, nineteen or twenty. Some of the others looked so young, maybe thirteen or fourteen. She found herself relaxing a little bit as they went for the suitcase. She followed Andrea into another section of the building off the common room. This section was also a big room cordoned off with partial walls and curtains to make small sleeping areas. Privacy did not appear to be an important factor.

She noticed Andrea kept glancing at Roberta's jeans and frowning. Her new roommate finally said, "I guess they didn't tell you that we aren't allowed to wear pants here, only dresses and skirts. The Salvation Army hasn't joined the sixties or even the twentieth century and doesn't approve of ladies wearing pants."

Roberta looked down at her jeans and T-shirt and thought about everyone she had just seen in the common room. She realized no one had been in jeans, Roberta's uniform of choice. Her heart skipped a beat or two.

"Oh my gosh, no. Nobody told me. How embarrassing! Now I know why Major B looked at me so sternly. I only have one skirt in my bag; the rest of my clothes are jeans and shirts. We packed a few of my sister's old maternity outfits, but most of those are pants and tops too."

"Don't worry about it. There's lots of extra clothing here, especially maternity clothing. It doesn't look like you'll be needing those for a while, however. We all share, and it's not exactly like a fashion show around here."

They had come to a curtain in the far corner of the vast room. Andrea pulled it back, exposing a cozy area with two beds and two small dressers. "Here's our room. We're lucky to have a window; some rooms don't. My bed is here, yours over there. You can have that dresser next to it."

Roberta finally dared to take a good look at Andrea. Her stomach was huge, but she didn't seem at all embarrassed to be so big and awkward. *Will I look like that? Yuck!* Roberta watched as Andrea slowly eased herself down on the bed, using her hands and arms to help her. She already liked Andrea. Setting her suitcase down on her new bed, she started taking out her few possessions and putting them in the dresser.

"I hope you aren't worried about us. Right now, the gals here are pretty good and some of them lots of fun. When I first got here, some bad-news girls or, should I say, unpleasant girls lived here. They were weird and maybe even a little wacko. The worst are gone now though. Nobody is here forever, and you can usually avoid the weird ones.

Right now everyone is pretty cool. You'll like them, most of them, anyway."

Roberta put her empty suitcase under the bed and sat down, sinking a little into the mattress, her shoulders following suit. For the first time in months, Roberta didn't feel so alone.

"Do you smoke?" Andrea asked.

Roberta thought that question a little strange. "Once in a while but not regularly."

"Great. Come, I'll show you the smoking room. Better change into that one skirt though."

As Roberta changed clothes, Andrea explained, "There are two smoking areas here, an indoor and an outdoor area. These are the only places we're allowed to smoke. But the main thing is the majors never go into them, so we have privacy there. With the fan going, we can talk without them eavesdropping. You have to watch out for Major B. especially. She's always looking for ways to lecture us."

"I kind of thought she was the one to avoid. She wasn't very friendly. I got the feeling she didn't like me either."

"I guess she isn't too bad. She mostly keeps to herself and leaves us alone. I don't think she likes any of us. She's probably afraid if she gets too close she could catch our disease, pregnancy."

Roberta chuckled. The two girls left the sleeping area and headed back to the large common room. Andrea chatted on. "Unfortunately, only four girls are allowed in the smoking areas at one time. Sometimes you have to kick somebody out to get your turn."

"Why only four?"

"The majors would tell you it's some kind of fire regulation, but I think they don't want us having too much fun. You don't have to smoke while you're there. You can just sit around and have a good time until somebody else wants in."

They headed to a door in the farthest corner of the common room. The Monkees were now on the radio. Roberta's relief was so great that she felt like dancing to the music.

The smell of the smoking room hit her nostrils well before they got there. In fact, she could almost feel the smoke bellowing out as Andrea opened the door. The room was very dark, with one little window high up on the outside wall. Inside two very pregnant girls were laughing so hard that tears were visible in their eyes. Roberta and Andrea sat on the two remaining folding chairs. Ashtrays stands were the only other items in the room. "Hey, Andrea, what's happening? Betsy was telling me a story about the lies she had to tell her family. I thought I was bad with the lies. Who's your buddy?"

"This is my new roomie, Roberta. I'm showing her around."

"Hi, Roberta. Welcome to the Army Armpit. You're going to love it here."

"Thanks. I'm not sure I'm very excited to be here, but this room looks fun. The chairs are certainly comfy."

"Ha, aren't they just far out? I'm hoping to take one home with me. You sure don't look pregnant. I know; you told lies just so you could join us in this wonderful place."

"I wish. No, my mother was anxious to get me away so no one would find out our little secret. She couldn't sit by and wait for me to start ballooning."

"Got it. Join the liar's club of Colorado."

Roberta soon adjusted to life in the "Army." She liked most everyone, as Andrea had predicted. Complaints of the discomforts of pregnancy were major topics of conversation. The upcoming birthing of babies was rarely a topic, however. Nor did they discuss giving up the babies. Roberta was happy to avoid those topics.

Not having to keep her pregnancy a secret, she found her clothes were suddenly too tight. Her body spread out like slow-rising bread. She dove into the shared clothes box for things to wear. Eventually she felt a fluttering movement on the surface of her rising abdomen, like a butterfly had been planted in the bread dough and was trying to escape. She told Andrea about this new phenomenon. Andrea laughed. "Guess what? You're going to have a baby. Wait until it starts kicking the heck out of you."

Although the exercise would have been good for them, the girls were not allowed to walk around the neighborhood. They even had to get permission to take a bus anywhere. The only other alternative to going anywhere was taking a taxi, and no one had the money for that. Keeping a low profile was an Army priority. Local boys enjoyed driving by whistling, yelling, and pointing if they saw one of them pregnant. Sometimes they would go around and around the block several times.

Everyone had a regular daily job. Roberta requested kitchen duty because it took up a lot of time. She was lucky enough to get the job right from the start and kept it until the end.

The kitchen girls sneaked food whenever they could. One day Andrea made fudge in the kitchen while the others were busy setting the tables and doing other small tasks. The cook had run upstairs to use the phone. "I'll be gone about a half hour, but you girls know what has to be done. I'll leave you to it."

Andrea worked fast, and they gobbled it fast. As they cleaned up before cook came back, Roberta said, "You know, the fudge didn't really taste all that good. In fact, it was more like thick chocolate soup with lumps of some kind of overcooked vegetable, maybe peas. It was fun, but you know, Andrea, I wouldn't put cook's assistant on your résumé just yet."

Other girls had duties like sweeping and vacuuming the floors, cleaning the bathrooms, and dusting. Major T. was their supervisor, but she wasn't the sharpest knife in the drawer, and working for her was difficult.

The round Miss Pinkerton could be fun, but she was also moody. Her bad moods were to be avoided if possible. Roberta learned it was best just to keep her distance. She wasn't that much fun.

Best of all of the regular staff was Poppy, hired to do the laundry. She was sixty-eight years old but dressed like she was twenty-three in bell-bottom jeans and caftan shirts. Her hair was long and straight, usually in braids. On her own time every week, she piled as many of them as she could into her old, multicolored van and took them to a ceramic shop, where they bought molded pottery to paint. Poppy always made stops at the ice cream stand, the fudge store, or the doughnut shop, sometimes paying for it all, never appearing embarrassed to be with the pregnant Salvation Army girls.

Roberta went into the home's office and called her parents collect every Sunday evening, silently crying during the conversations. Her parents didn't seem to want to hear about her days in the home, so her mother did most of the talking, telling about what they were doing and telling stories about Kibby and the kids.

She thought she might get a call from Peter at some time, but she never did. She didn't know how he would get the phone number, but she was hopeful. Roberta was sad to think it was all over between them. Peter had been a part of her life for a long time. *I guess he moved on. I made my nest; I have to live in it.*

—⁓—

Every two weeks was clinic day at the Army Armpit. Once a girl was six months pregnant, she had to attend every clinic to have an "examination." At her first clinic day, memories of her previous visit to Kibby's doctor were still vivid and kept Roberta fearful of things to come.

"Okay, Roberta, here we go." Andrea took her hand and lead her to the third floor. "Take off all your clothes, and put on one of these hospital gowns. Don't even try to keep your underwear on. Then follow me. You're going to love this."

Roberta did as she was told following the other pregnant girls to stand in line in the hallway. A few folding chairs were up against the wall for the most pregnant to sit on. Roberta sat on the cold, hard floor, draped only in her skimpy gown.

Andrea warranted one of the chairs but bent down to whisper to Roberta, "Just before it's your turn, go get one of the cups there on the table. One of them has your name on it. Take the cup, go into the bathroom beside the table, and pee into it. I hope you didn't just go. Nothing worse than not having enough pee."

"This is dreadful. What do I do then?"

"Leave your full cup on the table, and get back in line."

Major B directed traffic. "Hurry up. Dr. Dayton is your doctor today, and he only has so much time."

Betsy, sitting next to her, whispered, "The docs in town take turns volunteering their time for this clinic. You never know who's going to be the doc of the day. Some of them are nicer than others, but nobody is that bad. Don't worry."

After doing pee duty and waiting for a couple of hours in the dark, dingy hallway, Roberta shuffled into the exam room for her turn. She lay down as directed with her feet in the dreaded stirrups. The exam itself was quick and embarrassingly impersonal. The doctor said nothing to her but made comments to the nurse, who took notes.

Roberta felt like they were cattle being moved through a hallway chute and into the clinic room. She was tempted to let out a "Mooooo" but kept her mouth shut. Major B would come unglued if she made a noise like a cow. They would have to laugh about the image later in the smoking room.

—m—

Roberta wondered why no information was ever given to the girls to help them understand what their bodies were going through or to prepare them for childbirth. The nurses might have taken on that task, but they didn't. The majors and Pinkerton certainly wouldn't be helpful. They probably had more fear of childbirth than the girls did. Everyone seemed to have their head buried in the sand.

It was Andrea who told Roberta that once in a while, a girl would return to the Army to give birth a second time. Why hadn't they been told about birth control, or at least given a lecture on abstinence from intercourse? "Just feed those girls, herd them around, and send them back to where they came from." That was the Salvation Army way.

A few months before Roberta got to the home, the babies had been delivered on the third floor instead. That entire floor had been a kind of minihospital with a delivery room, a nursery, and a room of beds for the girls after they delivered. As they were cleaning up one night in the kitchen after dinner, Andrea said, "We used to be able to hear the girls' screams while they were in delivery. It was awful. I had to put a pillow over my head so I wouldn't hear them. Then later, we could hear baby cries. We knew then it was over for that girl."

"I guess I'm glad they changed the way they do things. I don't think I'd like that."

"Yeah, I'm glad all that stopped too. Now we go to the hospital once the nurses think it's time. We come back here after a few days but stay on the third floor."

A nurse employed by the home was present at all times on the third floor. Unlike the majors, they did not live there and were not members of the Salvation Army. The unwed mothers were permitted to go up to see the nurses one or two at a time for any kind of health issue. The nurses were good listeners and a comfort for many an insomniac but seldom were seen on the floors below.

Roberta had been at the home for over four weeks before there was ever a baby delivery. In one day two girls, including Andrea, had their babies. Roberta stayed with her roommate, holding her hand and rubbing her back until she went off to the hospital. When Andrea returned three days later, an invisible wall appeared between them.

The same thing happened with the others who went off to deliver. For weeks they had talked to each other about almost everything, and suddenly they didn't know what to say to each other. Andrea didn't share any of details of her delivery or what it was like leaving her baby behind. But then, Roberta didn't ask either. She only saw Andrea once more before she was gone for good, leaving a blank space in her days.

—∿—

Roberta saw the social worker alone in her office on three occasions during her stay at the home. Mrs. LaFontaine was like a breath of fresh air in a closed-up closet. She was attractive, warm, charming, intelligent, funny, and professional. She dressed in beautiful suits and gorgeous dress shoes—nothing hippie about Mrs. LaFontaine. Like with Poppy, Roberta was reminded that people existed in this world who weren't unwed mothers or crabby old maids. She treated Roberta like an adult.

Mrs. LaFontaine was who the girls went to with their more serious problems, personal or within the home. Roberta enjoyed hearing about Mrs. LaFontaine's life and family. She made it easy then to talk about herself. Mrs. LaFontaine's main role was to handle the adoptions. She dealt with the paperwork and matched the babies with adopting families. "Where would you like to see your baby go, what kind of family?"

Roberta did not have much to say. "I don't know, a good family, I guess. Maybe a family that values education, that is kind and likes to have fun." All Roberta knew was she could not provide a family for the baby. The baby itself was not real enough for her to imagine it in another home.

"Are you still okay with giving up the baby?" Mrs. LaFontaine asked on every occasion.

"Yeah, sure. It's fine."

—∿—

One sunny, breezy afternoon, Roberta and three of the other unwed mothers were sitting in the outside smoking area when Mary burst in. "Guess what? I'm leaving this place today and…I'm getting married!"

Mary had turned eighteen the week before, and her baby was due in less than a month. "Mom and Dad can't tell us what to do anymore. We're both eighteen now, so we're going to tie the knot."

"Wow! That's truly exciting! But where're you going to live? What'll you do for money? There's going to be three of you very soon, and you won't be able to work." Roberta wanted to tell her she was doing something very stupid and was cruisin' for a bruisin'.

"Jeff's brother and sister-in-law said we can live with them for a while and Jeff just got a great job baggin' and stackin' at a grocery store. He'll make good money, and then we can move out. Come help me pack so I can get out of here."

Mary's good friend went to help her while the others talked about their concerns. "Can't they see that it's never going to work? Frankly I see a divorce and an unhappy childhood in the future."

Jeannette said, "Maybe their plans will work and they'll live happily ever after."

Betsy said, "Somehow, I don't think so. They have so much working against them. It looks to me like getting married is just an act of defiance on their part."

Roberta added, "Yeah, their parents didn't want them to marry, so, by golly, they're going to do it. Who knows? If my parents would have insisted that Peter and I not marry, maybe we would have done the same thing." They never heard from Mary again.

The Mary and Jeff story was not the only excitement happening at the Army about that time. Just the week before, Judy went to the smoking room for help. "I've told you before that my parents don't know I'm pregnant and that they would throw me out of the family if they knew. My chances of ever getting through college would be over. They think I'm here in the city because I have a great job that is a part of my college program. I've told them I work every day so can't come for a visit."

"Yeah, you told us, but what's the problem you have now?"

"Well, my brother just called and said there is a big family reunion on the weekend and I'm expected to attend. No excuses. In fact, my brother was told to come get me and bring me to the reunion."

Judy was almost six months pregnant, but she was a stocky, big-busted girl and didn't look pregnant yet. Roberta and the other unwed mothers helped her wrap her stomach with ACE bandages as tight as she could stand. "Uh-oh, that isn't going to work. That really makes you look pregnant. It's too bulky."

"Hey, J. C. has a large-size girdle that I bet you could get into without too much trouble." Someone went to borrow the girdle, and everyone else dug into their clothes and the shared clothes box for anything that might conceal her pregnancy. She tried on at least twenty different outfits.

In the end, Judy went with the girdle and a skirt hemmed at her knees. A peasant-type blouse with big puffy sleeves came down to the top of her thighs and well over the skirt. They ironed her long hair to give her a hippie look that went with the outfit. They all agreed she looked pretty darn good. They coached her on how to stand, walk, and sit so that her posture helped hide her secret. She was forbidden to dance, even if the Beatles were playing.

That night Roberta and two others waited with great anticipation for Judy to get back from the reunion. Many laughs were had as she told the story of pulling off the day. "My brother, of course, was a huge help. I couldn't have done it without him. He nudged me constantly to remind me to walk a little slumped over. He kept me sitting in one chair most of the day, filling my plate frequently and delivering it so nobody could get a good look at me. Let me tell you, it was great eating all the food he brought. I'm stuffed."

In July, Roberta wanted to do something special to celebrate her twenty-first birthday. One "Army mate," Serena, was already twenty-one and old enough to drink alcohol, so they made a plan. They dressed up in their best maternity dresses, ordered a taxi, and rode in style to a hotel downtown. They enjoyed every minute of drinking a cocktail and eating a steak dinner, ignoring the people staring at them—two very pregnant young women out on the town on their own.

Soon after her birthday, with the help of Mrs. LaFontaine and the Youth Opportunity Center, Roberta got a temporary job just outside the city. She walked to the bus stop early in the morning, got on the bus, and rode it for about twenty-five minutes to a farm implement company. She worked in the office doing menial paperwork tasks. The work was boring, but she enjoyed getting away.

Her parents were paying $200 a month for her board and room and another $200 for the delivery of the baby. Roberta didn't like to think of all the money that was being paid out because of her mistake. Contributing a little to the bills gave her some peace of mind.

She soon learned to take a book to read during lunch and coffee breaks so that she didn't have to participate in small talk. Making up little stories to satisfy everyone's curiosity was stressful. Several times she had forgotten about a lie she'd told, and then a later story made no sense. Everyone looked at her in confusion. Questions were the worst. "Have you picked out the baby's name yet? Where does your husband work? When did you get married? Why did you and your husband move to Denver?" Reading a book in the corner by herself was easier. After four weeks on the job, despite the wonderful air-conditioning, she was ready to be back in her protective cell. She left with little fanfare.

Strange as it seemed, Roberta was becoming more and more anxious about leaving the home. She had learned to live with the food, and she had gotten used to not being able to go wherever she wanted. Life had gotten comfortable in many ways. The only people expecting her back in Washington were her family. She hadn't kept in touch with any of her friends because of the lies. Fear crept into her dreams and thoughts, the same fear of the unknown that she had before.

In the middle of October, Roberta gave birth to a baby boy, legally named "Baby Boy Kindle." By then, her closest friends had all delivered and left the Army, so she went through the whole ordeal with little support. Back pains started late one night, but she wasn't sure she was in labor. She waited for what seemed like a long time before going up to the third floor. The nurse sat with her until early morning, when her water broke and the pains started coming close together. The nurse declared it time to go to the hospital.

The real fun had just begun. The nurse from the home helped check Roberta into the hospital and then left her in their care. A hospital nurse put her off in a room by herself, gave her a thin gown to put on, and left her lying on a hard table to deal with the pains. She was on her own, cold and uncomfortable.

Finally another nurse came and gave her a blanket, but only after she asked for it. The hours ticked on; every once in a while a nurse, a different one every time, it seemed, returned to see how she was doing. The blanket gave her something to hug and hang on to when the pains took over her body. They came and went, came and went, each one unforgivingly dreadful. Her abdomen became so hard she was sure it would crack open like an egg. She pleaded for help, but none of the nurses showed any empathy for her. Roberta thought she might die. At times she wished she would.

She was not told why, but a nurse eventually wheeled her into another room. She was hopeful that because the pains were almost constant, she was soon to give birth and be rid of it all. Like she had always done while riding a roller coaster, Roberta screamed as a way to deal with the fear. Sometimes the screams were with words, pleas to whoever the nurse was at the moment: "Please help me. This baby needs to come out. I can't take any more of this."

Roberta sobbed when she heard one smirking nurse say, "Whoa, can she ever belt them out! Do you think anyone knows we're in here?"

For the first time in all these past months, Roberta lost all confidence in the decision she had made. *I was so wrong to do this. I should have had an abortion, or I should have married Peter. At least he would have helped me. I wouldn't be doing this alone.*

And then it was over. Roberta had no idea how long she had been in labor or what time of the day or night it was. If a doctor had come, she hadn't noticed. She didn't know any of the doctors anyway. She just knew that with one big push, the pain was pretty much gone.

No one told her if the baby was okay or not. She had heard a baby cry and assumed everything was all right. All the attention was on the baby, and she thought she heard whispers of a baby boy. Without a word, she was wheeled into a room and fell into an exhausted sleep.

—w—

Roberta had been told previously by the returning unwed mothers that she would be in a private room because the hospital didn't want the unmarried girls mixing with the legitimate mothers. At the time, she had thought it would be great to have her own space. Now she felt like an unclean freak. She woke up in the morning alone in her room at the end of the hall.

Roberta had also been told that she would be given a chance to see her baby through the nursery window if she wanted. Her thoughts on the subject had been divided. She was afraid she would fall apart if she saw it, but she also didn't want to be sorry later that she didn't.

Roberta began to hear another sound coming from down the hall, the sound of a baby not just crying, but wailing. The cries continued without pause for a long time, when a nurse brought in her breakfast on a tray. This nurse was different from the others, puffing up her pillows and straightening the sheets. She raised the bed, looking directly into her eyes. "How are you feeling today, honey? I heard you had a rough time of it yesterday."

The rare kindness made Roberta want to cry, but she dug into her breakfast. When the nurse returned to get the food tray, she gathered up enough courage to say, "Do you think I could see my baby now?"

The nurse glanced up at the ceiling, sighed, and thought for a moment. She looked back at Roberta. "Are you sure you want to?"

Roberta was thinking the nurse would take her down the hall to see the babies through the window. "Yes, I really do want to."

"Of course, sweetheart. Forget the rules. Give me a minute." Instead of helping her up to walk down the hall, the nurse hustled out of the room.

Ten minutes later, Roberta heard that same wailing baby coming down the hall. It cried all the way until it was laid in her arms. The baby went silent, looking wide eyed up at her.

Roberta's heart filled as motherly instincts consumed her. She felt an overwhelming love for the tightly swaddled creature. She had no idea she could feel this way about a baby.

"I did this?" she said to the nurse. Roberta, for the first time in all these months, was proud of what she had done. The nurse was looking down on them, but could only nod her head. Roberta slowly unwrapped the baby blanket and saw that, indeed, she had given birth to a boy. He was beautiful, he was perfect, and she had created him.

The nurse let her hold him for no longer than ten minutes as she puttered around the room, trying to look busy. Finally she said with a soft voice, "I'm sorry, Roberta, but I have to take him back to the nursery. I can be in a lot of trouble if they miss him."

Roberta turned to the baby in her arms. She looked into his dark eyes. He appeared to be looking just as intently at her. She wanted to think the look in his eyes said, "It's okay. I understand. I'll be all right." With that thought, she was able to release him to the nurse.

"Thank you," was all she could whisper. After they left she turned her head to the wall and let the tears silently streak down her cheeks.

Roberta walked down the hall to look at the babies in the nursery a number of times before she left the hospital. She saw all the mothers grouped in their rooms talking with each other, laughing, and some even feeding and holding their babies.

Sometimes the mothers and fathers were at the window with her. "Which one is yours? What's his name? When do you get to take him home? Where is your husband?" They were usually so excited and willing to talk about themselves that they didn't notice that she never answered their questions.

—⟋⟋⟋⟋—

Roberta returned to the "Army" after two nights in the hospital. She now understood why the girls before her were seldom seen after delivering their babies. She was glad she didn't have to go back to her old room and talk to the others. She wanted to forget the whole ordeal and go home. The nurses were kind and didn't ask questions. Major B came to see her but only briefly, as if it was on her to-do list for the day.

She visited Mrs. LaFontaine, the social worker, for the last time. She was kind as always, but also very businesslike for this visit. The purpose of the meeting was to sign the papers releasing herself as mother of Baby Boy Kindle. "I'm sure you remember, Roberta, that the adoption wouldn't be final for six months. You've never indicated that you might want to keep the baby. But if you do change your mind, you have to do it in the next six months. Do you understand?"

"Yes, I understand and, no, I won't change my mind," Roberta said with a steady voice. "But can you tell me if the baby is with his new family?"

Mrs. LaFontaine smiled. "I can tell you that he went to them after three days in the hospital. They're a very happy family right now." Roberta could only hope Mrs. LaFontaine was telling the truth. Believing that he was in the care of a loving family made her feel proud. She had created a beautiful baby boy for a family who wanted one.

Roberta signed the papers, confident she had done the right thing.

CHAPTER 10

ROBERTA LEFT COLORADO AND THE Army a week after giving birth to Baby Boy Kindle. She again flew alone, but this time without tears. She was now a different person; the spunk and defiant attitude had been squeezed out of her like a partially deflated beach ball. She had thought the worst would be over once she left Colorado, assuming everything would quickly return to normal; the deflated ball would just fill up with air again. However, more difficult times lay ahead.

The first few months were wonderful in many ways. The lies were less frequent mostly because she didn't look up her old friends. The food was amazing, as were movies and TV viewing. She wore her old clothes—pants, jeans, and bell-bottoms—with glee. The variety of things to do seemed never ending. Strangers no longer looked at her with scornful expressions; she could walk the streets shame free.

Kibby and Richard helped her find a room to rent in a basement not far from where they lived. The room was dungeonlike with concrete walls and no window. The bathroom was down the hall, but she had it to herself. Her dad presented her with a little TV for her room, but she frequently kept the landlady upstairs company, watching her big TV. The lady was pleasant enough, allowing Roberta to use her kitchen to prepare meals. The rent price was right, so she ignored the smell of mold and the perpetual dampness in her room.

Kibby helped Roberta pore over the help wanted ads in the paper until they found a few interesting job potentials. She was twenty-one now and had quite a few past employment experiences to put on her résumé. The courses she had taken in bookkeeping, typing, and dictation helped. She ended up with an interesting but not very high-paying job, the only girl in the office of an encyclopedia sales company. She rode the bus for about forty-five minutes every morning and evening to downtown Seattle and back.

Roberta spent many an evening and weekend afternoon with her sister, playing cards and watching movies on TV. They became better and then best friends. She loved being Bart and Lisa Anne's aunt. She didn't miss having other friends because she wasn't ready for them and their questions about her summer and fall. Small talk with anyone was excruciating, and she avoided it. She went to her parents' home in Rockford for Christmas but never ventured out of the house for fear of running into Peter or old friends.

—◊◊◊—

And then it hit: a delayed reaction to the reality of having given birth to a baby, a beautiful baby boy. And she had given him away! She had held him in her arms and still given him away! She didn't know who had him or where he lived.

One evening Roberta got herself so wound up, she had to call Kibby, who came immediately to be with her. "I don't know what he looks like, Kibby Jane. Does he have curly hair or green eyes like his dad's? Is he healthy? Is he a good baby? Are his parents good to him? Do they love him? I need to know all this stuff! But...I'll never know."

Kibby held Roberta's hand and listened to her talk and sob. "I want to change his diapers and feed him. He's on my mind almost every minute of the day. I can't erase the scene in my head of holding him in that hospital. I find myself crying over the littlest things; sometimes things that don't have anything to do with babies or motherhood. TV commercials make me cry."

"I'm so sorry, Roberta."

"You know the worst thing? My arms ache to hold him. The whole thing is physical for me. This has got to be worse than if he had died. I know he's out there, but I can't have him; my arms can't hold him."

Roberta sat on the bed; Kibby across from her on the only chair. Her sister somehow managed to look strong and be strong for her. Roberta appreciated all of it and tried to absorb her strength.

Kibby said, "Is it hard for you to be around Bart and especially Lisa Anne? She's not much older than the baby. Maybe you shouldn't spend so much time with them. I could come here more often instead of you coming over to the house. We could go more places."

"Except neither one of us has any money to do things or to pay a babysitter. Besides, I love being with the kids. I don't know what I'd do without all four of you. Richard must be getting sick of me being around so much."

"Richard is not sick of you. He loves it that you keep me company when he's gone to work so much. And remember, you give us a chance to go out once in a while when you babysit. Don't worry about that for a minute. You come to our house anytime."

Roberta stood and paced the room for a few minutes before sitting down again, the tears finally drying up. "I feel so ashamed of what I've done. How could I just give away a baby, a baby that I made in my own body? I carried him around inside of me for nine months, for Pete's sake. I was the bad girl getting pregnant, but this is the final act as the bad girl. Oh, Kibby, did I do the right thing?"

Roberta was surprised when her sister replied, "If you only knew the number of times I asked myself that same thing the first year I was married and had Bart."

"What? You weren't sure you wanted to get married?"

"Oh, yeah, I had many doubts back then. And now when I'm alone with the kids all day and when Richard works night after night, I still ask myself what happened to the wonderful career I was going to have. But you know, I just have to look in on the kids and, yes, I did the right thing. It'll come to you too. Your hormones are in charge of your emotions right now."

"But did I do the right thing? I didn't do what you did."

"Of course you did the right thing. Marriage was not for you, not right now. Someday, you'll have other babies. You're not a bad girl; you're the ultimate good girl. You've been brave, and you've given a couple a chance to have a family."

—— ⁓ ——

As time went on, Roberta felt less sad and guilty. The Army Armpit experience seemed more like a dream than a reality. The pain remained but felt less like a sting and more like a dull ache, an ache that she felt in her arms and chest.

Roberta's parents never, ever asked about her experiences or the delivery or how she was coping emotionally. They went on like nothing had happened. Maybe they felt like that was helpful, that talking about it might dig up feelings that should be left alone. "I guess I really don't want to talk to them about any of it," she eventually told Kibby.

—— ⁓ ——

Kibby looked for interesting and cheap outings for the two of them. She talked Roberta into having a free facial at one of the big department stores downtown. They had "the works," which included a facial massage and a slathering of special creams guaranteed to make them look young forever. Their faces were treated to all the makeup a woman would ever want. At the end of the appointment, they hardly recognized each other, somehow holding back the giggles in front of the beautician.

Eventually they faced reality and climbed back into Kibby's little beat-up Corvair to head home and claim the children. When they drove out of the car park, it was raining by the bucketful. The Corvair's windshield wipers didn't work well at the best of times; visibility that day was close to nonexistent. They made the decision to stay off the freeway and stick with the main streets. Halfway home they heard and felt a loud "bang"—a flat tire! Kibby managed to get the car safely to the curb as the downpour continued.

Roberta yelped, "What was that?"

"Oh my gosh, Roberta. We have a flat. Thank God we didn't take the freeway." Kibby turned to look at her sister sitting in the passenger seat and burst out laughing. "Oh my, what's this gorgeous, Hollywood-looking creature doing in my broken-down old Corvair?"

Her laughter, of course, was infectious. Neither one of them could speak until Roberta finally said. "You should talk; you look like you just stepped off the red carpet at the Oscars."

Suddenly Kibby stopped laughing and stared wide eyed out the passenger window on the other side of Roberta. "What the heck?"

Roberta turned her head, fearful of what her sister might be looking at. When she did, the rain was, of course, pouring down the window, but on the other side was a police officer getting soaked. He started tapping on the window, so Roberta rolled it down two inches. "What're you lovely ladies doing here on the side of the road? This isn't a good place to be in all this rain. It's very difficult to see you here; I'm afraid another car is going to sideswipe you."

Kibby yelled over the pounding rain, "Maybe you can't see in all this rain, but we have a flat tire, and there's no way we're getting out to change it. I don't think we know how anyway."

"No, of course you can't change it now. Can I just give the two of you a ride somewhere, and the tire can be dealt with later?"

"That would be wonderful. We have to hurry home to get my two children. My husband can deal with the car when he gets home."

That is how the two gorgeous babes from the suburbs found themselves in the back seat of a cop car. The outing had proved to be a very interesting diversion, one they talked about for years.

In time Roberta Jo grew bored with her desk job and decided it was time to seriously go back to school. She went back to her original major, not secretarial training. She went back to study and prepare for a career, and not to party. She made sure she lived with other girls who were also serious students.

She began to get straight As and after two years graduated with a bachelor's of science degree in speech and hearing science, making her dad proud and letting her mom breathe a sigh of relief.

Her last year at college, Roberta met Ken, who became her husband soon after graduation. He came from a well-educated, fun-loving family from New York State. Helen approved of him; Roberta Jo had finally found someone who looked like he had promise.

The year after the wedding, Roberta and Ken sold their cars and stereo and traveled in Europe for nine months, hitchhiking and carrying their few possessions in heavy backpacks. They had a grand time, exploring numerous countries, working the winter in a ski area in Bavaria, and renting a house for a month in Greece. On their return, Ken went for his master's degree, and they eventually moved to Canada, where good jobs were plentiful. They moved often, Roberta taking whatever jobs she could find.

Roberta told her husband early on about the baby she had given up. She thought he deserved to know what a terrible thing she had done. To her surprise, he said he didn't think less of her. She didn't tell anyone else though for another ten years or more.

And, yes, Roberta had another baby, Ashley. At twenty-eight years old, she was more than ready to be a mother this time. Ashley was the love of her life, calming the recurring ache in her arms. For Roberta's little family, Canada was a great outdoor adventure. They skied, both downhill and cross-country, hiked, backpacked, and camped, activities readily available in the Canadian Rockies. Ashley went everywhere with them.

When Ashley was almost four years old, Roberta started wanting another child, maybe a boy this time. However, her marriage was not looking good. Her husband was not as in love with fatherhood as she was with motherhood. Ken wanted to have more adventures, and a growing toddler was making that more difficult.

She could see the writing on the wall and went back to taking her birth control pills. If she got pregnant, she was probably going to be a single mother of two. The man who she thought was her best friend and the love of her life became a cruel stranger. Her heart was broken, but she finally gave up trying to hold something together that no longer existed and again went back to school to be able to make a decent living.

Andrew, Roberta and Kibby's beloved father, had died the year before Ashley was born while Roberta still lived in the United States. Roberta had quit her nurses' aide job, and Kibby had left her small children with friends and Richard to go to help care for Andrew the three months before his death. Roberta missed him. She hadn't been ready to be without a father.

And then every year in October, Baby Boy Kindle's birthday month, the ache in her arms and heart returned to haunt her. She would wonder what he looked like now and if he was loved. As Ashley grew and went through developmental milestones, she wondered if her baby boy had gone through them at the same age. She wondered if he was having a birthday party and if he played sports. Mostly she wondered if he was a happy boy growing up in a good home. She never shared her sadness with anyone during this month. Her mother had never wanted to know anything about him, and her sister was busy raising her own children.

In her grief for her father, she wondered why she lost the males in her life over and over again. Grief for Baby Boy Kindle, her father, Ken, and sometimes even Peter was stacked up in her heart like a pile of heavy books. *Did I do something wrong?*

In 1977, while Roberta was going back to school because her marriage was failing, she made a new young friend, Lilly.

"Hey, Roberta. Are you in there?" Her neighbor, Lilly's mother, was pounding on the back-door screen.

"Hey back, Patricia. Ashley and I are in the living room playing dolls. Want to join us? We'll let you have any doll you want, won't we, Ashley? Well...maybe not Ken. He's Ashley's favorite because that's her dad's name."

Roberta and Ashley were sitting on the floor with Barbie dolls, doll clothes, and doll paraphernalia spread out around them. Rod Stewart was quietly singing "Tonight's the Night" in the background.

Roberta was over thirty years old now. She hadn't noticed any crow's feet at her eyes, but her hair was starting to show some gray. She would have to have help from a hairdresser soon. She was heavier than she had been in her twenties but still slim enough. Her best features were still her blue eyes, a contrast to her dark hair.

"Are you kidding? I'd love to play Barbies with you two." Patricia smiled at Ashley and gave her a quick pat on the head. The four-year-old was too involved with her play to say anything back.

After playing dolls for a few minutes, Roberta talked Ashley into taking them outside for a while. The two women went into the kitchen for a cup of tea. The radio station played Andy Gibb's "I Just Want to Be Your Everything." Roberta suspected that Patricia had something serious to talk about, and her hunches were correct. Patricia's daughter, Lilly, only sixteen years old, had just told her mother that she was pregnant.

"I'm so angry at Lilly, I could just spit. I know I haven't been very nice about the whole thing, but I'm just so damn mad. I don't know what we're going to do. She's already three months pregnant, for God's sake. She waited for more than two months before telling me."

"I'm so sorry, Patricia. How about a beer instead of tea? Alcohol always helps me deal with life's problems. I don't think tea is strong enough for this conversation."

"That would be great. Drowning my sorrows in beer is an excellent idea. You know, we had such great hopes and dreams for Lilly. She's so smart and capable. Well, forget the smart. Maybe she isn't so smart after all. How in the heck did she let this happen?"

"Have you told Randy?" Roberta asked once they were curled up on the couch with their beers.

"Oh God, that's next...telling her dad. And you think I'm mad. The shit is going to hit the fan at our house."

Roberta and Patricia were not close friends but had a pleasant, neighborly relationship. Roberta had always wondered who wore the pants in the family. Randy, Lilly's dad, was very strong willed and could put his foot down pretty hard. But he also drank a lot, Roberta suspected. Patricia appeared to be superpassive, a doing-what-her-husband-said kind of gal, but had fooled her more than once, demonstrating great strength running the household. Roberta liked that side of her.

Roberta did not say anything, but Lilly had already come to her with the news that she was pregnant. Over the last year, Roberta and Lilly had connected. They had gone shopping together for clothes and occasionally to a movie and lunch.

Lilly was the quiet child of the family of four children, but she also had a rebellious streak. She was tall and lean with the personality to match, strong willed and of few words, unless she had something important to say. She always seemed to know what she wanted and wasn't afraid to tell anyone what that was.

The following day, Lilly came to Roberta to report her father's reaction to the news. "Dad actually didn't say much after Mom told him. Can you believe it? He just said he was disappointed in me and I was a disgrace to the family. I guess that's enough, eh?"

Lilly continued, "Get this. He said I'd always been the quiet one. He said Grandma told him that you can never trust the quiet ones." Lilly started sobbing. "What does that mean? Are they saying that I can't be trusted, that they have never trusted me? I made a mistake. I didn't get pregnant to be mean. They're making me feel so evil. Like I'm a failure or something."

Roberta went to the couch to sit beside Lilly, hoping to comfort her in some way. "Lilly, you're not a failure. You're right; you just made a mistake, and now you're going to have to deal with it, that's all. No doubt your life is going to take a turn here, but you're still going to do wonderful things, and you're going to have a wonderful life. You just can't see it now."

"Do you really think so? I've made such a mess of it so far."

"Do you want to tell me about how you got pregnant? You don't have to, but it might help to talk about it."

Lilly took a big breath and thought for a few moments, "Okay. It's no big secret. Jacob and I have been together for months now. You know his family has always been friends with my family; well, I guess, they're more like friends of a family friend. Anyway, my parents know him and liked it that I was dating him. That's what they told me anyway. We did a bunch of kissing and stuff right from the beginning. It's just that he kept telling me we should go all the way. He said everybody else did it. We should do it too. He said he wouldn't tell anyone."

"I'm afraid all the guys say that. It's a ploy to get in the girls' pants. You aren't the first one to hear that stuff and fall for it."

Lilly hung her head down, avoiding Roberta's eyes. She curled up in a tight little ball beside Roberta. Roberta was afraid she had made a mistake suggesting Roberta tell all, except she noted that Lilly was no longer sobbing.

The next thing out of Lilly's mouth, however, brought back the sobbing. "Ya know the worst part? The creep threatened to date my sister if I didn't have sex with him. He said Terry would probably do it with him if I didn't. I was so jealous. Terry has lots of boyfriends; she didn't need to steal mine!" Shame had now become anger, but Roberta thought that was a good thing.

"Oh, that was mean of Jacob. I can see why you caved in to his wants. This is hard for you to tell me, isn't it? I promise I'll never share this with anyone else unless you want me to."

"Thank you, Roberta. You're a good friend."

"Okay, now I have something to tell you, something that I have told very few people my whole life. It all took place a great many years ago."

Roberta went on to tell Lilly about how twelve years ago, she had also gotten pregnant. "Much like you, I caved in and had sex with my high school sweetheart." Roberta was now the one tearing up. "I loved this boyfriend very much. We had dated each other off and on for years, but I wasn't ready to marry him."

Roberta got up and went for the Kleenex box. "The hardest part was telling my parents. They were disappointed in me as well. My mother said some cruel things that I'll never forget. I tell you all this, Lilly, because I want you to know that you're far from the only young girl that has found herself in this position. You're going to get through this, just like I got through it years ago. Your parents may be saying things that feel mean to you right now, but they're good, kind people, and they're going to do all they can to help you, just as my parents did for me."

Roberta was not ready to tell Lilly the rest of her story, the decision she had made back then. She didn't want to influence, in any way, Lilly and her family's decision.

"Oh my gosh, Roberta. You got pregnant when you were my age, and you weren't married? I don't believe it."

"Well, believe it. The very same thing, except that I was older than you are now. There were tough times for sure. But I survived."

"But what did you do? Ashley isn't that old. She couldn't be the baby you had then."

Roberta took a big breath, not at all sure that she was handling this correctly or in the best way. "Someday, I'll tell you the rest of my story, but for now, you need to find out what your options are for solving your problem. You have to make the decision with your parents. You can tell them my story if you want. I may do it myself later, if I think it might help them or you. For now, tell me what you think you want to do."

Lilly's body had uncurled after hearing about Roberta's past. She took a Kleenex from Roberta, blew her nose, and said, "I don't know what I want to do. I guess I'll do whatever Mom and Dad tell me to do. Neither one of them want me to marry Jacob. Thank heavens for that. He was an okay boyfriend, but I certainly don't want to marry him! Yuck! He doesn't want to marry me either, I don't think."

"Have you told him you're pregnant with his baby?"

"I told him when I first thought I might be pregnant. He looked at me as though I was a freak. Later, when I told him that it was for sure, he acted just as weird. You'd have thought I had some disease. I haven't heard a word from him since. That's a good thing, though. I don't really want to hear from him."

"Well, it looks like getting married is out. What options other than marriage have your parents talked about?"

"Mom keeps saying that I need to go to a doctor, not our family doctor, but some other doctor. I don't want to go. I've heard other girls talk about having exams 'down there.' It sounds awful."

"Well, go home; talk to your mom and your dad. Don't be afraid to ask questions. You want to know and you deserve to know what they're thinking. Remember that I'm always here to talk. But also remember that your mom and I are friends, too, and we're probably going to be talking about all of this. I can keep secrets between you and me, but I can't lie to her. Do you feel any better now after talking?"

"Oh yes. Can I come back tomorrow? We're supposed to have a big discussion at home tonight. I may want to talk to you afterward."

"Yes, of course, you can come every day if you want. This's a good time right after you get home from school. Usually Ashley is busy playing outside with her buddy."

Lilly did come back the next day. "Mom is making an appointment with *that* doctor, so I guess I have to go see him. She also told me not to tell my sisters that I'm pregnant yet. It's all a hush-hush secret."

Roberta didn't see Lilly or Patricia again for almost a week, when Lilly told her that she went to see the doctor. "When we drove into the parking lot at the doctor's office, Mom said that when I saw the doctor,

I needed to act like I was crazy, terribly upset that I was pregnant. She said I had to convince him that I couldn't have the baby. I was to tell him that I have to drive my sister to school every day and a baby would mess up both our lives, so we might as well end both of our lives right now. Mom said I had to do it. I had to convince him that the baby would be the end of my life."

Roberta had given Lilly a Kleenex, which she was now shredding to pieces. "I was so shocked that I didn't even answer her. I just got out of the car and went into the doctor's office. It was awful, Roberta. I didn't understand what Mom wanted me to do or why. All of a sudden, I had to play the crazy girl role? You said to ask questions, but I didn't know what to ask them."

"I didn't know what to ask the doctor either. And then...I had to take off *all* my clothes and lay down on this table with my legs spread apart. Can you believe it? He was a stranger! I was so embarrassed. I couldn't believe my mom and dad wanted me to do this. It hurt like heck too."

Lilly and Roberta were sitting on the front porch, watching Ashley play with her friend. It was a beautiful spring evening. The leaves were about ready to pop their new spring-green leaves. Lilly's eyes were open wide, her face pale and looking thinner than ever. She had gone through three Kleenex. "Somehow, I got through all that. I think I kind of blanked out cause I don't remember much of it. Afterward, I put my clothes back on and went to sit in his office like he had told me to do. I didn't say a word to him. I wanted to run out of the building."

Roberta remembered her similar scene when she was twenty years old and then the many Army clinics, like they happened yesterday. She didn't share the memories but let Lilly talk on, holding her hand and occasionally squeezing it to show her support. "I couldn't say any-thing like Mom wanted me to say. I couldn't get my mouth to work to say anything. He asked if I wanted to have this baby or if I wanted to get married. All I could do was shake my head yes or no. He told me I was definitely pregnant. Duh! He said everything was healthy; the baby was healthy, and so was I. Who cares, eh?

"I finally got out of there, and I went back to the car to Mom and Dad. Mom kept saying, 'Did you act crazy?' I told her I did because I thought the doctor might think I was crazy. But I hadn't said a word the whole time. I'm just glad all that's over with. I'm thinking Mom is the crazy one."

"I'm glad it's over too. You were a very brave girl to do all that. I'm proud of you."

Patricia came over the next day. Ashley was watching *Mr. Dressup* on TV. "Hey, Roberta."

"Hey, Patricia. Time for another beer?"

"Sounds good. I could use one about now." They settled down at the kitchen table out of Ashley's earshot. "I know Lilly has been over here talking to you. I want you to know that I'm glad she comes. You're a good friend. I hope you're okay with it."

"Oh, I'm better than okay. You bet. I'm glad to be here for her. I was worried, though, that you might not approve. I'm glad you do."

"I certainly do. I don't know if she told you, but Randy and I took her to a doctor to consider an abortion. I think it was a horrible experience for her. She was pretty shook up afterward. But we thought it might be a good option. The doc told us later that she was too far along to perform an abortion. Probably just as well. I don't know if we could have followed through on that anyway."

Patricia seemed to have no idea how traumatic it had been for her daughter. *You'd have thought Patricia would have at least gone in with her. She's only sixteen.* Roberta kept her thoughts to herself.

Patricia went on to say, "So I've been doing a little looking around and found an unwed mothers' home in the city. She could go there and give the baby up for adoption. Randy and I drove by and took a look at it, but it looked horribly institutional. I also found out it's expensive, and I don't think we can afford it."

Roberta tried to keep her composure. She wanted to scream, "No, no, no." She bit her tongue and pressed her lips together to keep the words from bursting out.

"I asked Lilly what she wanted to do. She didn't even answer me. None of us want her to get married, abortion is out, the home looks too expensive. Randy would still like her to give the baby up for adoption, but I don't like that idea at all. What's left, eh? I can't believe this is happening. We're about out of options."

"It sure looks like it. Do you think Lilly could stay home with you and have the baby? She could still give the baby up for adoption."

"That's about what we're left with. I'll let you know soon what we decide. Or maybe Lilly will want to tell you what we decide. Right now, I've got to get home. Thanks for the listening ear and the beer."

"You're welcome. I'm so glad you're okay with my visits with Lilly. She always looks so frazzled when she first gets here and is so much calmer after she tells me what's going on."

Close to a week later, Lilly came to see Roberta again. "Tell me what's happening, Lilly. You look kinda beat up." She also looked like she had lost weight instead of gaining weight with the pregnancy. Dark circles were around her eyes.

"I don't feel beat up. I don't feel much of anything. I'm kinda numb. Mom keeps asking me what I want to do about the baby. I don't know! I'm sixteen years old. I don't know what to do about a baby. I just want to do whatever they think I should do. Mom keeps saying she just wants to get rid of the problem."

"What does that mean, get rid of the problem?"

"I guess they just want me to give the baby up for adoption. We can't afford for me to go off somewhere and have it, so I guess I'll just stay home and have it."

"What does your dad have to say about it?"

"He doesn't say much of anything. He just drinks a lot and stays away. When he does say something, he's very loud about it. I'm glad when he stays away so he isn't here to be mean to all of us. I don't get it. He can be the best dad ever some days. Now Mom says I have to go to school and tell the principal. She won't go with me. She says I got myself in this predicament; I have to deal with it."

Roberta cringed. She didn't understand why Patricia was so un-supportive. "Would your sister go with you, do you think? Would that help?"

"Are you kidding? Terry is furious about the whole thing. She hates me right now. She wouldn't be any help at all. The others haven't been told yet. It's still a big secret." Roberta wanted to offer to go with her to the school but was afraid she would upset Patricia.

The next week Lilly reported that the principal told her she could no longer attend school. "He said they can't have pregnant girls run-ning around the school giving the other girls the idea that it's okay to have a baby when they aren't married.

"Now, Mom says no matter what, I have to have the baby before school starts in September again. That way, I can go back to driving Terry and me to school. Like I really have any kind of control over when the baby comes." Roberta let Lilly vent her feelings without tak-ing sides.

"Mom won't even let me out of the house. When I do go shopping or something with her, we have to go to the city so no one'll see us. You'd think I had leprosy or something. She isn't even going to take me to the doctor again. The doctor I went to reported everything was okay, and that's good enough."

This last news broke Roberta's heart. The poor sixteen-year-old was going to get no more preparation than she had gotten when she gave birth to Baby Boy Kindle. She started thinking maybe she could provide Lilly with some information on pregnancy and childbirth, be-ing careful not to step on Patricia's toes. Roberta went to the library and checked out all the books she could find.

When Lilly showed up, Roberta was prepared with pictures of fe-tuses. She talked about labor and delivery, and they practiced breath-ing and relaxation exercises. Lilly wasn't always attentive, so she made the sessions short.

Lilly's sister brought home her school work every day, and she fin-ished out the school year with her class. Friends did not come to visit. Patricia gave her work to do around the house, but she was bored much of the time. She came around to see Roberta and Ashley almost daily. Roberta tried to make it fun by playing games with Ashley, and they frequently watched movies on TV.

About the eighth month of pregnancy, Lilly shared that her mother was having a change of heart. "My parents have turned their bathroom into a kind of nursery. They came home with a small crib, a baby carrier, baby bottles, and even diapers. Can you believe it?"

"What do you think they are planning to do?"

"Who knows? I just do whatever they want me to do. I'm just responsible for having the baby before school starts in September. Heaven help me if that doesn't happen." Secretly, Roberta was relieved that it looked like Lilly was not going to give her baby away for adoption.

In mid-August, Lilly gave birth to a healthy boy, James, who came home from the hospital with Lilly. The baby stayed the nights in his grandparents' bathroom so they could care for him and Lilly could sleep. When she came home from school, she cared for him until bedtime and on weekends. Lilly was definitely the mom. Randy and Patricia appeared both proud and thrilled to have a little grandson. Lilly's sister, Terry, was the unhappiest of all the family members. She reportedly was embarrassed to attend their old school, so she moved out of the family home and in with friends.

Lilly brought the baby over to see Roberta. "The delivery was awful. I know you told me it would be bad, but it was more than bad. I remembered most of what you taught me, but I couldn't always to do the breathing and relaxing. There was one nurse who did a lot to coach me. She was very kind. She would get close to my face and whisper to me to breathe and to stay calm. That helped a lot."

"Was your mom in there with you?" Roberta asked.

"No, Mom didn't come into the labor room with me. I don't know why. She watched through the window. It helped to know she was close, but I would have liked her to be in the room with me."

The kids at school didn't appear to know anything about the baby. Maybe the teachers had told them to not say anything. One visit, Lilly told Roberta, "I was at the mall in the city with James in my arms. I saw two of my old girl friends from school walking right toward me. I would have hidden in a store, but it was too late; they saw me and waved, all friendlylike. One of them asked who the baby belonged to. I had to tell them the baby was mine. I thought they knew; I thought everyone knew. But the girls were dumbfounded and just turned and walked away."

Lilly was a good mother despite her young age. When little James was just three months old, one of Lilly's sisters set her up on a blind date. She told Roberta that she thought it was a great idea because the guy, Don, was also very tall.

The first date evidently didn't go well. Lilly said he was a jerk. "He spent most of the evening bragging about himself and his accomplishments. He didn't ask anything about me."

Roberta was shocked that Lily had told him right off that she had a three-month-old son. But a few days later, he called and asked her out to a movie. "Of course I said yes. I would do just about anything to get out of the house for a while."

The day after the movie date, Lilly went to see Roberta. "You won't believe this, Roberta. My second date with Don was fantastic. He was so different when it was just the two of us without friends around. He was so interested in me. He didn't mind at all that I had a baby. In fact, he wanted to know all about James. And he's so cute, taller than me even."

"I'm so happy for you, Lilly. Did you make plans to see each other again?"

"Yes, we did. He wants to meet James next. My parents are even happy about him. They know his parents and like them."

Lilly came to see Roberta less and less but reported that she and Don were continuing to see each other. "I'm just happy to have a friend who likes me and wants to be with me."

"I like your attitude. This is all great news. Keep me posted, and maybe I can meet Don one day."

Roberta thought, *I wasn't always sure, but I'm thinking Lilly and her family did the right thing.*

Part Four
Disclosures: 1987

When you come to the edge of all the light you have, and must take a step into the darkness of the unknown, believe that one of two things will happen to you: either there will be something solid for you to stand on, or, you will be taught how to fly.

—Patrick Overton

.

CHAPTER 11

"OKAY, DINNER'S READY. WHO'S HUNGRY?" Roberta had laid out the usual Friday night fare of makings for tacos. She liked the ritual because she didn't have to think about what she was going to cook. It was the only time she allowed the family to have dinner in front of the TV.

They would be watching shows like *Full House*, *The A-Team*, and *The Cosby Show* since Ashley would be present for taco night. Roberta and her husband had just installed a huge satellite dish in the side yard of their small acreage. The variety of available TV shows was astounding, but they also had to filter out what was inappropriate for fourteen-year-old children.

Roberta was not in her usual Friday night let-down-your-hair-mood, however. She had been a little blue the last few days, and she knew why...it was October. After dinner, Roberta still couldn't shake the melancholy that covered her from head to toe like a giant bunting bag. Later that evening, she laid in bed for a long time, unable to sleep. Ashley had gone to bed hours ago, and Stan, Roberta's fiancé, next to her was already snoring.

All of a sudden, a light bulb went off in her head. *I've had it with this sorrow thing every year! Baby Boy Kindle will be twenty-one years old in a few days. He's not a baby anymore; he's not even a child. Besides, having a baby out of wedlock is no longer a social crime. Giving up a baby for adoption isn't a crime*

175

either, last I heard. I'm going to tell my secret to whoever I want. With that decision, she rolled over and went to sleep.

The next morning Roberta woke up, immediately remembering her vow of the night before. She gave Stan a shake and said, "Okay, big guy, I've made a decision. Do you want to hear it?"

"I don't know, do I? I have a feeling I'm going to hear about it whether I want to or not."

She and Stan had been living together for three years and had just decided they would get married. The wedding was planned for the day after Christmas, just over two months away. Roberta had always said that she would never marry again. She had pushed Stan to move in with her three years ago; that was enough. Their present living arrangement seemed to be working all right. They had purchased a house together two years ago, and that had felt like a commitment similar to marriage. However, Stan had romantically asked her to marry him this summer while they were on vacation, and she couldn't, and didn't, say no. It had been his idea, not hers, and that made the difference.

In the first year of dating Stan, Roberta had told him that she had given birth to a baby. By coincidence, he had gotten a girlfriend pregnant about the same time. His girlfriend had also given the baby up for adoption. He did not, however, have the same emotional tie that she did, not having experienced a baby growing inside his body.

Roberta continued her conversation with Stan. "Maybe you remember that the baby I had is going to be twenty-one this month. I want the secret to be finished."

"Okay, I get it. There's no reason it shouldn't be out in the open now."

"I want to tell Ashley about the baby. But…here's the biggie. I need to tell her now because"—Roberta took a big breath—"then I want to see if I can find him. He will legally be an adult. I no longer have to worry about his adoptive parents getting upset. But what if I find him right away and he shows up on the doorstep? Ashley has to know about him before that happens."

Stan yawned, giving up the idea of going back to sleep. "I see your point, and you're absolutely right. Tell Ashley first. But how about you? Are you ready to have him show up on your doorstep?"

"Oh, I'm so ready. I can't think of anything better to happen to me right now. Just think, 1987: the year we got married and the year I met my son!"

"Wow!"

"How about you, Stan? Are you ready for this to happen? That means you'll not only have a stepdaughter; you'll have a stepson." Stan had been married before but did not have any children of his own.

"I can handle it. Bring him on! But could we have a cup of coffee first?"

Roberta wanted to add the question of how would he feel if his daughter showed up at the doorstep, but she didn't say anything. That was a different issue that didn't need to be dealt with right now, or ever.

—◆—

Roberta was nervous about telling her daughter. *Will she think less of me? Would this give her permission to be sexually promiscuous?*

Nervous or not, she couldn't wait. Later that morning, she gave Ashley a chance to get up, wake up, and have some breakfast. Roberta then knocked on her daughter's bedroom door. With permission granted, Roberta entered her daughter's room trying not to look around at the piles of clothes and dirty dishes. "Ashley, I have something to tell you. Do I have your attention? Because this is something that's really important to me."

"Okay, Mom, let her rip. You have my undivided attention. I'll even turn off my stereo."

Roberta sat down on the unmade bed and watched Ashley turn off Michael Jackson belting out his latest. Her daughter curled up on the bed beside her. She sat on her hands so Ashley wouldn't see them shaking. "Okay. Twenty-one years ago, almost exactly, before I ever met your dad…I had a baby."

Ashley's facial expression did not change. She look intensely at her mother, though, seemingly interested in what she had to say, but not shocked in any way. Roberta decided that was a good sign and continued. "I was very young, and there were so many things I wanted to do with my life. I loved the baby's father; we had been high school sweethearts. But we decided not to get married. He wasn't ready either. I gave the baby up for adoption." With the last bit of news, Ashley's eyes popped open wide. Roberta could see the wheels turning inside her head. It was so like Ashley to not speak her thoughts right away.

Roberta let the news soak in a few minutes before adding, "That means you have a half brother out there somewhere."

"Cool. I always wanted a brother."

"So you're okay with this news? I'm sorry I couldn't tell you sooner."

"Why couldn't you?"

"Having a baby when you weren't married was a big deal back then and had to be kept a secret. I had to swear to my parents that I wouldn't tell anyone, and I pretty much haven't all these years."

"I'm okay with it, Mom. But why did you decide to tell me now? I don't get it."

"Well…I've always wanted you to know but didn't know when was that best time. Now that he's going to be twenty-one, I want to try and find him. Once I try, I might find out something immediately. I don't want that to happen without you knowing about him first. Do you understand?"

"Yeah, I do understand. Thanks, Mom. I'm wondering, though, is this hard for you?"

"You know, right this minute, no." Roberta threw her hands up above her head. "It feels wonderful! It feels like a weight is lifted off my shoulders—not just telling you, but I feel I'm telling the world. Thank you, thank you, Ashley, for being so receptive to the whole thing. That helps a lot." Roberta brought her hands back down and around her daughter into a giant hug.

Ashley broke away from her mother's embrace. "Is that why you have been so big on sex education all my life? Is this why I know more about having babies and not having babies than anyone I know?"

Now it was Roberta's turn to be wide eyed in surprise. She sat up straight and looked at her daughter. "You do? Well, I guess having that baby is why I talked to you so much about sex. When I was a kid, I didn't know much about how babies came about, and I didn't want it to be that way with you. I'm thrilled that you feel you're the most informed of all your friends."

"Yeah, I could just about teach a sex ed class." They both laughed at the thought.

Not wanting to lose another sex ed opportunity, Roberta said, "I guess right now is as good a time as ever to tell you that if you ever find yourself in the position that you think you'll have sex with a guy, I want you to come to me first."

"What do you mean? Why would I tell you first?"

"I feel very strongly about protecting you from having a baby before you're ready. Now you know why I feel that way. I've been listening to our friends, the Bateses and the Campbells, talk about their kids and birth control. They did everything they could think of to make sure their kids, even the boys, didn't get pregnant before marriage. I want to do the same."

"How do we do that?"

"I'd like to take you to our doctor and get you birth control pills when you think it is time. That isn't to say I want you to have sex before you're in a serious relationship. I would rather you waited until you're truly in love and ready to commit to someone before you have sex. But before you do have sex, we need to fix you up with birth control pills."

"Wow, okay."

"No questions asked, just tell me you need to get to the doctor. Or, if you want, you have my permission to go to the doctor on your own. Understand?"

"Okay, I get it. But I don't think I'm going to need anything soon."
"Good, I like it that way."

—⁓—

Roberta didn't tell anyone else about her son; telling Ashley seemed to be enough. She did send a letter to the State of Colorado Health Department to find out how she might find him. She received a reply that she needed to apply to the adoption registry in that state. Although adoption records had been sealed in the past; now anyone could apply. The registry would match her with anyone who disclosed the same information: her maiden name and the place and date of the baby's birth. She would be notified when and if there was a match.

Roberta promptly sent away for the application. When the form came, she learned that a contact person needed to be named in case she could not be located. She could understand the reason for such a contact person. Three and a half years was the longest she had ever lived at the same residence. She decided that her mother was the best choice as the contact person. Helen had lived in the same house she had lived in for over forty years and wouldn't likely be moving soon.

Roberta and Helen never talked about the baby, but they were going to have to now. Roberta was nervous about bringing up the subject; she never knew how her mother would react to anything. She opened a can of cold beer for courage, sat down, and dialed her mother's number.

"Hi, Mother. What's happening in Rockford?"

"Hi, Roberta Jo. It's great to hear your voice, and there's lots happening here. I just booked my flight to China. Can you believe it? I'll be gone for three weeks traveling with a group of college alumni. It should be a great trip."

"What! You just got back from Israel, didn't you?"

"No, that was three months ago. Besides, I don't leave on this trip for another six months. This one is going to be a photography trip. I've just bought a wonderful new camera, and Beverly is giving me lessons on developing my own film. She has all the equipment at her house, so I don't have to purchase my own. I'm also hoping to be able to do my own photo developing for the historical preservation work we're doing here."

"Wow, Mother, you're one busy gal." Roberta could see Helen had not slowed down since turning seventy.

"Did I tell you we got the local library building on the National Historical Registry and are now working on some of the lovely old homes in town?"

"No, I knew you were working on it, but I didn't know anything was that final. Congratulations. Speaking of registrations, I have something to ask of you." Roberta was afraid that if she didn't rudely interrupt her mother, she would never get a word in edgewise. Helen avoided using the phone, but when she did get on, she was compelled to keep the conversation going.

"Great. Enough about me. What do you need?"

Roberta took a big swig of beer before answering. "I guess you remember the baby boy I had years ago and gave up for adoption."

"Yes, of course I do."

"Would you believe he's now twenty-one years old? And because of that, I've decided to try and find him." Helen didn't say word, an unusual event. Getting no response, good or bad, from her mother, Roberta was forced to say something. "What do you think?"

"Has it really been twenty-one years?"

"Yes, it has."

"Well, I think you need to do what's important to you. I know it wasn't easy for you, giving him up. I think it a good decision that you try to find him. How can I possibly help?"

Roberta relaxed back into her chair. "I found out that I can apply to an adoption registry in Colorado to put my name and information on file. Then if he or, I guess, his adoptive parents try to find me, we'll be matched."

"And what does that have to do with me?"

"They need a contact person in case I have moved and they can't find me. You know how much I have moved around?"

"I'd be happy to be that contact person. What do I have to do?"

"Oh, nothing really. Just know that you could be contacted if I can't be found. I'll try to remember to keep the registry informed, though, when I move."

"No problem. Give them my name and address for sure." Helen evidently had no more to say on that topic. "I wanted you to know that the sale of your father's business is final. It's such a relief to not have that responsibility anymore. I had fun running it after he died, but it began to take up too much of my time. It was getting hard to take off on my trips."

"I understand. I best get off this phone now. Sounds like you're having a ball. I'm so happy for you."

"Thanks, Roberta Jo. I love you. Bye."

Stan walked into the room where she sat finishing her beer, thinking about the call. "Well, how did it go?'

"It went well, I think. No bombs from Mother this time. Whew!"

Stan went to get his own beer and sat down beside her on the couch, "Congratulations. What now?"

"I guess I can send off the paperwork to the registry. And maybe I should call my sister and let her know what I'm doing. No, I guess that won't work. I just remembered that Kibby is off to San Francisco again on a buying trip for her store."

"Off again? Your sister sure landed a great job at that kitchen store. Didn't you say she is now a manager doing most of the buying?"

"That's right. I'm so proud that all her wonderful cooking has led to a career."

"You know, you and your sister have done not too badly for a couple of small-town hicks who both got knocked up at twenty years of age."

"Hey, watch what you're saying. You made a baby back then, too, remember?"

"Yeah, I know; I'm just giving you a bad time. I'm proud of the both of you, that's all."

"We are both late bloomers, for sure, and we have had our buds knocked back a few times, but watch out! The petals are now open; we're on our way!"

Roberta had also made an interesting career for herself since her divorce from Ken. She taught school for five years but found the classroom was not her thing. The school district had asked her to be their speech therapist. Having summers and holidays to spend with Ashley had been great. She would have to get her master's degree someday, but that would have to wait.

—⟋⟍—

Helen hung up the phone after talking to Roberta, sat back in her chair, and let her mind drift back to when Roberta Jo had gone off to have the baby to be given up for adoption. She remembered that Andrew always wanted to tell the girls that she too had gotten pregnant before they were married. He had gone along with her wishes to keep it all a secret, but she knew he thought they would have appreciated knowing it.

Maybe he was right and I was wrong. They both would have been comforted knowing we had made a mistake too. But it wasn't just the pregnancy. It was the abortion. I just couldn't tell them that part.

But now Helen wished she had told them back then. It seemed too late. She thought they would probably be angry to hear it now. *But maybe I should just do it. If I'm regretting it now, it might just get worse. Oh, Andrew, I wish you were here to tell me what to do!*

—⟋⟍—

Roberta sent in the adoption registry application and waited for a reply with news of a match. Nothing happened; a reply never came.

After a month, she realized a reunion with her son was not going to happen. She was respectful of Baby Boy Kindle's wishes, so she did not seek out private investigators who could be hired to look further. *If he doesn't want to be found, I don't want to push it.*

But fear lived in the back of Roberta's mind that her son maybe resented her or was angry because she had given him away. The word "abandonment" floated around in her head. The fear that he had had a horrible childhood smoldered there as well. Maybe he would have been better off with her if she had gotten married? Maybe he wasn't even alive?

Roberta tried to imagine Baby Boy Kindle as the adult that he now was. Sometimes when she was among a lot of strangers, she would look around and try to imagine which one could be him. *Would he look like that guy sitting over there on the bench? Would he be balding, like Daddy did at such a young age? Would he look like my nephew, Bart, or like my cousin Jason? Would he have a stocky build like many of the men in the family, or would he be tall and slim like Mother's dad and brother? Surely, I would recognize him. He is my son. Of course, I would recognize him!*

Kibby was still the best sounding board a person could have. She had voiced her approval of Roberta's decision to try and find the baby. And now she got it that Roberta was sad that she had heard nothing back from the registry. "You've done all you can. You've got to leave it up to whatever happens now."

"I know you're right. But I'm so impatient. I got all geared up for finally getting some answers and to have this wonderful reunion with my son. But nothing has changed."

"Roberta, you have to have patience, something you have never had a lot of. You want things to happen right now. Don't let this get the best of you. You get so restless and discontent with the world when things don't go the way you want. You have a wonderful husband, daughter, and career. Take pride and joy in all that, and be happy."

"You're right. I need to hear all that. I'm going to step back and I'm going to enjoy what I have. I love you, Big Sister."

—◆—

A few weeks later, Kibby called Roberta back. "Hi, Roberta Jo. I've been thinking a lot about our last phone conversation, and then the most coincidental thing happened."

"I'm all ears."

"I don't know if you ever met my friend Casey. She used to work at the store. I don't think you did meet her. Anyway, I hadn't seen her for almost a year, so we got together to have lunch the other day."

"I remember you talking about Casey. Wasn't she the one who never married and is ten or so years younger than you?"

"Yes, that's the one. Well, she told me this incredible story of what she has been through since she left the store. Would you believe she just found out that her mother is really her aunt?"

"What?" Roberta figured she needed to sit down for this conversation and did so.

"That's right. Her real mother is in a mental hospital and has been for years. Casey had been told all these years that this woman was her aunt. Can you imagine? So, of course, the woman who raised her is really the aunt. I thought of you, I guess, because her real mom got pregnant when she was young and unmarried and didn't want to keep the baby. Anyway, the woman who Casey thought was her mother had not been able to get pregnant with her husband, so she and her husband raised the baby—Casey."

"Whoa, that's quite a story."

"But there's more. Casey is furious. She was raised with two brothers-cousins that her aunt eventually was able to conceive. Her whole life has been turned upside down, and she is holding a bucketful of anger. She hasn't talked to her mother, a.k.a. aunt, now for most of this past year. One of her brothers-cousins has been very supportive, but the other has been a real creep."

"What about the man who raised her as her dad. Is he in the picture?"

"He has been an alcoholic for years, and she had pretty much separated herself from him since she left home. The couple has been separated off and on for years. I guess he doesn't have much to say about the whole thing. Casey blames the whole deception on the woman who raised her."

Although it was an interesting story, Roberta was wondering what it had to do with her. Kibby finally said, "Okay, the reason I wanted to tell you all this is because Casey decided to try to find her biological father. Her mom-aunt gave her enough info that she eventually did find him. He had long ago moved to New York State. I got real excited, thinking of you trying to find your son, when she told me all this."

"I understand now. Has she been able to meet him?" Roberta's adrenaline was pumping.

"She did! She talked to him quite a few times on the phone and then went to meet him and his family. They got along very well, I guess. She also met her two half sisters. The story doesn't end there, however. She got along well with the sisters, finding they had all kinds of things in common. One of the sisters became especially friendly with Casey. I think her name is Diana. She and Casey continued to communicate regularly, like maybe every week. Diana even came to visit Casey in Seattle."

"Then, get this…the second sister began to get wildly jealous of the relationship and made threats to Casey. It's been bad. She has accused Casey of making up the whole lost-daughter story so that she can inherit some of their dad's money. Diana has had to back off of their friendship."

Roberta asked, "What about Casey's biological dad? Is he doing anything to straighten things out?"

"That's just it. He died a couple of months ago. Now she isn't hearing from anyone and doesn't know what to do. She's afraid to call them because they might continue to think she is after an inheritance. She lost most of her first family, and now she's lost her newly acquired family."

"Wow, you're right. That's an incredible story."

"The main reason I wanted to tell you this is because I know you want so badly to find your son. But beware—there's always the possibility that you might open a can of worms. Maybe no news is good news."

"I get what you're saying. I guess she thought she was doing the right thing the whole time, huh?"

CHAPTER 12

A FEW MONTHS LATER, ROBERTA was enjoying a leisurely Saturday morning after an especially trying workweek when the phone rang. "Well, hi, Mother. You must have known I'm sitting here having a cup of coffee. Get a cup, and we'll have it together."

Roberta's "Helen radar alert" started beeping. Her mother rarely initiated a phone call to her or her sister. Roberta knew something was up.

"Sure. I'll drink one with you. Give me a minute." Roberta was glad she had picked up the kitchen phone with its twenty-five-foot cord so she could stretch it to a comfortable chair in the living room. Now she could look out at her front yard, where the much-anticipated spring was beginning to show its face. With the Rocky Mountains in the background, the view was stunning.

Helen soon returned. "I wanted to talk to you about something important. I just came back from your sister's house after telling her something that now I need to tell you."

"Sounds serious. Are you okay?" Roberta thought maybe she needed something stronger than coffee for this call, perhaps an added splash of brandy.

"Oh, I'm fine. It's not that anything is wrong. I just wanted to tell you girls something that has been on my mind lately." Roberta knew at that point that her Helen alert had been accurate.

Helen continued, hardly taking a breath. "I wanted you to know that your father and I made a decision years ago that was very important to us at the time. Not everyone would agree that it was a good decision. We certainly had our doubts through the years, but at the time, it was the right decision for us. We kept it a secret all this time."

"Okay. Now I'm really curious, and you have my full attention."

Roberta heard her mother take a sip of her coffee. She was glad to have a moment to brace herself. "When your father and I were engaged to be married, we made a mistake, and I got pregnant. The Second World War was out there and threatening to drastically change our lives and our plans. We weren't ready to have a baby, and most important, we were not yet married. Pregnancy before marriage was very much frowned upon way back then; it was nothing like now. Our families would have turned their backs on us and never spoken to us again. So, for all those reasons, I had an abortion."

Roberta held back a gasp. If Helen said any more, gave any more details, she did not hear them. She certainly didn't notice that her mother's voice was very shaky during her last sentence. The mountain scene in front of her blurred.

She couldn't believe it. Her mind spun almost out of control. She and Kibby had both gone through hell when they were twenty and had gotten pregnant. And their mother didn't say a word about having been in the same predicament when she was their same age? She had spoken unkind words and made her feel like a slut while secretly having the knowledge that she had made the very same mistake? Roberta's stomach was twisting, rising to her throat.

"Roberta Jo, are you still there?"

A few more awkward moments of silence occurred before Roberta was finally able to speak. She wanted to slam the phone down onto its cradle and scream every swear word she knew, but she resisted, speaking as calmly as she could. "Yes, Mother, I'm all right…I guess. I'm just very surprised hearing your news. I don't know what to say."

"Okay, well, I wanted you to know since I had just told your sister and needed to get it off my chest. I feel so much better now. It was such a big secret for such a very long time. I guess I don't have anything else to say. I hope I haven't upset you. Give my love to Stan and Ashley. I'll talk to you later. I love you. Bye."

Helen didn't even wait for Roberta to sign off with her own good-bye. She was left holding the receiver to her ear.

Finally returning the phone to its cradle in the kitchen, Roberta went back to sit in her chair and stare out the window. The view of the Rockies was spoiled. The beautiful spring day had turned back to ugly winter gray. She felt betrayed. She felt angry. Oh, she felt angry. Forget it—she was furious beyond words!

Her mother had always preached to them about lying. "Lying will get you nowhere. The truth is hard; lying is harder in the end," had always been Helen's mantra. Yet her mother lied to her at a time when she had struggled harder than ever before. It would have been so helpful to know her parents had made the same mistake. And she had done the same thing to Kibby. Where was Daddy back then? Why didn't he think that it would be helpful for them to have this information? He had always been so good at defending them when Helen was angry or upset.

Roberta heard Stan come into the room behind her. He slowly sat down beside her without saying anything. He took her hand and held it for a few minutes before saying, "I heard you talking on the phone. Was it your mother?"

Roberta turned to look at him. When she could finally open her mouth, she could only cry. Her anger came out in gasping sobs as she tried to tell Stan of her mother's shocking news. The words came out in a garbled form. Stan had to keep asking her to repeat herself.

"You know what? I have to call Kibby."

"I understand. Do it right now."

Roberta went for the phone again, her hand shaking so badly that she had trouble dialing the numbers. "Hi, Kibby. It's Roberta Jo."

"Mother just called you, didn't she? I can hear it in your voice."

"Yes, she did. What a slap in our faces. I don't know if I can ever forgive her for this one."

"Can you believe she had an abortion back in the forties? An abortion! That was scandalous in the sixties. Hell, it's still scandalous. Think about what it must have been like in the forties. She's lucky she lived through it. Women died from bad abortions. And she and Daddy decided that together? My gosh, think of it, they had me a year later... what did you say to her?"

"Nothing. I couldn't get anything out. She just told me and then said goodbye. It was all very abrupt and cold."

"That's about how it was here too. She blurted it out to Richard and I just as she was getting ready to leave. The kids were running around, and we couldn't talk about it."

Roberta stood up and started pacing. "That's Mother for sure. Remember, she doesn't do emotion or affection well."

"Yeah, I remember, all right. We're always so surprised with her inability to do hugs and affection. Why?"

"Probably because we're hopeful." Roberta caught a sob trying to escape her whole body.

Kibby said, "I'm just so angry. It feels like she just made this news up to shock us or something. I know it would have been hard for them to tell us back when we got pregnant, but for Pete's sake, it was all hard! We needed to know."

"Do you think that when I told her I was going to look for Baby Boy Kindle, something broke loose in her head? Maybe that was what made her decide to tell us her secret."

"You got a point. Something set her off. She has had the secret for fifty years!"

"She said she felt so much better that she had told us! *She* feels better! I'm so *glad* for her. Phooey! Didn't she know this news would affect us big-time?" Roberta felt her stomach rising again and knew she had to get off the phone soon and do something else.

The sisters said their goodbyes but Roberta sat for a while longer, staring out the window. She had forgotten that her mother thought it was ridiculous when people went around hugging each other. Then she had met Ken's family, and they were big huggers. Helen liked and admired the family, and soon she became a hugger herself. She went through the motions anyway. Somehow the warmth didn't ever come through.

Roberta also remembered that Helen used to be an incredible prude. When she and Ken first got married, her mother got angry at Ken for swearing or telling off-color jokes. She had asked Roberta to have a talk with him to tell him to filter his language for her sake. *Wow, sometimes Mother is the one who needs a filter these days. She loves to shock people with her "colorful" language and actions.*

Roberta remembered that her friend, Mary, had turned her on to smoking marijuana after they had moved away. Ha! What had happened to that prude? Somehow she had been replaced by this adventuresome, traveling, community-involved, entrepreneur, modern woman who enjoyed her own swearing! And now an abortion. *I love and certainly admire my mother but never know what to expect from her.*

Roberta finally got out of her chair, changed her clothes, and did what always worked for her in times of stress: she went for a long run with the dog.

Late that following summer, halfway through 1988, Helen, Kibby, and Roberta made an unprecedented road trip together. Helen drove to Roberta's house in Canada and spent a few days with her family. Then Kibby flew in, and the three of them took off for Vancouver and Victoria. Roberta and Kibby took turns navigating and driving Helen's little 1984 Honda Accord. Helen sat packed away in the back seat to babysit their purchases as they shopped across British Columbia before heading back east again.

The trip was everything the three hoped it would be. On occasion, they got the giggles so bad Helen feared she would pee her pants. They bought look-alike shirts in Victoria and wore them until they were dirty.

One night in a restaurant, Helen started choking just as the waiter stopped to take their orders. Roberta continued giving her order, as Kibby put her hands above her head to demonstrate for Helen what she needed to do to remedy the choking. Roberta looked across the table to see her mother and her sister, dressed alike, with their hands high over their heads. She lost it and couldn't stop laughing. The giggles were contagious, and the other two lost it as well.

The waiter stared wide eyed at the three weird ladies. " Uh. I'll tell you what, I'll be back in a few minutes. It seems you're not ready to order after all."

They sunbathed on the beach in Vancouver, shopped in GasTown, spent a day at Butchart Gardens, spent a day at the British Columbia Museum, and had high tea at the Empress Hotel. They ate tons of ethnic and seafood and drank their fair share of beer and wine. Helen insisted on doing everything the girls did. Roberta and Kibby did sneak in a few long walks on their own to get some exercise and to mull over how it was going with Helen.

"Maybe we should bring up our thoughts and anger about her abortion. What do you think?" Roberta said to her sister.

"I thought of that too. But you know, we're having such a great time. I would hate to spoil it," replied Kibby, always the diplomat of the two. "It wouldn't really change anything if we did bring it up."

"You're right! We're getting along so well. Forget it, bad idea."

"I'd like to know the details of the abortion experience, though; it must have been terrible." Kibby signaled her sister to cross the street to enter a beautiful public garden that had opened out in front of them.

"Yeah, but most of all, I would like to know *why* they had an abortion and couldn't tell us way back when we were in trouble."

"Don't even go there, Roberta. We're never going to know. Besides I've come to realize Mother has no idea that she hurt us so much."

"Yeah, I think you're right. Instead, let's focus on these huge cedar trees. I wonder how old this park is. Can't you visualize the artist, Emily Carr, having picnics and sketching here in the early nineteen hundreds?"

When they got back to the hotel, they talked to Helen about doing a similar trip every five years or so. They figured Kibby's and Roberta's daughters could be part of the reunion when they got old enough. Helen insisted, "Okay, but they can't go with us until they are old enough to drink alcohol legally."

The trip changed things for the three of them. They became friends, not just mother and daughters.

CHAPTER 13

A YEAR AFTER ROBERTA AND her husband moved back to the United States from Canada in 1992, Stan was diagnosed with cancer. Because they were so new in their Oregon community, Roberta had little support in helping her deal with his illness and, eventually, his death.

She thought about moving back to Canada where her friends lived or to Washington where her family was. But she had taken her dream job after finally finishing her master's degree in speech-language pathology. The first year on the job had been a huge challenge, but she loved it. It actually became her therapy, helping her through the loneliness. Ashley was out of the house, attending university in Victoria.

Just a few months before she and Stan moved to Oregon, they had been walking down the street in Vancouver on their way to a restaurant. They had just returned from a James Taylor concert at the Pacific National Exhibition Hall, still smiling from the experience when they heard a woman yelling, "Stan, Stan Travers, is that you?"

They both had turned around to see a women about their age signaling to them. "Yes, I'm Stan Travers, but I'm afraid I don't know who you are."

"I'm Betty Jean! Remember me from Edmonton over twenty years ago?"

By this time, the woman had caught up with them on the sidewalk. Roberta watched her husband's face go pale. After a long hesitation,

Stan replied, "Oh my gosh, Betty Jean. Of course I remember. How did you even recognize me? And how are you?"

"Well, I have to say, I have been thinking about you a lot lately. A mutual friend told me that you were living in Vancouver for a while and in this area. I guess in the back of my mind, I thought I might run into you. I live just a few blocks from here."

"What a coincidence though." Stan turned to Roberta. "Oh, I'm sorry, Betty Jean, meet my wife, Roberta. We're just on our way to Wild Catch, the restaurant just up the hill." The two women shook hands, but Roberta had no idea who this Betty Jean was.

"I figured that was where you were headed. I just came from there. My husband already went to his car, or I'd introduce you to him. Stan, do you think I could get your phone number? I'd like to call you soon and explain why I've been thinking about you. Maybe we can even get together and catch up on our lives."

Stan pulled out a pen from his pocket. "Sure, let me write it down for you. We're only going to be here at this number for a few more weeks, as we're moving to Oregon."

"Okay, I'll call soon. Here's my business card, too, in case you want to get ahold of me. I'm looking forward to a good conversation. Nice meeting you, Roberta."

Stan and Roberta had been left standing on the sidewalk with their mouths hanging open. "Now, what was that all about? Should I be jealous or something? Your face went white when you first saw her."

"No, don't be jealous. You do know who that is, don't you?"

Roberta shrugged her shoulders. "I don't have a clue, although the name sounds kind of familiar."

By this time they were in the restaurant, so Roberta waited until they were settled at their table with beers in front of them. The place smelled wonderful, very garlicky and fishy. "Okay, who the heck is Betty Jean?"

"Betty Jean was the college girlfriend that I got pregnant while in Edmonton. Remember, I told you about all that when you told me about the baby you gave up? She had never been a serious girlfriend, and I never questioned her decision to give the baby up for adoption. I certainly never wanted to marry her, and she didn't seem to be expecting that. She went away, and I never heard any more from her or about her until ten minutes ago."

"I do remember, of course. What do you think she wants to talk to you about after all these years?"

"Let's see. It was about 1965 and this is 1992. That was twenty-seven years ago. I guess there could only be one thing she wants to talk to me about."

"I'm thinking the same thing. I'll bet she has found your son or daughter, and she wants to tell you about it. Or maybe she even wants you to meet him or her." Roberta was quiet for a long time but finally said, "I have to ask you this time; are you ready for that to happen?"

Stan didn't answer. Roberta decided to keep her mouth shut and wait to see what happened next. She was not a part of any of this anyway and needed to back off. She sipped her beer and studied the menu in front of her instead.

Within a few days, Stan got that call from Betty Jean and found they had guessed correctly. Betty Jean had located the baby girl she had given up twenty-seven years before. Stan learned that the daughter, Laura, had attended college but had recently been drifting with no direction, trying to figure out what to do with her life.

Betty Jean and her daughter had become good friends, and because their reunion had been so successful, Betty Jean was anxious for Stan and Laura to also meet. Stan told her on the phone that he had to give it some thought and would get back to her.

Stan had given Roberta the details of the phone call but still didn't share how he felt about meeting this newly found daughter. He did say that his parents would be upset to know he had fathered a baby all those years ago. He was fearful of their reaction.

Roberta was more than a little jealous that Stan's child had been found. But Stan only lived for a little over a year after that; for three months of it, he was very ill. Being introduced to a daughter that he had heard nothing about for twenty-six or more years was not a priority and never a topic of conversation. Roberta later found in his wallet the business card that Betty Jean had given him and couldn't help but think he hadn't totally ruled out meeting her.

—〰—

Stan had been gone for four or five months when Roberta got a call from Betty Jean. "Hello, Roberta. This is Betty Jean in British Columbia. Do you remember that we met on the street in Vancouver soon after I was reunited with my daughter, Laura?"

"Yes, I certainly do remember. How are you, Betty Jean?" Roberta was back to work, trying to achieve some normality in her life. She took one day at a time and was not ready for any surprises, including anything that this Betty Jean had up her sleeve. She felt tempted to hang up the phone, but she curled up in Stan's old recliner and waited for what was to come.

"I'm fine. But I've heard from a mutual friend that Stan recently passed away after a brief illness. I'm so sorry. Please accept my condolences. He was much too young. Life does have its surprises, doesn't it?"

"Yes, it does, and thank you. You're right; forty-eight years of age is way too young." *Damn. Why did I pick up this phone? I don't want to talk to this woman.*

"I understand this is still a very difficult time for you, but I'd like for you to think about doing me a favor."

Oh my Lord, what now? Do me a favor instead and say goodbye. Roberta sighed and said, "What can I do for you?"

Betty Jean's voice became so soft, her words were like whispers inside a funeral home. "Laura, of course, is disappointed that she came so close to meeting her biological father and now he's gone. She'd like to meet Stan's parents, her biological grandparents. I'm wondering if you could make their meeting happen. Even if you were to just break the news to them, and we could go from there?"

This woman's soft funeral voice was making her sick to her stomach. She began pacing back and forth in the living room. "I just don't know. Stan and I didn't talk much about his child."

"He never did call me back, even after I left him messages on the machine."

"I don't think I can help you, Betty Jean. He did tell me he couldn't tell his parents about her. You know, Stan didn't have any other children, and he was an only child himself? It would be a great shock to them. I'm sorry; I need to honor his wishes. Anyway, none of this has anything to do with me."

Betty Jean was silent for a long time. She said a quick goodbye and whispered, "Thank you." *Well, that's done; hopefully, nothing more will come of it.*

—⁓—

But that wasn't the end of it. Six months later, Roberta got a call from her mother-in-law, Stan's eighty-four-year-old mother. Roberta had become close friends with Stan's parents, Eldon and Ida though his illness and death. They took care of each other in many ways. Roberta visited with them in Canada as often as she could, and they seemed to trust her. So it wasn't unusual for Roberta to receive a call from them.

Ida sounded very tense right from the beginning, however. "Hi, Ida. How are you two? Is your arthritis giving you a break these days?"

"Oh, I'm doing okay. Eldon has a cold, so he's taking it easy. But I'm calling you about something else. Yesterday, I was washing my hair, and Eldon had gone for a walk. The phone rang, and I would have just let it go, but I was worried about him since he hadn't been feeling well. I didn't think he should be out walking, but he went anyway. So I wrapped a towel around my dripping hair and answered the phone. It was a young woman who claimed to be our granddaughter. I had to have her repeat everything over and over again. I didn't have my hearing aids in, of course."

"Oh my gosh, Ida. What a surprise and shock for you. What did you say to her?"

"She gave me her name and phone number and said she would call back later. I wrote down the phone number but not her name, and now I don't remember it. I told her not to call back but to wait to hear from me. But now I'm afraid to tell Eldon. He'll be so upset and probably angry. He seems to get angry about everything these days. What do you think I should do? Do you think she's just after our money or something? Do you know anything about this?"

Roberta had never heard Ida so upset, even after all that they had gone through together. "You know, Ida, I have known about her. Laura is her name. Months ago, I got a call from her mother, Betty Jean, because they wanted me to tell you about her. I told the woman that I couldn't tell you because it had nothing to do with me. I'm so sorry, Ida. I guess I should have told you. I had no idea that she was going to call you like this. It probably would have been better if I had told you instead of hearing it like you did. What can I do? Are you going to tell Eldon?"

"I think I have to. I haven't been able to think of anything else. I don't like having a secret from him like this."

Roberta was again sitting in the old recliner, sipping coffee from a mug. "Of course you don't. Do you want me there to help?"

"No. I can't wait any longer. I just wanted to know if you knew anything about her. Do you think she could possibly be Stan's child?"

"I'm pretty sure she is, Ida. Stan had just found out months before he died. She was adopted out to a family there in British Columbia. He had talked to Betty Jean but avoided her after that. He was very fearful of letting the two of you know about her."

Ida let out a big sigh, pausing before continuing. "You know, I remember Betty Jean from when Stan was dating her. I met her once or twice back then. He was still living with us while he went to university. I thought she was a little strange then. Stan didn't want to continue seeing her, but she kept hanging around with him and his friends. Did Stan know back then that she was pregnant?"

"Yes, that's what he told me. He said she never expected anything from him but was going to give it up for adoption. That was the last he ever heard from her. He told me soon after we started dating."

Ida's voice sounded stronger. "Well, it sounds like she's really Stan's daughter. I think that makes it easier to tell Eldon. He should be home soon. I'm going to do it the minute he gets here. I'm glad I called you."

"I'm so sorry, Ida. What a shocking way for you to find out. Please call and let me know how it goes with Eldon. Let me know if I can do anything to help."

"I will. Thanks."

In her next call, Ida reported things getting even worse. Eldon was indeed suspicious and angry. Roberta asked to talk to him, hoping it would help. "Surely Stan would have told us something in all those years," Eldon said, his voice getting louder with each sentence. "And why now does she come forward, waiting until Stan is gone? She could have contacted us when he was alive, even if he didn't want to meet her. She's looking for a monetary windfall. That's what this is all about. I just know it."

Roberta decided she couldn't get in the middle, any more now than before. She drove to Canada as soon as she could get away, to see if she couldn't at least calm the situation. Eldon wouldn't talk about it with her. When he went out for a walk, she and Ida sat down with a cup of tea and discussed what had been going on. Ida gave her some surprising news.

"Would you believe Betty Jean had the nerve to show up at our door last week? She gave us a sales pitch about getting to know this 'Laura.' The woman is more weird than I remembered from years ago. She gets so soft-spoken that I can't hear her, so half the time I don't know what she's saying. Eldon finally just walked out on her, walked right out the front door. He thinks she's in on a money scheme. He's probably right. Don't even try to get him talking about it. He just gets more wound up. He's going to have a heart attack if he gets any more excited."

Roberta was also worried about Eldon's health; he looked frail. The couple had enough on their plate trying to sell their house so they could move into a retirement home.

When she got back home Roberta gave Betty Jean a call and told her that she had to give up hope of trying to get Laura together with them. She wanted to tell her to give it up for good but settled for suggesting she give it some time.

Betty Jean responded, slipping into her funeral voice, "It may be too late."

"What do you mean? Too late for what?" Roberta was thinking this woman was as wacko as Ida said.

"I'm sorry to have to tell you that Laura tried to take her own life last night. She took a whole bottle of pills. Fortunately, she's staying with her parents right now. Her mother heard her moaning and went in to check on her. They got her to the hospital in time. She's going to be okay."

"Oh my gosh. I'm so sorry but glad she's okay. What happened to set her off?"

"She has taken it so hard that the Traverses thought she was trying to get money out of them. Laura's the most honest person I've ever known. She would never take advantage of anyone."

"What a mess this has become. I guess Stan was right in thinking his parents wouldn't take this well. They'd feel so bad, though, if they knew they made Laura that upset. You have to promise me that you won't contact them about this. In fact, you can't contact them at all. Eldon has a bad heart, and right now, he's doing way more than he should be to get ready to move. Will you please promise me? And will you please ask Laura, when she's well, not to contact them for the same reason?"

"Of course. I'll do my best."

"If she ever indicates that she'll try again, please have her call me first. Okay?"

"Yes, I think that's a good idea."

"Let's do our best to keep it from getting worse for any of them. Just count your blessings that Laura and you have done so well to reunite. That has to be good enough for now."

"Thank you, Roberta. We'll talk at another time." Roberta hoped that talk would never happen but had a feeling she hadn't heard the last of Betty Jean or Laura.

———◊◊◊———

Sure enough, about a year later, Betty Jean gave Roberta another call. She hadn't lost her funeral voice. "Do you think we might be able to work out a way for the Traverses to meet Laura? She's had a very good year. She finished getting her teaching credentials and is having a successful first year teaching middle school. She loves it and is living in a little condo of her own. She's so much more stable than she was a year ago."

"To be honest, I don't understand why you are doing all this reaching out, Betty Jean. Why doesn't Laura contact me herself? I thought that was what we agreed should happen next, if anything." Roberta was getting angry and let it show in her voice.

"Yes, well, Laura's afraid to reach out. She doesn't want to upset anyone like happened last time. I just want the Traverses to have what I've had the last few years. Laura and I have such a wonderful relationship. I want that for the three of them, especially since they've lost their only child."

"Tell Laura that when she's ready, she and I can get together and decide what to do. It shouldn't have anything to do with you anymore. Please don't call me again, and certainly don't call Eldon and Ida. Eldon's not well. They don't need this."

Another year later, Laura called Roberta and asked if they could meet and maybe Roberta could share photos of Stan. She wanted to know more about him. They had lunch together when Roberta went to Canada next. Roberta put together some photos and a few other items to give her. They had a wonderful lunch, talking for hours and finding they had much in common including the same birthday. Roberta was relieved that meeting with the Traverses was never discussed. She thought maybe she had done the right thing after all.

CHAPTER 14

IN 1994 SOME OF THE women in the Kindle family held a women's mini-reunion, a two-day affair at Aunt Ellie's (Andrew's sister) in California. In attendance were another sister, Ada; Helen; and Florence, Helen's old friend and Andrew's cousin, who had been responsible for introducing Helen to Andrew. The younger generation included both Roberta and Kibby and three of their cousins. Roberta and Kibby had grown up with one of the cousins, Kay. The other two cousins were Patty, Roberta's old Colorado buddy, and her sister, Rhonda, who had been Kibby's Colorado buddy.

Roberta expected the reunion to be as fun as Kindle get-togethers usually were. Arguments could also be a problem, but the women stayed on their best behavior that weekend and had many a laugh. They spent most of their time at Ellie's on her gorgeous redwood deck nestled in the trees. They sipped wine and shared the stories of their lives.

Helen, Roberta, and Kibby had flown to Oakland a few days before the reunion started to spend time with Kay. Cousin Kay had never married but had become a successful paralegal. Afterward they returned for another night at Kay's house. The women were sitting around having a glass of wine when Helen dropped one of her bombs.

Roberta and Kibby were sitting on the couch listening to a conversation between Helen and Kay. "I thought you might want to know,

Kay, that I had an abortion just before Andrew and I got married. I told the girls a few years ago, but I wanted you to know too. It was wonderful to get it off my chest after all those years of keeping such a huge secret. Times have changed so much. It isn't such a big deal now, getting pregnant before getting married. But it was then, believe me. In 1940, having sex before marriage was not acceptable. Andrew and I felt the only option we had was abortion. However, I guess we always wondered if we did the right thing."

Roberta's and Kibby's jaws dropped. They looked wide eyed at each other. Roberta thought she was hearing things, listening to her mother reveal the big secret again in such a lighthearted way. Kibby gently put her hand on Roberta's shoulder.

But Helen wasn't finished. "Kind of interesting, don't you think, that my two girls also got pregnant when they weren't married? You know, I'm sure that Roberta gave up a baby for adoption when she was very young."

At that point Roberta jumped up and left the room, not wanting to blurt out what she would regret later. She grabbed the bottle of wine and headed for the bathroom. Kibby followed her. They huddled together in the tiny room of their cousin's house, one sitting on the toilet and the other on the bathtub's edge. They passed the bottle back and forth; their wineglasses hadn't come with them.

Roberta was wild eyed. "Since when does my mother get to tell *my* secret? She's the one back then who said it was a secret that had to be kept from everyone. Then she just throws it out there. You'd think she could have at least asked me first if it was okay to tell anybody else. Does she know how much guilt and shame and embarrassment I hold for that time in my life? Still...twenty-eight years later! It's not a story for her to tell. Hell, how many people has she told?"

"I'm so sorry, Roberta. I'm sure she has told a lot of people. You heard her; she feels good getting it all off her chest, our secrets as well as her own. I know she told Aunt Ellie and Florence because I heard them talking about it when we were just at Ellie's."

The two sat in silence for a few moments, passing the bottle, trying to gather their wits. Roberta wished they had brought in two bottles. Kibby finally spoke up. "There's something else I have to tell you that I overheard at Aunt Ellie's when we were there."

"Oh no, I can imagine. What else did our mother tell?"

"It's not so much what she told, but what Aunt Ellie told her. They were talking about you giving up a baby for adoption. Would you believe Cousin Patty also gave up a baby for adoption just a year or so before you?"

"You're kidding! I had no idea. Patty and I haven't seen each other in all these years since high school. She must have gotten pregnant just right after that."

"Patty was also sent away to have her baby, but she was so miserable, she and her mother went and hid away at their family vacation cabin." Kibby held up her hand to stop Roberta from responding. "But that's not all. Aunt Ellie told Mother that she wished she had known about you two girls and your problems back then. She said she would have taken you into her house to have the babies in California under her roof. She was really upset that Patty and you had been sent away and hidden. She said she would have enjoyed having you there."

Roberta stared at her sister, tears forming. "Oh my gosh, that's so sweet of Aunt Ellie. That would have been wonderful to have come here instead of being shoved off to 'the home.' Aunt Ellie is such a kick; she would have made it fun. Did Patty hear about this? And does Patty know I had a baby back then?"

Kibby grabbed the bottle from her sister and took a swig. "That I don't know. Patty wasn't part of this conversation. It was just Mother, Aunt Ellie, and Florence talking. I was eavesdropping."

Roberta changed the subject back to Helen's big mouth. "Well, how about you, Kibby? Do we have to tell everyone that you got pregnant before you got married too? People have guessed at it, no doubt, but do we have to announce it at this late date? And announce it so lightly, like what we're having for dinner?"

"No, it took me by surprise, too, when she said that. It was a very hard time in my life and a huge decision to make. I don't want to hang out the dirty laundry now any more than I did then. I don't think we should say anything to Mother here, though. It'll just make Kay feel uncomfortable. Let's go out and pretend it's all okay...again."

"You're right; let's go. Kay doesn't need to be in the middle of our family dirt and hurt. Besides, the wine in this bottle's all gone." Fortunately, when they went back into the room, the subject had changed, and the sisters could pretend they hadn't been upset.

Helen settled back in her seat on the airplane on her flight home after the reunion. She was not happy with herself. She knew now that she had made a mistake in telling Kay about her abortion. Furthermore, she had made an even worse mistake when she mentioned Roberta's and Kibby's pregnancies before they were ever married.

I saw the girls dash off to the bathroom. They were angry; I just know it. Will they ever forgive me? Should I call and apologize? No, not this time. They're big girls. They'll get over it and feel better for having told all the secrets; just as I have.

CHAPTER 15

WHEN ROBERTA GOT BACK HOME from the California reunion, she couldn't quit thinking about Cousin Patty and that she had also given up a baby. She gave Patty a call.

"Hi, Patty. This is your long-lost cousin in Oregon. Can you believe it?"

"Oh my gosh, what a surprise. It was so fun seeing you in California after so many years."

"Wasn't it, though? I had a ball. But, you know, I didn't feel you and I had much time to talk. So I have a proposal. Do you think that in the next few months we could get together? Just you and me? I would love to reminisce our past adventures from high school days. But I have to confess, there's something else I really want to talk about."

"Okay, you've got me curious."

"Well, Kibby told me you had a baby and gave it up for adoption, just as I did. She overheard Mother and Aunt Ellie talking about us. I haven't been able to get it off my mind since I got back. I'd really like to talk about our experiences. What do you think?"

Patty quickly replied, "I think that's a great idea. I've been thinking of you too. We have a bunch in common, don't we? Besides, I agree; it'd be fun talking about old times."

"I have some free flying mileage coming to me. How about if I fly into Denver for a weekend, and we can really get into it? That's if you don't mind having me for a houseguest for a few days."

"Great, sounds like fun."

—m—

A month or so later, Roberta flew to Denver. Patty was divorced and living on her own. Her two children were grown and long gone, so the gals had the house to themselves. Conversation was a little strained in the beginning, but with a little help from a bottle of tequila, licks of salt, and squeezes of lime, they began a "true confession fest."

The last time they had been together alone, they had listened to The Beach Boys, Ritchie Valens, and Buddy Holly. This night they listened to Mariah Carey, Sheryl Crow, and Bon Jovi. They stretched out in the living room, shoes kicked off, feet on the coffee table. Roberta started out and told Patty the details of when she got pregnant, telling her parents, going away to the home, and the aftermath, including her wishes to someday meet her son.

They both shed a few tears but basically held it together. "Okay, your turn. Another drink, and then you tell me your story."

"Well, I guess in some ways, our stories are similar but in some ways so very different. Let me start by saying, you were so lucky to have the parents you had. I can remember that you and your mother seemed to always talked about everything. My parents didn't ever sit down and talk to me about the importance of going to college, about sex, going out in the world or anything. I thought I was supposed to be a housewife and a mother, the end. Not you. You had plans and dreams."

Roberta knew that to be true. As angry as she and Kibby were at their mother at times, Helen had always been there for them, to talk and to help deal with their problems.

Patty sat up to the edge of her chair. "Most important, you had a say in making the decision of putting your child up for adoption. That was huge. I had no choice. I was told what to do right from the beginning. My experience was so shameful to my parents, especially my dad, because of his position in the community as a family physician. There were never any other options presented to me. I just had to be hidden away. That was the master plan."

Roberta thought for a moment before responding but decided she had to say what was on her mind. "I think I might have given you the wrong idea of my mother's actions at that time. She pretty much ran the show. Sure, I made the decision to not get married and to do the adoption thing, but from then on, I just followed instructions. And believe me, there was a lot of secrecy and plenty of shame involved."

"I guess I can believe that. Helen is a take-charge person, all right. I can see that she could run the show."

"You got that right. I don't know if you knew that Mother had an abortion before she and Daddy got married."

"You're kidding." Patty sat up even straighter and stared at Roberta. "An abortion?"

"Sorry to shock you, but, no, I'm afraid I'm not kidding. I thought you knew, or I wouldn't have been so blatant in my bringing it up. Mother has been telling everyone the last few years, ever since she decided to come out of the closet, so to speak."

"But that was way back there. I didn't know they even did abortions back then."

"Oh my gosh, yes. Women have been having abortions of all kinds since the beginning of time. They weren't legal, of course, and many women died. Mother was lucky. Kibby and I don't know the details of her story, but we do know she went to who she thought was a real doctor. We've been so angry since we found out that we're afraid to bring it up again with her."

"When did she tell you?"

"Not until about six or seven years ago."

"But that was way after you gave up your baby and Kibby was married and had a baby. She didn't tell you when you guys got pregnant and weren't married?"

"Unfortunately, no; they didn't tell either one of us when it would have been so very helpful."

"No wonder you're angry."

"Tell me about it." Roberta tried not to, but she began to feel mad all over again. She decided she'd better change the subject. "But enough of that. Tell me more about when you had your baby."

Patty took a big breath, poured them another tequila, and continued with her story. "My dad had my doctor call the father of the baby and insist that he marry me. Can you believe that? We weren't in love. We just had a lot of fun together. Too much fun, I guess. In the end, the guy called me and offered to do the right thing and marry me. He had since joined the military, so he asked me to go with him to California on his motorcycle. It sounded very exciting but also very scary. I was only nineteen years old. I said no."

"So what did you do?" asked Roberta.

"Like you, I was shipped off to an unwed mothers' home. I give my parents credit; they did the best they could to help me adjust to that place. They made sure I had my car, and my dog was boarded nearby so I could go visit him. But the place was awful. It felt like we were there to be slaves to do housekeeping and then sit around to wait out our time. I didn't make any friends. I remember going to see my dog, sitting on the floor of the kennel with him, crying and crying."

Patty went for the box of Kleenex. "I finally convinced my mother to let me come home. We ended up spending the remainder of the time, the two of us, hiding at our summer cabin in the mountains. Dad stayed at home and worked. I don't even remember him ever coming to visit. I guess it was too shameful to warrant a visit. It must have been hard for my mother to hide away like that. She was supportive, but we never talked about what we were doing. And who was supporting her? How many lies did she have to tell her friends?"

"Sounds awful. The time must have dragged. I, at least, made friends who were in the same position. We had some fun together."

Once Patty started talking on the subject, she couldn't stop. "My parents decided I needed counseling. Ya think? It was considerate of them, I guess, but I remember sitting there with the counselor and never saying a word. I felt nothing. I couldn't or wouldn't even see myself, let alone talk about myself. I was just a body that moved around in space and had no meaning, like a ghostly cloud of nothing.

"I remember having to hide somewhere in the house when anyone came to the house. If we went anywhere in the car, I had to lay down on the seat. It was like I really didn't exist. Frankly, I didn't want to exist.

"Finally, the day came that I went into labor. We went to my doctor, and the next thing I knew, we were at the hospital. Just like you, I spent hours and hours alone in a drab little room all by myself. I remember asking where my parents were and was told that they were in the lobby. Why weren't they with me? My dad is a doctor, for Pete's sake! An occasional nurse came in to check on things. Not once did they talk to me about what was going on with the labor process and what would happen during the delivery. Certainly no one asked me if I was scared or worried. I was alone and terrified.

"Eventually the doctor came in and said they were taking me to the delivery room. I was so scared; the closer we got to this room that they were talking about, the more fearful I was. I eventually lost it. I screamed and begged the doctor to put me to sleep. They finally did; I remember nothing about the delivery."

By this time, both Roberta and Patty had tears running down their cheeks. They decided they better lay off the tequila and have something to eat. They hugged each other and told each other they were sorry.

After walking to a restaurant, they talked only of their present lives and how they spent their time. Back at Patty's house, they made a pot a coffee, and Roberta got the conversation rolling again. "Did you see the baby?"

"No, I never saw or held the baby. At some point, I think I saw my parents, but I was soon alone again. No one talked to me about anything. Then some lady came in and said I had to sign the birth certificate. She asked if I had a name for the baby, and I told her I didn't even know if it was a boy or a girl. How could I name it? There was a place in the paperwork for the father's name, so I told her his name.

"The signature meant for the mother was the only other part I remember. Right from the beginning, my dad had told me to make up a name for myself. I had used a couple of names in the past months. To be honest, I don't know which name I signed. I was told that later I'd have to go to court and sign the adoption papers. Adoption papers? I didn't know what she was talking about. No one had ever talked about adoption. I was just doing what I was told. I was just the 'shameful daughter'; apparently I had no rights, no voice, no existence.

"Days later, when I did go to court, the judge showed no compassion or concern. He made me feel ashamed. The paperwork had little pieces of paper that covered up each place that referred to the baby's sex. I was told to read every page to see if I agreed with the adoption. I scanned through the pages but didn't really read the words. I finally saw one place that didn't get covered up, and it said female. So I knew for the first time that I had had a baby girl. But I was numb, didn't feel anything or think anything. Being the obedient child, I just signed the papers with the name I saw at the top of the pages.

"Somehow I've buried all of this so deep. I've built a wall of denial around me. It actually feels good right now, getting it out."

Roberta went to the kitchen and poured them another a cup of coffee. She then moved to the couch to sit closer to Patty, putting her hand on her cousin's shoulder. "I'm glad it feels good. Go on. I know there's more."

"I never even asked if the baby was okay, but it haunted me enough that I called the doctor weeks later and asked him about the birth. The doctor assured me that the baby was normal and healthy. I accepted that and went on with my life.

"Years later I got married and had two wonderful children. I continued to suppress any thoughts or feelings about the first child, the child that I never saw, never told goodbye. There's a deep sadness within me that has continued all these years. I never really grieved properly for that child."

Roberta was beginning to understand that Patty's present-day thoughts for her adopted child were very different from hers. She asked, "Have you ever told anyone about the baby?"

"Only when I felt I had to. I told my husband. He didn't get it, but I was okay with that. I never, ever talk to my sister or my parents about her."

Roberta finally asked, "Would you like to find your daughter?"

Patty slumped down on the couch. "I was afraid you were going to ask me that. To be honest, I'm afraid to look for her. I know she was healthy when I had her; that's enough. Plus, I don't think it would be easy looking for her. I'm not positive of her birthdate, I don't remember the doctor's name, and most important, and I don't know for sure what name I gave."

"I'm so sorry that you have had all this bottled up inside all this time, Patty. I don't know what I'd do if I couldn't talk to Kibby about my son. She's such a sounding board for me."

"This is the first time I have told anyone the details of the whole experience. I'm so envious that you can talk to your family. I realize I have so much anger, especially for myself."

"Tell me, do you think you did the right thing back then?"

"Probably...I was so young. But then I wasn't given a chance to choose anything else, was I? But what else could I have done?"

The women sat in silence for a few minutes before Patty continued. "The shame and guilt and anger turned inward defined me as a person back then and continues to do so, to a certain extent. I embarrassed my parents. I was so bad that I couldn't even use my real name at the home or the hospital, or even to a judge. It's weird that I have always been very self-confident as a mother and as a nurse, but as a person, my self-esteem can be so fragile. Actually, it really sucks at times. I think it all stems from the guilt and shame from almost thirty years ago. Why didn't I stand up for myself?"

Roberta felt the need to change the subject again; Patty was being too hard on herself. "Did you know that Aunt Ellie told mother that she had wished she knew you and I were pregnant back then? She said she'd have taken us in to have the babies."

"Yes, I did hear about that. I guess my sister heard them talking at the reunion. Isn't that great of her?" said Patty.

"And it would've been so fun to be with her. It certainly would have been a hundred percent better than what we both went through."

"That's for sure."

The cousins talked on again and off again those few days about their different experiences. But they also talked about the adventures they had as teenagers. Roberta thought they had a lot of laughs. She tried not to talk much about her need and wish to find Baby Boy Kindle. Patty felt differently, and that was okay.

—ɯ—

Roberta was working in her yard, pulling weeds, digging up overgrown plants, and placing them in barren parts of the yard. The weather was perfect for such chores, sunny but cool. She stood up and looked around, thinking how she had turned it all into an amazing yard, a far cry from what she and Stan had purchased four years before. She heard the phone ring inside the house and raced to get it before it went to the machine.

"Hey, Roberta Jo. It's your sister."

"Oh, wow. What a treat. What's happenin' in your part of the world?"

"Lots of work. But that's okay; I love it. But I got a brilliant idea this morning."

"Of course you did. You're always brilliant."

"I have to go to San Francisco in two months to buy for the store. Remember I told you about that fantastic spa that my friend took me to last time I went there?"

Roberta sat down in a kitchen chair, happy to take a break. "Yeah, I remember. I was so jealous. It sounded fantastic."

"Well, how about you meet me there after my buying, and we'll have three or four days of bliss—massages, wraps, and steam baths, whatever looks good?"

"Are you kidding me? I'm definitely in for that."

"Can you get off work okay?"

"No problem. I have lots of vacation time coming. But I have another idea to add to that."

"Like what?"

"I have a surprise. I'm buying a convertible this week! I have wanted one ever since I had to give up my '57 Chevy in the sixties."

"Oh, that's exciting. What did you buy?"

"It's a brand new, forest-green, 1997 Chrysler Sebring with a black top. I haven't seen it yet. It's being delivered soon."

"Beautiful. So tell me your idea."

"How about if I drive to northern California while you're doing your buying, and I'll meet you at the spa? We could drive up the coast afterward in the convertible, staying at different places along the way. You could come home with me, and then I'll drive you to the airport to fly home."

"Now, that's a plan! Let me see if I can iron out the details at work and if I can get reservations at the spa. I'll get back to you soon."

"Perfect."

Roberta and Kibby worked out the details and had a wonderful time, with the spa being everything Roberta thought it should be. The massages and wraps were her first; they would not be her last. They rode bikes, went on short hikes, and hit a few wineries. Then top down, hair blowing in the wind, pretending they were twentysomething instead of fiftysomething, they drove from one coastal town to the next, finding for a motel every evening. Their old anger at Helen came out in conversation only once during the week and a half. Roberta had decided life was too short to spend any more time on that topic.

Part Five
Baby Boy Kindle: 2011

Hope is the thing with feathers that perches in the soul, and sings the
tunes without words and never stops at all.

—Emily Dickinson

CHAPTER 16

"OKAY, YOU QUILTERS. THIS IS an aha moment," Roberta hollered out at a quilt retreat in Newport, Oregon. She proudly held up her completed full-size quilt top, the project she had been working on for over a year. "What do you think? Is it a finisher?" In the background, dune grass stretched out revealing a peek at deep blue ocean waves and their white caps.

The quilt buddies agreed that it was indeed worth finishing. The twelve of them had been at the retreat house for two full days with two more days to go. They went to the same place every year. They ate a lot, laughed a lot, and did a little bit of shopping, walking, and wine drinking. Oh, yes, they did quilt…a lot.

Roberta was now sixty-six years old, her hair a silvery gray. The color gave away her age, but she didn't care anymore. She was content enough in her own skin. She had retired seven years before, and quilting had become her passion.

As always, while quilting, Roberta's thoughts went to the past and the people in her life. Her personal life had been problem free for many years now, and she was thankful for that. She sometimes found herself waiting for the ax to drop again. The first thirty years of adulthood had come with such a great number of disappointments and trials. In her forties, she had lost a husband to cancer. In her thirties, a second husband had left her to raise a young daughter alone. In her twenties, she had lost a father to cancer and had given up a baby. Efforts to find her son had still gone nowhere. It suddenly hit Roberta that he would be forty-four years old by now.

Roberta folded up her completed quilt top and sat down in contemplation of what she would do next. Despite all her past sorrows, she felt her life had been wonderful. She had lived in Colorado; Washington; Maine; Oklahoma; New York State; Alberta and British Columbia, Canada; and now, Oregon. She and her first husband had spent nine months traveling in Europe, renting a house in Greece for a month, and working in a hotel kitchen in Germany for a month. What an adventure that had been.

Most important, she had given birth to a wonderful daughter who was the love of her life. Ashley had been her rock and was now a young woman having her own adventures.

To put the icing on her life's cake, after ten years of living alone, she had met a man who had turned her head. He was fifty-nine and she fifty-seven when they got married. Roberta retired early to marry Bruce and move to his farm outside the city. She loved living on the farm and having so many things to do outside. They had cows, pigs, chickens, a huge garden, Christmas trees, and, her favorite, two dogs.

Ashley was the one who first pointed out how her three husbands were so different from each other. Her first husband, Ken, had been quite hyper, flipping from one interest or hobby to the next. For him, life was always greener on the other side of the fence. She no longer held any resentment toward him, however. After all, he had given her Ashley and had continued to be a good father to her.

Husband number two, Stan, had been the opposite of hyper. In fact, he had been laid-back to the point of being a little lazy, certainly not a handyman. Roberta had learned that she was better off doing jobs around the house herself rather than put up with broken light bulbs and half-finished plumbing. Stan had been a people person, though, always helping friends solve their problems. Unfortunately, much of the time he spent helping his friends had been at a bar drinking way into the night. However, he had been supportive of Roberta's role as a mother and of Ashley's accomplishments and a top-notch administrator, both at his job and at home.

Stan's sickness and death had affected Roberta deeply. She had been a social recluse for years after he died, with no patience for small talk or making new friends. She had been content with doing most everything on her own and spending extra hours at her job.

As Roberta cleaned up the area around her sewing machine, she realized that life was not fair. Some people seemed to float along, their spouses and children being successful, healthy, and loyal. Others kept getting knocked down by "bad stuff."

She had learned to take the "good stuff" and wear it on her chest and put the bad stuff in her pocket. Every once in a while, she knew to take the bad out of her pocket, examine it, have a good pity-party cry and stick it back in the pocket. Roberta even took her dad out of her pocket once in a while. And, of course, Baby Boy Kindle came out every October.

Husband number three, Bruce, was definitely different from the other two husbands. He was not hyper like number one, but he was very busy doing what he liked to do, and that was almost always outdoors. He was certainly not an administrator; in fact, he was not even a good delegator. His motto was, "If you want it done right, do it yourself." Bruce always wanted it done right, immediately, and with no help.

Roberta had again thought she would never remarry but decided that a few good years with Bruce was worth it. If he died first, her great fear, she would just have it put that in her pocket as well.

Her sister had been right years ago when she told her she was too impatient…or was it too restless? For the first time, Roberta felt content. Before, contentment seemed to be a type of failure. Discontentment and restlessness had always seemed to be richer. Now she was finding that life was better lived in a more tranquil, repetitive pattern. It had taken nearly sixty years for her to figure that out.

Besides quilting, hard exercise had also become a passion for Roberta. She was proud to claim she had completed twelve sprint triathlons and two two-hundred-mile bike rides, all since turning fifty-five years old. Physical exercise kept her mentally healthy; quilting gave her mental challenges and an active social life thanks to this busy quilt group she belonged to.

———m———

Fellow quilter Andrea chided from behind her sewing machine, "Okay, Roberta, snap out of it. Now that you finished that quilt top, what's next? You have two more days to quilt." The living room of the rented house looked like a sweatshop with sewing machines, ironing boards, design walls, and fabric everywhere.

"I guess I better make a trip to the quilt store and look into starting a new project. This one has been in my face for so long, I don't know where to start. Who's up for a shopping trip?"

Sandy hollered, "I hear your phone ringing, Roberta. You better get that first. Maybe it's Bruce telling you not to spend any money. We all know you do exactly what he tells you to do."

"Are you kidding me? I've got my own money. That'll be the day he tells me how to spend it." Roberta picked up her cell phone sitting beside her machine. "Oh, hi, Bruce, it is you. We were just talking about you."

"Of course you were talking about me. Women can't help but think of me once they meet me."

"Right! Dream on."

"No, I just wanted you to know that the mail lady just tried to deliver a notice of a registered letter for you. She wouldn't let me sign for it. You have to go to the post office when you get back and get it yourself."

"Any idea who it's from?"

"No, she wouldn't let me look at it. Have you got a boyfriend you haven't told me about?" Roberta could hear the smile in his voice.

"Wouldn't you like to know, big boy? I guess we'll both have to wait until I get home to find out. Meanwhile, I'm going shopping at the quilt store to spend some bucks. Time's a-wastin'. See you in a couple of days."

—m—

That night the ladies sat around the living room relaxing after dinner, some of them doing handwork on their quilts. The conversation went to their mothers. Most of them had learned how to sew from their mothers. Roberta was no exception. "My mother was a wonderful seamstress at one time. She made beautiful clothes for my sister and me, and made all my dad's shirts."

"Didn't you tell me that she wrote a book?"

"Yes, she wrote and published two historical books, one about the two counties she lived in and one about a large cattle ranch. She also got into historical preservation of local homes and buildings and helped start up a small history museum. Mother had to learn to use a computer to do the writing, which was no small task for a woman in her seventies. Once the books were published, she had a great time giving talks to different groups, clubs, and schoolkids, and going to book signings."

"Does she still live on her own?"

"No, about seven years ago, she moved to a retirement home in Seattle to be close to my sister. She's ninety-four now but healthy as a horse. She loves her margaritas and her warm Bud Light. We have to limit her to only one margarita per hour, as she can down one in ten minutes. Would you believe she still goes to the pool and swims a quarter to a half mile at a time?"

"My gosh, Roberta, your mother is amazing. She sounds more like a woman generations younger than she is."

Roberta nodded. "For sure."

"What about your sister, Kibby? Has she been as accomplished?"

"As a matter fact, she has. She is the buyer for a gourmet cooking store in Seattle. Would you believe she has a personal shopper who picks out clothes for her. I always feel like a country bumpkin when

I'm with her. Her husband, Richard, made a name for himself as a designing engineer. He's won international awards for his designs. I'm proud of them both."

Andrea looked up from her sewing. "Tell the girls about your NPR that you do every few years with the women in your family. I love hearing about it."

"Oh my, you may be sorry you got me started on that. NPR is this reunion that my mother, my sister, my niece, my daughter, and I do every three to five years. We pick a destination where no one has to be a hostess. We usually rent a whole house so we can play games and hang out for four or five days.

"Where have you gone?"

"Well, let's see. First just Kibby, Mother, and I went to Vancouver and Victoria, Canada. Then when my niece, Lisa, was old enough, we went to the mountains in Idaho. When Ashley was old enough, we went to Spain, if you can believe it. That trip was a bit much for many reasons. Mother had trouble walking any distance; Lisa missed her four-month-old son at home; and Ashley left early to do an extended tour of Europe with her boyfriend. Next we came to the Oregon coast and stayed in a little beach house in Yachats. Then Santa Fe, New Mexico. Somewhere in there, we went to the wine country of California. They were all a hoot. The last venture was to the mountains of Colorado."

"What great fun. What kinds of things do you do when you get there?"

Since the women continued to be so interested in this topic, Roberta continued. "In Spain we did some of the usual touristy stuff, including a bull fight and a flamenco-dance play of Cinderella, if you can imagine that. In Idaho, we went to an old-time melodrama where the audience is encouraged to take part in the production by booing and cheering. Lisa was a riot and kept us in stitches. Mother couldn't be beat, so the two of them became a cheering and booing section all of their own.

"Of course, in California we visited a different winery every day, coming home with a few bottles to drink later. While we were here at the Oregon coast, we talked a lot about getting tattoos, even Mother. We spent hours discussing the design and where we'd have it put. We convinced Mother to have MIA for 'Missing in Action' on the missing breast area where she had had a mastectomy. I actually think she would have done it."

"What do you mean? Why didn't you do it?"

"We found a listing for a tattoo artist in Yachats, but when we called, he was not open on weekends. We had waited too long to call." Roberta got up to refill her glass of wine. "Anyone else want more?"

When she sat down again, Andrea asked, "Where are you going next?"

"I don't know. Mother is almost ninety-five, so getting her anywhere is difficult. We haven't talked much about a destination. I guess there's a chance that the next one will be just the four of us."

Bea asked, "I want to know why you call it NPR. It doesn't sound like anything related to National Public Radio."

"Would you believe, Mother named it NPR, which stands for 'No Penis Rendezvous.' She says the rules are: to be able to go to the reunion, you have to be of drinking age, and you can't have a penis." Roberta watched the shocked look on some of the faces.

"Mother loves to shock people with her off-color language. Her nickname for Bruce is 'Son of a Bitch'. That all started the first time she met him. He was teasing her about something, so she started the son of a bitch thing and it stuck. He loves it."

Later that night, Roberta lay in bed thinking about Helen and her mother-in-law, Stan's mother. The two women were so different. Eldon, Stan's father, had died six years before, and Roberta had become Ida's main caregiver. The ninety-nine-year-old had never learned how to write a check, let alone manage numerous investments and bank accounts. Roberta had had to take charge of her financial estate, health care, and living arrangements.

One good thing was that Ida had let Laura, her granddaughter and Stan's adopted daughter, into her life. Laura lived much closer to Ida than Roberta did, so the two of them worked as a team caring for her. Laura had recently married and continued to teach. They had become good friends.

CHAPTER 17

WHEN ROBERTA GOT HOME FROM the retreat, one of her chores was to stop at the little post office and pick up her registered letter. "Hi, Jessie, I hear I have a registered letter. It's a great mystery."

Jessie handed her the letter, and she signed for it. They stood and chatted for a few minutes before Roberta had a chance to glance at the return address. When she finally did, she stopped midsentence, knowing immediately what the letter was. She somehow was able to finish the conversation and break away from the postmistress. She walked blindly back to her car, her heart beating at a rapid rate and legs wanting to collapse. The return address on the envelope was the State of Colorado Bureau of Vital Records and Health Statistics.

She sat in her car, ripped open the envelope, and read the letter, tears streaming down her cheeks, breaths coming in large gulps. Roberta Jo had waited twenty-four years for this letter, and now it was in her hand.

Dear Mrs. Samuelson:

On 10/13/87, our records indicate that you filed a registration with the Colorado Voluntary Adoption Registry. Your registration indicated a desire to be reunited with a male child born on 10/14/1966, in Colorado Springs, Colorado, and subsequently adopted.

Based upon a review of our records and recent filings, it appears that a match has occurred. State law provides that I inform parties that a potential match has occurred, and afford each party the opportunity to formally withdraw from the program prior to notification of the other party.

If you desire to withdraw from the program and not proceed with notification, please inform me within thirty days of the receipt of this letter by written and notarized request to withdraw. If a withdrawal notice is not received from either party, I will proceed at the end of the thirty-day period to notify each party by certified mail.

Twenty-four years! Roberta had resigned herself to the fact that she would never know anything more about her son. She had given up the right to knowledge of his life. And now! She was about to find out everything. She was about to have the answers to her forty-four-year-old questions.

Roberta dropped the idea of doing her other errands, turned around, and went back to the farm. She found Bruce just coming back from the barn, and yelled at him to come into the house and sit down.

Once they were sitting in their chairs by the big window overlooking the garden and barns, Roberta finally spoke. "I picked up the registered letter, all right. Our lives are about to make a turn. Are you ready for this news?"

"Yes, I guess I am. It must be big. You're white as a ghost, and you've been crying. Go ahead; tell me."

Roberta's face contorted as her eyebrows arched and she pulled her lips inward. She could see Bruce bracing for a new show of tears. Roberta held herself together long enough to blurt out. "I've been matched with my son, the son I told you about years ago, the son that I'd given up ever knowing anything about."

Bruce sat up straight. "Oh my, this is big. Is it a letter from him?"

"No. He has registered, just as I did. We have to wait for thirty days to be sure we still want to go through with the match. If we don't contact the agency, they'll send us the contact information."

By this time, Roberta no longer felt the need to cry but, instead, sported a smile that covered her whole face. "Can you believe it? He is forty-four years old. Maybe I'll actually meet him! I'm just sure it's him that has registered. For some reason, he's now reaching out to me after all these years."

Bruce leaned back again in his chair, waiting until he could finally get more than a word into the conversation. "Of course, I remember the story that you had told me years ago. But I was pretty certain you would never know any more about him. This is going to be interesting."

—m—

The couple talked about the letter and its implications almost every day for the thirty days while they waited. Sometimes they talked seriously, sometimes Roberta teared up, sometimes they even laughed about it. What they couldn't figure out was why he was reaching out now. Why, at age forty-four, did he finally want to know something about his birth mother?

One day Bruce chuckled and said, "Maybe he's just getting out of prison and is looking for someone to take care of him, a 'sugar mama' of sorts."

"Thanks a lot. I'd rather like to think that he's running for the office of governor of Colorado, and he thinks it'll help his campaign if he connects up with his birth mother," replied Roberta, the optimist of the two.

Bruce got serious again. "Maybe he thinks he has some terrible illness, and he merely wants to know his genetic history. Maybe he doesn't want anything to do with meeting you or getting to know you. You have to prepare yourself for anything."

Roberta sighed. "Yeah, I guess so."

The only other person Roberta told of the letter was her sister. Kibby, of course, said she was pleased to hear the news and excited that she might someday meet a nephew.

Approximately four weeks later, another registered letter arrived. After another trip to the post office, Roberta waited this time until she got back home to open it and read it to Bruce.

Her eyes flew first to the bottom of the letter. "David! His name is David!"

"Okay! Now go back and read it all to me."

Dear Mrs. Samuelson:

We have completed the thirty day waiting period after our notification to you that we have found a match with your application for the Adoption Registry. You have not indicated that you wish to cancel your request for the information to be released. This letter is to notify you of your son's current name, his address, and how he may be reached by telephone. Your son will receive the same information concerning you via certified mail under today's date.

If you have any questions about this information or procedure, please call at the number on the letterhead of this letter.

Your son's name, address and phone number are:
David Hiatt
Pinecrest Road
Woodland Park, Colorado
719-326-4965

"Just like that! 'Your son,' the letter says. Like, of course, I have a son. One little piece of paper, a few lines of typing after all this time. It looks so simple...oh my gosh, Bruce, he has a name. What do I do now? There are no rules to follow."

—⁂—

Roberta decided to write her son a letter. She had some things that she felt needed to be said to him. She didn't know if she would be able to say them on the phone when or if he called. She wrote the letter immediately and mailed it before she could think twice.

Dear David,

Today I received my second letter informing me that you had gone on the registry to find me. And now you have. Where do we go from here?

Well, I am your biological mother. As you know, my name is Roberta Samuelson now. I was born Roberta Jo Kindle. I am now married to a wonderful man, Bruce Samuelson. We have been married eight years. I have a daughter, Ashley Warrington, who is thirty-six and lives in California with her husband, Mark.

Enough of the details; there is so much more. But what I most want to say in this letter is how thrilled I am to hear from you. I first registered with the Colorado registry when you were twenty-one years old. I always knew I could hear from you at any time, but I also knew I might never hear from you. The dream of connecting back with you has come true for me.

The second thing that I wanted to say in this letter, because it is so important for you to know, is that giving you up for adoption those forty-four years ago was the hardest thing I ever had to do in my life. It was physically and mentally painful for a long time. I had my reasons that someday I would like to share with you, but first and foremost, I want you to know that I did not give you up lightly. I was upset for years and continued to think of you often. Especially on your birthday each year, I thought of you, wondered what your life was like and what kind of person you were.

I wonder now what your motivation was to try and find me and if you are feeling as positive about the prospects of a relationship in the future.

I realize we might talk by phone before you receive this, but I want you to receive it in the mail as well.

With sincerity, Roberta

That evening the phone rang. She knew who it was, so she made herself comfortable in her big chair before answering. "Hello."
"Is this Roberta?"
Roberta was able to say, "Yes, it is."
"Well, this is David. I guess you recently got a letter much like mine."
Roberta motioned for Bruce to sit down beside her. Her voice and wide-eyed facial expression told him that this was the phone call they were expecting. She needed to feel Bruce beside her, but the conversation also needed to be private, between only the two of them.
"Hello, David. Yes, I got my letter, and I'm more than a little nervous right now. I don't know how to do this. I've waited for so long for this moment. I did write you a letter yesterday and already mailed it off to you. It doesn't say a lot, but it says what I absolutely wanted and

needed to say to you. I wanted to make sure it was said." Roberta felt she was blubbering without really saying anything at all.

David's voice sounded almost a shaky as hers felt. "I don't know how to do this either. But let me start by telling you a little about myself. I live on a small acreage just outside of Colorado Springs. I've been married for eighteen years, and we've lived here for sixteen of them. My wife, Leslie, is a high school teacher. We have two sons, a twelve-year-old and a sixteen-year-old. We moved to this small town because it was a better place to raise the boys.

"I work for the Federal Aviation Administration at the airport in Colorado Springs. I was in the air force for a few years but didn't really like the military, so I dropped out when I could, joining the Air Guard Reserves. They gave me good training, so I was able to find a great job. Whew! I guess that's enough about me for now. Tell me something about you."

"Wow, I don't know where to start. Let's see." Roberta gave him a short rendition of her life from the time she was twenty-one years of age to the present.

"I'm sorry to hear you've had some hard knocks."

"Yes, I have. But my husband, Bruce, is sitting here beside me holding my hand so that I can keep going with this conversation. By the way, there won't be a test regarding the details of my complicated life. Feel free to ask me questions later if you missed some or all of it. I have trouble enough keeping it straight. I guess I should add that I'm now retired and living on Bruce's small acreage where he has a hobby farm. He's retired as well."

David said, "Where did you grow up?"

"I guess I did leave out all those early years. I was born and raised in eastern Washington State. I was sent to Colorado to have you, but I never really lived there."

"Weird that I've never lived anywhere else but Colorado, except when I was in the military."

By this time, Bruce had left the room, as he was not hearing the other side of the phone call. He told Roberta later that she looked comfortable handling the call at this point. Her breathing and facial expressions had returned to normal. He went back to her side when, from the next room, he heard, "There's something I need to know before we go any farther."

"Sure, what do you need to know? Anything."

"I need to know why you've chosen now to finally find you birth mother. You really don't have to answer that if you don't want. I would understand."

David was quick to reply, "Sure, I can answer that. I see why that's a big question for you. I have to tell you first that my mother died years ago when I was in my early twenties. She was in a train and automobile accident. I still miss her very much. My father never remarried and hasn't been well for years. He has Parkinson's disease, and I don't think he ever got completely over my mom's death. She pretty much ran everything in their lives. A year ago or so, he had a stroke, which has really debilitated him. I had to take over his affairs, paying the bills, taking care of the house, all that. One day I was looking for some papers for his house, and I found my adoption papers. Up until then I had no idea I had been adopted. I have a sister, and I found her adoption papers as well."

Roberta looked at Bruce in shock. "You have got to be kidding, David? You just found out you were adopted?" Roberta repeated what he had said for Bruce's sake. They hadn't ever thought of this scenario.

"That's right. I found out about five weeks ago. I went to the state looking for some answers and further proof, I guess, and that's how I got routed to the adoption birth registry. I knew within minutes that there was a match between us. I still haven't gotten my head around the whole thing."

"Do you have any idea why your parents decided to keep it from you?" By this time, Bruce stared wide eyed at her.

"I have no idea. My dad has dementia pretty bad now, and I don't want to ask him about it. He might not even understand what I'm talking about. He's confused most of the time. I have talked to an aunt that my parents were close to. It seems most of the family knew we were adopted but promised my parents they'd not say anything to us. I'm guessing I'll never know why they thought it had to be such a secret. My aunt never understood their reasoning."

David went on, "You know, I never felt like I was a lot like my family, especially my sister. I used to tease her that she was adopted. Weird to find out we were both adopted. But I knew something wasn't quite right. Was I damaged by any of that? Probably not."

Roberta and David talked for another hour or so before saying their goodbyes. They both expressed an interest in meeting up soon and would work on that later. They each promised to send photos of their families and David, photos of when he was a child growing up.

Roberta said she would do what she could to locate David's biological father. She had a good idea where he was. Peter should know that she had connected with his son, and David should have a chance to contact Peter, if that is what he wanted to do.

After Roberta hung up, she sat back in her chair for a long time. Bruce had gone out to the barn by then. She could see him out repairing a fence. She was glad to have the house to herself for a while. She wanted to reflect on all she had learned about her son.

Her son! David sounded wonderful. How could she be so lucky? He didn't just get out of prison after all. He is a grown-up, responsible young man. Young? No, he is forty-four years old. He has a great job and a great family. And to think he had never known he was adopted, all those years. He must be reeling at the idea of it all.

CHAPTER 18

ROBERTA WAS IMPATIENT FOR THE photos to get there. When they did, she found it hard to look at the ones of David as an infant. *That's him! No doubt about it. That's the baby I held way back then. That's the baby I gave away.* Her heart stuck in her throat, tears always waiting to flow.

She enjoyed the photos of when he was growing up; when they had gone camping and fishing and around the Christmas tree, and the more recent family photos when they were on trips. Shock waves went through her brain. *No way. How could the baby that I've pictured all these years be this same young man...and with a family.* She could intellectualize it but had difficulty putting it into reality. She kept going back to the photos, awestruck, but in a very good way. The tears that did flow were happy tears.

"Can you believe it, Bruce? I'm going to tell everyone I know that I have a son. They will all know my dark secret. It's a revelation."

Roberta starting with her next quilt gathering. Her friends were sitting around in chairs in Betty's living room doing various handwork. "Okay, ladies, I have news, and it isn't about a quilt."

The women looked up, dropped what they were doing, and gave her their full attention. "Everyone sitting down? This is a big deal in my life, and I want to share it with you."

Roberta's voice was shaky, but she started in, eager to get it out. "Forty-four years ago, I got pregnant. I was only twenty years old. I

238

was in love but not ready to get married. So I made the decision to have the baby and give it up for adoption. It was one of the hardest things I ever did in my life. When that baby became twenty-one years of age, I decided to look for him. That was twenty-four years ago. I was never able to find him and had quit trying."

No one said a word, but Roberta had more to say. "Well, a few weeks ago…I found him! Or, I guess he found me. We have talked on the phone, and it's been wonderful. He's just the greatest guy. We plan on meeting sometime this summer, and I can't tell you how excited I am."

Roberta looked around the room. Her friends were sitting with eyes wide, some with tears pooling in them. When they could talk, they told Roberta how happy they were for her and were anxious to hear more news as it developed. Roberta couldn't wipe the smile off her face. She sighed. *I did it; I told my secret.*

She then told other friends. She told Bruce's relatives; she told anyone who she thought might be remotely interested. And of course, she called Kibby, and she called her daughter. Both were excited to hear the relationship between Roberta and her newfound son (who no longer needed to be called Baby Boy Kindle, but could be called David) was going so well. And she called Helen, who was now ninety-five years old.

"Hi, Mother. It's Roberta Jo. How are you today?"

"Oh, hi, Roberta Jo. I'm okay. No more aches and pains than usual. I didn't get to swimming this week. I set the alarm clock wrong one day and just couldn't get up the second day. Now I'm sorry I didn't make myself go. I always feel better afterward."

Roberta took a big breath. "I have some news for you, Mother…I don't know if you remember, but way back in the sixties, I gave birth to a baby boy and gave him up for adoption. Do you remember?"

There was a long pause before Helen answered. "Yes, I think I do remember. That was a long time ago, wasn't it?"

"Yes, it was a long time ago. Forty-four years ago, as a matter of fact." Roberta tried to ignore the lump in her throat and the shakiness of her voice. Helen's hearing was not good, so she had to practically yell on the phone.

"The news is that I've been able to find him, and we have talked on the phone. He lives in Colorado, where I went to have him. He has a family there and sounds like a wonderful man. We're going to try to get together somehow this summer."

"Well, that is news. Now who was his father?"

Interesting that Mother should ask that right away. Roberta was tempted to say she was never sure who the father was but held back her sarcasm. Instead she yelled, "Remember, it was Peter, the boyfriend that I had for so long in high school and college. His grandmother was a good friend of Grandma's."

"I think I remember. I'm happy for you, Roberta. I'm happy that he has turned out well. You be sure and tell me how it goes when you meet him. And tell him I would like to meet him someday. Did you tell me his name?"

"No, I guess not. His name is David, David Hiatt." Roberta assured her mother that she would hear all about it. They chatted for a few more minutes, and then Roberta could tell Helen was tired and had had enough. She wasn't sure Helen remembered the story of David's birth, but she had done what she wanted to do: put Helen in the loop. No more secrets.

Roberta got Peter's address from a friend and fired off a letter to him. She had tried to call his phone, but no one ever answered. She wasn't comfortable leaving a message. In the letter, she reminded him of the birth and told him that David had just located her after finding out that he was adopted. She asked Peter to call her or email her so she could share their information.

Peter called her a few days later, and they had an interesting, cordial conversation—a little catch-up on life and then a sharing of the information about David. All was strange and a little strained but uneventful and unemotional; it was much more comfortable than she had anticipated.

Roberta was sure Peter had given little thought to their son through the years. He told her that he had never shared the secret with the two children that he had raised. She understood why he did not have the same emotional attachment, just as she had understood her second husband's attitude toward his newfound daughter.

The mother-and-son connection successfully continued by email and by phone. The summer plan was for Roberta and Bruce to drive down the coast to where the Hiatts frequently vacationed at a campground in their travel trailer.

Over and over, Roberta heard from David that he had had a wonderful, happy life growing up. His parents had been good parents, providing many good family times. David also repeatedly thanked her for going through with the adoption. She wondered if he was saying thank you for not having an abortion, but giving him life. He never put it in those words, however. Maybe she had done the right thing all those years ago.

CHAPTER 19

JULY QUICKLY ARRIVED. ROBERTA WAS beside herself with excitement as she and Bruce drove down the Oregon coast. She was about to meet her *son*. "Now remember, he's not a baby, as I've pictured him all these years. He's a grown man," she said to Bruce.

"Who are you trying to convince, me or you?"

As they got closer, she felt a calming sensation come over her, like she was in slow motion and at great peace with the world. She looked out the car window at the huge evergreen trees and glimpses of ocean passing by. She felt she had never seen anything so beautiful. She smiled nonstop, both inside and out.

Roberta and Bruce checked into the motel where they were staying the two nights. Then, all that was left was the drive to the campground where the Hiatt family was waiting.

The drive took all of five minutes. They followed the numbers on the campsites until they found the right one, got out of the car, and walked toward the family of four watching and waiting around a campfire.

Roberta felt she must be a part of a movie scene. She recognized them because she had been staring at their photos for over two months. She felt that she more than recognized them. She felt she knew them and had known them for a long time.

They all hugged and made cordial comments, no one quite knowing what to say to each other. Oddly enough, the meeting was not uncomfortable. It didn't matter what anyone said. There were no rules; there was no protocol, so they said whatever came to mind. Roberta did not wish to be anywhere else but right there. She liked to think they felt the same way.

Family resemblances were not remarkable. Roberta thought David might possibly look like her dad had at that age. He and her oldest grandson certainly had Roberta's and Andrew's blue eyes. Maybe she just wanted him to look like her dad. Other than that, there was little likeness between mother and son and grandsons. Nobody cared; it wasn't important.

The six of them talked sitting around the campfire for hours that day. They shared stories of their lives and experiences for a while, but then the conversation would get back to what they were doing and how epic it was.

Even the two teenage boys, Roberta's grandsons, appeared to hang on to every word that was said. They didn't appear interested in going off and doing something else. Eventually, they all went to the beach and flew kites, a favorite family activity. David tried to teach Roberta how to fly a two-string kite, but she had a difficult time focusing and never got the hang of it.

Roberta and David's wife, Leslie, found many things in common: swimming, walking, biking, and reading. David and Bruce were instant buddies as well. They talked trucks, farms, and cows.

They drank beer, sipped wine, and ate around the campfire until bedtime, when Roberta and Bruce drove back to their motel. The next morning they returned for breakfast and then went to town for some tourist activities. They still had more to talk about and continued to do so through the day and again at breakfast the last day.

The three days they spent together, Roberta fought the constant urge to hug David every five minutes but was afraid he would think her weird and clingy if she gave in to it. Her eyes couldn't get enough of him. Sometimes, she just went and stood by him so that she could at least touch him, kind of like having a new boyfriend. The physical emotion was not sexual but so very intense. She didn't speak of it, as she didn't know how she could put it into words. It might have made everyone uncomfortable if she had tried.

Whatever it could be called, she was in love with this new son of hers. Roberta kept thinking how strange it was that she felt like she knew him so well, yet there was no history between them. They were starting new history from scratch.

David wanted to know the circumstances around how he had come to be. Roberta told him all she could remember. She held nothing back about Peter and their relationship, but she had her own difficulty understanding why they had not gotten married. So many others did get married when they found themselves in the same position. Her sister had. She didn't feel guilty, and she no longer felt like the "bad girl," but it was a question she couldn't fully answer.

"Hey, Kibby Jane."

"Oh my gosh, Roberta. How did it go? I've been thinking of you all weekend."

"Oh, Kibby, it couldn't have been better. They're the most fantastic family. David is gorgeous. I want to believe he looks like Daddy did at that age, but I'm probably making that all up. Maybe he looks a little like Bart. Or maybe I'm making that up too. He has Daddy's and my eyes for sure; so does his oldest son. I really liked David's wife, Leslie, too. We all talked for hours. I couldn't be happier."

"I'm so excited for you. I didn't think all this would ever happen. I guess I'm the pessimist. You were always sure it would."

"Well, maybe not. I had given up too. I'll talk to you soon; I just had to let you know it went so well."

Roberta also called her cousin Patty. The two cousins had talked on the phone occasionally through the fifteen or so years since they had spent that disclosure weekend together. She thought Patty deserved to know what was going on, even though she still didn't want to find her daughter.

"I am so happy for you," said Patty. "I know you've been wanting this for such a long time. I guess I still don't want to do the same, but I want to thank you for suggesting that book. I bought it but didn't read it until just recently. And you know, I feel a big relief knowing there were so many other girls who went through what we went through. Do you remember that many of the girls didn't have happy endings when they got together with their babies? I guess I'm still fearful that I won't have a happy ending either."

"I understand completely, Patty. Maybe you'll want to find her someday. Right now, you do whatever feels right. I'm glad the book helped."

—⟋⟍⟍—

David told Roberta that he wanted to meet as much of her family as he could. So that next spring, a little family reunion was arranged at Kibby's vacation home. He met his half sister, who was pregnant at the time; Ashley's husband, Mark; his aunt, Kibby, and her husband, Richard; his niece and nephew, Lisa Anne and Bart, and their families; and his grandmother, Helen.

The long weekend went well, celebrating Kibby and Richard's fiftieth wedding anniversary as well as the two new members of the family. Mark had not met everyone before either. Roberta was only disappointed that Helen spent a good deal of the time sleeping, not feeling well enough to join in.

The Hiatts and the Samuelsons got together every summer, at the beach or at one of their residences. As time went on, and they put down more and more history; David seemed less like a new boyfriend and more like the son he was.

David told Roberta he wanted to call her "Mom." She was thrilled, though not sure she deserved the title. Sometime later, he asked her if she might make a quilt from his military clothing, badges, and so forth. She eagerly took on the task, and as the quilt developed, she felt she was maybe earning her own "mother" badge.

Sitting in the sand at the beach one summer, Roberta asked David if he had talked to his biological father, Peter. "Yes, we've talked on the phone a few times. We have a lot in common, you know. We both have enjoyed restoring and working on old cars. Neither one of us ever wanted to go to college. We would rather work with our hands than learn from a book or lecture."

They watched the ocean sky filled with flying seagulls and other shore birds. Roberta never got over how they could swarm in one big mass, as if they were connected to each other. "That is interesting that you're both like that without ever knowing each other."

"Peter says his latest thing is working on and flying airplanes. And here I have worked on planes and in the airplane industry my whole career."

"Wow, that's more than a coincidence it seems."

"Yeah, but our relationship hasn't really gone anywhere. Now I only hear from him when I receive forwarded emails about cars or airplanes. Part of the problem is, I just don't have the time to develop any kind of relationship with him, what with work, family, and our little farm. But then I'm not sure that I even want it to happen."

Roberta thought that David was much more a "people" person than Peter, more sensitive and perceptive. From what Peter told her on the phone, he never did have the drive to make anything of his life like David had.

"Wow, David, you've had a lot on your plate and on your mind since we found each other, haven't you?"

David turned to face his newfound mother. "Yeah, but it has been worth it."

Roberta and Bruce went for a walk on the beach the next day before anyone else got up. The sand was littered with large jellyfish that had been dumped by the surf during the night. Bruce poked at them with his walking stick. Roberta told her husband about the conversation of the day before. Her mind went to how alike and how different her two children were.

"Don't you think Ashley's and David's personalities are much alike?"

Bruce gave her a questioning look. "What do you mean? I don't see that."

"They can both be very quiet and reserved when with a group of people. They aren't really shy, but appear to most people to be shy. But really, they are checking out all that's going on around them. Neither one of them are good at small talk 'cause they are busy thinking. When they're ready and know how they fit in the group, they can be as boisterous as anyone."

"Yeah, I guess I never really thought about it."

"The bad part of that is, they are lousy at sharing their deep thoughts. They hold it all in. I don't know about David because I don't know him as well, but Ashley can make some astonishing statement that blows your mind. You thought she wasn't paying any attention, but then you see that she had been one hundred percent present. She's done that over and over to me. I suspect David is like that because he has told me of the deep thoughts he has put together. His perception of Peter is a good example."

"That is interesting. They didn't both get that way because they grew up together."

"Isn't that weird? I also suspect that they will never really strongly connect with each other because they are that way. Besides, their lives are busy, they don't live close to each other, and their lifestyles and political views are quite different." Roberta sighed. "It's time to turn around back to the house. I'm tired, and the wind is picking up."

Also that weekend, David told the Samuelsons that his adoptive dad was failing both physically and mentally. "There is no way I can confront him about the adoptions, although I would really like to know why they were such a secret."

Roberta asked, "Do you think your mother would have told you and your sister once you were both adults?"

"Maybe. I'm thinking my father was the one who objected to telling the world that his kids were adopted. Maybe he felt less of a man not being able to father a child."

Some questions were still unanswered and always would be. Roberta had no complaints. Her biggest questions had been answered. She now knew where and who her son was.

Part Six
Having Done the Right
Thing: 2013

When I forgive other people, I let them go, I free them from my ignorance. And as soon as I do, I feel lighter, brighter and better…Forgiveness is a gift you give yourself. You are relieved of carrying that burden of resentment.

—Maya Angelou

CHAPTER 20

ROBERTA MADE A CALL TO her sister. "Hi, Kibby. How's Mother doing this week?"

"Not so good. She's eating and drinking almost nothing right now. I just found out from the nurses that she's lost thirty pounds in the last four months or so. She must not have been eating much all this time. She doesn't want to get up and sit in her chair or watch TV or do anything, really. She just sleeps in her bed. That's not like our mother. She doesn't even want to get up for the bathroom and has become seriously incontinent. The home says they can't continue to have her there. She needs too much care."

"Oh my gosh, that doesn't sound good. What're you going to do? I want to help." Roberta was out walking the dogs on a logging road close to her home.

"Yesterday, I had a long conversation with her doctor. He thinks the best thing is to put her on hospice. There's a wonderful hospice residential facility here that she could move into right now. It's close by, and they can provide all of the nursing care she'd ever need. They have social workers, nurses, their own physician…everything. It's expensive, but there's financial aid available."

Kibby sounded strong and capable, but Roberta also knew her sister was good at faking strength on the phone. She had told Roberta before that she could secretly cry and nobody would guess it. "I think I need to come, don't you?"

Nine years ago, Helen had moved to Seattle, and Kibby had been handed the head caregiver role. She always said she didn't mind, but Roberta knew Helen's needs and wants were unpredictable, sometimes requiring hours of Kibby's time going back and forth between her home and Helen's home.

Helen could be appreciative, but she could also be demanding. When she needed something, she needed it *right now*. When she was ready to go home, she wanted to leave *right then*. Never mind that Kibby had a life of her own, and there were other things she would rather be doing than playing delivery woman or chauffeur.

The worst was when Helen needed to be moved. The decision as to where to move to was big, and the physical moving of all the furniture and "stuff" was also big.

"Well, I feel like I'm getting good advice and help. I'm not sure. Do you want to come?" Kibby replied to Roberta's offer.

Now Roberta's eyes were tearing, and she was not good at faking it. By this time she had stopped walking and was sitting on a log that had been left beside the ditch. "Yes, I do. I want to help you and I want to see her. I want us to do this together. Remember? We've talked about this before, Kibby Jane. We always try to do the hard things on our own. I have kicked myself to the wall for years that I didn't go to help you when you had cancer and all that surgery ten years ago. All three of us think that way—Mother, you, and me. You've already done enough on your own. Let the three of us do this together for once."

"You're right. I'd love to have you here with me. And since when did you get to be the social worker?" Roberta heard the relief in her sister's voice; the humor was a dead giveaway. "But I don't know what's going to happen. Mother may just be in a slump and will pull out of it. She's done it before, maybe not when she was this bad, but she's had slumps before. Then she's rallied. You could get here, and she'll be sitting in her chair, asking for a warm beer."

Roberta chuckled. "Now that would be wonderful. I'll take my chances that'll happen. Then we can sit down and have a beer with her. I want mine cold though."

"Oh, me too!"

"Now, I'm going to go find an airplane to get on as soon as possible. I'll buy a one-way ticket, and we'll go from there."

"Sounds good. Call and let me know when I'm to pick you up at the airport."

Roberta jogged back down the logging road and home. She went straight to the computer, booked her flight for early the next morning, and then went back outside to find Bruce. She found him weeding in the corn rows. "It doesn't look good in Seattle. I think Mother might be dying. I want to be there, so I've booked an airplane ticket for tomorrow. Will you take me to the airport? I don't know when I'll be coming back home."

She got all that out before letting out a big sob. It suddenly hit her that this woman, this living legacy, this powerful force in so many people's lives, was coming to the end of her life. She would soon be only a legend, no longer that dynamic strength.

—⟋⟍—

When Kibby Jane picked up her sister the next day, they drove straight to Helen's assisted living residence. The nurse at the front desk said she had only had a few sips of water and liquid nutrients all day, refusing everything else. The two sisters walked quickly down the hall of the residence toward Helen's room. Roberta was nervous about seeing her mother in such a broken down state. The world seemed to be in slow motion. The facility smelled just like all the other old people's facilities she had been in before: a combination of disinfectants, urine, and dinner cooking in the kitchen. Roberta couldn't help thinking that she had done all this before. And she had, taking care of her mother-in-law, Ida, in Canada, just a few years before.

Upon entering Helen's room, Roberta kneeled beside the bed so she could put her face close to her mother's. Helen opened her eyes for just a few seconds and looked at her and then up to Kibby standing beside her. She gave them both a bit of a smile before closing her eyes again.

Roberta squeaked, "Hi, Mother…we're both here."

Helen did not respond again, but Kibby talked on, using an extremely loud voice, as Helen undoubtedly didn't have her hearing aids in. "Mother, Roberta just got here to see you and to help out. Your doctor has asked that we move you to another place where you can get better care. They're coming soon to take you there by ambulance. Roberta and I think it's the best thing right now."

The sisters sat down in nearby chairs but went up to her every few minutes to let her know they were still there. After an hour or two, a young woman came in, introducing herself as the hospice social worker. She explained to them what was probably going to take place in the next few days as Helen's body slowed down.

Kibby and Roberta were insistent that Helen not be forced to eat or drink. Helen had always been a strong advocate of individual end-of-life wishes. For the last thirty years, she had told them over and over again that she did not want to live to be a frail one-hundred-year-old lady. She did not hear well, so any socializing had become difficult. In the last six months, she had stopped going for her weekly swim, and in the last few months, she had even stopped reading. Roberta was sure Helen had chosen to come to the end of her life at this time.

Kibby told the social worker, "It's so like her to want to take control of her death, just as she needed to always have control of her life,"

"I understand, if those are her wishes. People will bring food and drink, but only because that's the law. Feel free to not offer any of it to her. It'll be up to you. You need to know, too, that a few bites or sips of anything could sustain and prolong her life for many hours and even days."

The ambulance arrived and took Helen to the hospice facility. Everyone was respectful and kind. Her room turned out to be spacious with a large window, with sunlight streaming in. A couch and soft chair provided comfortable seating for family members and friends.

A food tray appeared but was placed on a table across the room from the bed. Roberta and Kibby snacked on it occasionally. They continued to go up to their mother, talk to her, letting her know they were there. "It's okay, Mother, if you want to go now. We'll be all right. We have each other. We'll miss you, but all this lying around isn't like you or how you have lived your life. It's okay to let go. We'll be here."

Kibby called her two children who lived in the Seattle area. Lisa chose not to come. She wanted to remember her grandmother as the vivacious woman she had always been. Bart had been especially attached to Helen but was not sure he would come visit.

A heavily accented nurse's aide made a huge fuss over Helen, cooing and clucking over her, wiping her face with a clean, moist cloth and combing her hair. She took a little barrette with a flower out of her own hair and tenderly put it in Helen's. "My granddaughter left this at my house this morning, and I just knew I'd have a use for it today. It looks very pretty on you, Helen. Don't you think so, girls?"

Kibby and Roberta didn't have the heart to tell her that it wasn't at all like their mother to wear a flower or even a barrette in her hair. They loved the gesture, however, so Helen unknowingly wore the flowered barrette until it eventually fell out onto the pillow.

Helen soon became very restless, physically agitated, turning over and over, kicking the bedcovers off. The sisters were concerned that she would eventually fall out of the bed. When they mentioned it to the nurse, they expected that cold, hard bed rails would be put up. Instead, they lowered the bed almost to the floor, where they placed a mattress to catch her if she did roll off. They could easily sit or kneel on the mattress to be close to her.

Helen did once open her eyes wide and gave her two daughters a huge smile. Roberta surprised herself and called her mother "Mommy," a name she hadn't called her since she was in elementary school. Wide eyed, she looked around at Kibby. "Did you hear what I just called Mother?" Kibby was only able to nod her head yes. Both of the girls were feeling in control of their emotions, but they knew it wouldn't take much to set them off.

In the early evening, they felt they might as well go home and come back the next morning. Helen had settled down and seemed to be asleep. They were confident that she was in good hands. So they went home and shared with Richard the events of the day. He, too, was upset. Helen had been a driving force in his life for the fifty-plus years that he had been with Kibby.

Late that evening, Bart called and reported that he had gone to the hospice residence and spent a couple of hours with his grandmother. He had lain down on the mattress beside her bed, held her hand, and talked to her. He reported that he told her that he had been so lucky to have a grandmother that took him traveling, shared books with him, and took great interest in everything he did. Roberta and Kibby were glad they had left so Bart could have that special time with her.

The next morning, the two women took their time getting back to Helen, stopping to do a few errands on the way. As they walked down the hallway to her room, one of the staff members spoke out to them. "Ladies, wait a minute; I need to talk to you." They didn't recognize her from the day before but waited for her to catch up to them. "I'm sorry, but I wanted to talk to you before you got to your mother's room. You need to know that she passed away earlier this morning. In fact, her death occurred such a short time ago that we haven't had time to give you a call. I'm so sorry. Feel free to go in and spend as much time as you like with her."

Roberta and Kibby stood stunned, paralyzed in their tracks in the hallway. Roberta thought they'd have a few days before she died. She regretted that they hadn't moved along a lot quicker that morning so they could have been there with her when she passed. She was relieved of that guilt when Kibby said, "It was like Mother to die privately, before we got here."

When they got to the room, Roberta saw how at peace she looked. The agitation she had demonstrated the day before had vanished. The sisters plopped down beside each other on the couch, neither one talking, each with their own thoughts. When she could, Kibby called Richard and her two children and gave them the news. Roberta called Ashley, David, and Bruce.

Bart soon joined them. The three of them sat and talked about Helen and her remarkable life. Helen was a woman who maybe didn't always do the right thing, but she did follow her dreams, maybe in a little different way that she had originally planned. She had been a mother and grandmother who encouraged them all to do the same. Helen was gone but would not be forgotten.

CHAPTER 21

TWO MONTHS LATER, HELEN KINDLE'S memorial event took place in Rockford at the museum that she had helped get off the ground years before. Kibby and Roberta organized and carried out the open house affair. Helen had asked that no service take place, as she was neither a religious nor a sentimental person. But she also had said the family could do as they pleased. If they felt the need to have some kind of closure, that was okay too. Kibby and Roberta kept it informal, a chance for family and friends to gather, to reacquaint themselves with each other, and to share their memories of Helen—no speeches, no eulogies, no prayers, no singing.

Panels were arranged on tables, displaying photos of Helen at different ages and stages of her life. Newspaper clippings about her and her accomplishments were tacked onto poster boards: swimming volunteer work, Girl Scout volunteer work, historical preservation, museum founding, and various awards given to her by the community. Many of her self-developed photographs of travels around the country and the world were displayed. The two historical books she had authored were there for everyone to see.

As people entered the room at the museum, the first thing they saw was one can of Bud Light sitting by an author's photograph of Helen. When Bruce and Roberta were setting up the displays, Bruce had insisted on placing it there since Helen loved her warm beer, always in a can.

One of the guests, the daughter of Helen's very good friend, sneaked in a large framed photo of Helen in a bathing suit, posing as if she were a model for the latest swimwear. She was probably in her forties when her photographer friend took the photo and promised no one would ever see it. Helen, however, would have laughed knowing that it had shown up at her memorial. In fact, Lisa, Ashley, Kibby, and Roberta grabbed the framed photo and stuffed themselves in a vintage telephone booth that was part of a museum display. How many Kindle girls can you get in one phone booth? The NPR girls at their best!

Catered appetizers and wine were placed on tables for the guests to enjoy. Later in the afternoon, Bart and David made a run to the liquor store for cold beer. After all, beer was the Kindle family drink of choice.

Cousins and aunts, uncles, nieces, and nephews saw each other for the first time in years. There were not many of Helen's friends attending; few had outlived her.

Roberta thought Helen would have loved being at her own memorial, a chance to visit with all the people from her life.

—⁂—

Roberta found her forty-year-old daughter, Ashley, sitting by herself on one of chairs on the far wall, shoulders slumped, staring at the floor. She went to sit beside her. "You look sad, Ashley. Are you thinking about your grandmother?"

"Yes, I am. I guess it just hit me that I won't ever see her again."

"It's okay to be sad. You're missing her, of course. Tell me your thoughts and memories. Maybe it'll help to talk."

"I was thinking about how she's done so much in her life. She's given so much to others, and she's seen so much. She's a huge role model for me. The women in this family are amazing. You're all so strong and successful. How can I possibly live up to all that?"

Roberta grabbed her daughter's hand. "Oh, Ashley, you already have. You've experienced so much in your forty years. You were forced to go through your parents' divorce. You've gone through the deaths of a stepfather, an uncle, and now two grandmothers. You worked hard for a bachelor's degree and a master's degree. You've had a number of wonderful, amazing jobs, giving so much to the children that you work with. You've done more traveling than most people your age, both by yourself and with family. Think of that whole year in Asia and the South Pacific with your dad. Your grandmother didn't travel at all until she was much older than you are now.

"And don't forget, you've married a wonderful man and given birth to an incredible little boy. Grandma was so proud of you. You are also an amazing woman and you've just begun; no doubt you're going to do many more astounding things in your life."

"Wow, when you put it all together, I guess I have done a lot. But, you know, I haven't always been strong through all that."

Roberta nodded. "But don't think for a minute that your grandmother sailed easily through her life. She had many struggles. She wasn't always strong, and she didn't always succeed in what she did. She had failures, and she had depression. What's important is what you *do* after the times that didn't go so well."

"You're right, I guess, Mom. Thanks. How about you? You have had some very hard times. I can remember you being incredibly sad, but you always seem to bounce back."

"It just looks like that to you. I've always been afraid of failure and criticism."

Ashley waved to her son across the room. "You have?"

"You bet. Maybe you've never noticed, but I always make sure I can do something before I really go after it and do it. I practice before I commit. For example, I played at teaching children at a small school for disabled before I started a teacher-training program. It took me twenty years of working with just my bachelor's degree before I had the nerve to go get my master's degree. I always overtrained in running, biking, and swimming to make sure I could put it all together for a triathlon."

Ashley stared at her mother. "I never saw all that."

"Almost all my jobs as a professional, I worked alone and liked it that way. I wasn't comfortable having someone always looking over my shoulder. Someone might notice I wasn't perfect. I played around with quilting on my own before I ever took a class where someone would be watching me. I'm still nervous taking a quilting class."

"I see what you're saying. But maybe it's all a good thing."

"Yes, it worked for me. That's very perceptive of you. You know, I did take one huge risk when I was very young. Just think, I could have just sat in Rockford all my life and never had a chance to do the wonderful things that I did. I've been thinking a lot about that the last few days. Do you see that man over there?" Roberta pointed to a man who was across the room from them talking to young friends of Helen's.

"Yes, I wondered who that was. I saw him talking a long time with David."

"Well, that's Peter, David's biological father."

"What? That was your boyfriend back in high school? The guy who got you pregnant?"

"That would be the one. David, Bruce, and I had lunch yesterday with him and his girlfriend. With all of us in Rockford, it was a good opportunity to introduce David to his father. It was a strange gathering, but it went okay. Sitting across the table from Peter after forty-six years was weird, believe me."

"Why is Peter here today? I don't understand that."

"Pretty strange, huh? Mother didn't ever like Peter, and I don't think they've had any kind of connection all these years living in the same town. Mother knew his brother and sister more than she knew Peter. Would you believe that my grandmother and Peter's grandmother became best of friends years after David was born? They would have been shocked to know they had the same great-grandson."

"Aren't you glad you didn't marry him?"

"You better believe it. What I was trying to say was: I could have married him and stayed in Rockford all these years. I did take a big risk back then. Thank goodness I had the courage to do that."

Ashley suddenly changed the subject. "Did I ever tell you about my friend Felicia and her husband, Matthew?"

"I don't think so. How do you know them?

"They're friends of ours in California. I mention it now because I was thinking about David and that he didn't know he was adopted all his life."

"Were these friends adopted or something?"

"No, but they have tried everything possible to get pregnant. They're almost as old as I am, so they don't have a lot of time left."

"What does that have to do with David's story?" asked Roberta.

"I was just thinking about how times have changed so much. Way back then in the sixties, David's parents also couldn't get pregnant, so they adopted David. But it had to be a huge secret for some reason. I don't get that." Ashley continued with a puzzled look on her face. "Well, anyway, my friends also decided to adopt, but they wanted to be able to choose their adopted baby's parents—or at least the mother. They also wanted to be a part of the whole pregnancy."

"Okay, how did they do that?"

Ashley strained to see if her young son was doing okay as he was passed from one relative to another. "It was expensive, but they had an agency find an unwed mother who was willing to give up her baby but also have them be a part of the pregnancy. The agency found a woman that met their specifications. They became close friends with her, having her over for dinners, going to her ultrasounds, going to prenatal classes to be able to coach her through the birth, the whole nine yards."

"Wow, I guess times have changed. It was all out in the open," said Roberta.

"Oh yes; we even spent time with her. We had showers for her and bought her maternity clothes. We really liked her. Felicia and Matthew promised her that she could see as much of the baby as she liked when it was born, as long as they were with her for visitations and the visits fit into their schedules. All was good."

"I'm thinking there is part of this story that's not all good."

"You got that right. When the baby was born, the woman's attitude changed totally. In fact, she booted them out of the delivery room while she was still in labor. When they went to see her and the baby just hours after he was born, she refused to let them hold the baby."

Ashley giggled watching her cousin Lisa chasing her son around the room. "They had thought she was legally obligated to give him up to them. But there was one little loophole that allowed her to change her mind up to three months after the birth. Their lawyer said that the loophole was required by law and had no choice but to put it in the paperwork. Felicia and Matthew had read that part but had forgotten it when they became such good friends with her."

"Oh, how awful for your friends."

"They're devastated even now, almost six months later. It's been like their baby died. The baby's room and clothes were all ready for him. They'd even picked out a name, knowing it was going to be a boy."

"Oh, my. Having a baby is all so complicated."

"You're right; it is complicated. Do you think you made the right decision about David back then?" Ashley asked.

"Yes. Other options didn't seem right for me at the time. Speaking of decisions and babies, do you remember the Baileys, the family that lived next door to us in Canada when you were young?" Roberta waved to two new arrivals as they passed on their way to the displays.

Ashley frowned, trying to bring up an image of old neighbors. Roberta said, "You were pretty young then. Lilly Bailey was the daughter. She had a baby when she was seventeen but wasn't married."

"I kind of remember Lilly. She'd come over and play games and dolls with me. We moved to another house before I was in middle school," said Ashley.

"That's right. Well, Lilly and her parents decided that she should keep her baby. Lilly and I were friends, and she came to see me often, to talk and later to get out of the house.

"As it turned out, she met a guy her age just months after the baby was born. They got married and had another baby of their own. I still hear from Lilly once in a while. It all worked out for her."

"Okay, Mom. Look over there at Lisa." Ashley dug her elbow into her mother's side and pointed to her cousin going for another glass of wine. "She's always so happy and ready for a good time. Everybody loves her. She's certainly sailed through life."

Roberta watched her niece, now walking over to Bart and David. Lisa had the biggest brown eyes imaginable. She was petite at just under five feet; it was hard to believe she was almost fifty years old with a teenage son of her own.

"Oh, I wouldn't say that. There's a lot you don't know about your cousin, Lisa Anne. She was a wild one in high school and after. Do you remember she came and stayed with us one summer? Her parents thought it might help for Lisa see there was more to the world than what high school life was offering her. After that summer, she got messed up in selling drugs and, I think, kicked out of school. Kibby and Richard were beside themselves for years over that girl's behavior. That was when Kibby became such an amazing cook. It was therapy for her and has been ever since. When your aunt Kibby is upset, you'll always find her in the kitchen."

"Wow, I had no idea. I do remember when Lisa came and stayed with us. We had great fun. She was like the greatest big sister ever."

"She met her husband, Leo. The marriage was scary because he didn't look like he had much potential. But somehow they were great for each other and made a good life together."

"What a story, I see her in a different light now. Speaking of light, I better go see how the light of my life, your grandson, is doing."

"Besides, you need to get something to eat and drink."

Ashley got up and went to rescue her one-year-old son. Kibby quickly took Ashley's place beside Roberta, handing her a fresh glass of wine. Kibby's hair was even more silvery than Roberta's. She wore it in a spiky style that fit her spunky, youthful personality. She was as petite as her daughter, a few inches taller, but shorter than Roberta. "Whoa, what were you two talking about? It looked very serious over here."

Roberta hugged her sister. "Thanks for the wine. It was serious. We started out talking about Mother 'cause Ashley was missing her. Then she got into how Mother and the other women in this family are such strong role models for her. I guess we've set the standard pretty high."

"That was a heavy conversation. Did you tell her about mother's abortion?"

"You know, I didn't. I don't think I ever have. Maybe this isn't the time or place to break that news to her. Did you ever tell Lisa?"

"I did, but she just took it in her stride. I don't think anything you tell these kids about their grandmother would shock them."

"Yeah, it's also two generations later. Having babies out of wedlock without fathers, or getting married after the baby is born, abortions—none of that is a big deal to them. A big deal would be a virgin after age twenty-five."

"That would be rare. Speaking of abortions, did I ever tell you about when I first knew Callie?"

"I don't think so. You and Callie have been friends forever, I know that."

Kibby took a big breath. "Callie was one of my roommates in college. She was a little promiscuous for that day and age but not off the wall. But she was date-raped by a friend of some friends. As it turned out, this guy had a history of that sort of thing. Well, Callie, pretty much went off the deep end, getting even worse when she found out she was pregnant. In fact, she tried taking too many pills one night. We think her counselor helped her have an abortion."

"No, I didn't know any of that. And here Callie's one of the stablest women I know. She's a federal judge, for Pete's sake, and a registered nurse and lawyer before that, right? She has practically been a member of your family all these years."

"Yes, she has."

"I don't think I could never have an abortion, but then, I didn't get raped either."

"She did what she had to do, and for her it was the right thing. I was so glad to see her here today," added Kibby. "She and Mother were great friends."

Lisa sat down beside her mother and her aunt Kibby in their chairs against the wall, handing them a plate of appetizers. "You two are too funny, sitting here like a couple of old biddies, gossiping away."

Roberta waved her hand at her niece. "Get out of here. We aren't gossiping; we are saying important things to each other. Like always. Thanks for the goodies."

Lisa walked away. "Did I tell you Cousin Patty called me a week ago?"

"No, you didn't tell me. What did she have to say?"

"It was the best phone call ever! Of course, she wanted to tell us how sorry she was that Mother had died. But the good news is that she's decided to look for her daughter. She doesn't want to be silent anymore. And she doesn't want to continue to feel guilty and ashamed of what she did way back in the sixties. She's angry now after fifty years of sadness and depression. She says she is also allowing herself to grieve for her firstborn daughter for the first time. Her head's in a good place."

"Wow. That's amazing."

Kibby nibbled on her appetizers. "Keep me in the loop. I'm glad she's had you to talk to her all these years. Speaking of unwed mothers, I have to tell you about the dream I had last night."

"Oh, please do. I love hearing about other people's dreams," said Roberta, wondering why her sister wanted to talk about a dream right now. She was feeling like she should get up and get back to talking to the guests.

Kibby squirmed in her chair. "I dreamt about when you and I went through Mother's things two months ago. Remember we got it all done quickly?"

"Of course I remember. You had done most of the work of getting rid of stuff when she moved to the assisted living facility."

"Yeah, well, the dream left reality when we uncovered a writing that she had done the last months. Remember how she was always writing those one- or two-page essays about different people or events or just her thoughts on some subject?"

"Yes, I think we all have file folders full of those writings."

"Well, in this dream we found a one-page writing, sort of like those, except that it was more like a letter to you and me."

"Oh, interesting. What was in the letter?"

Kibby continued her hands becoming more and more animated. "It was more or less an apology to you and me for not telling us about her abortion when we had each gotten pregnant. She said she didn't really know why she hadn't told us. Daddy wanted to tell all but she didn't. She had regretted it all those years. She wrote that's why she was so relieved to finally tell us in the eighties."

"Oh my gosh! What a dream. I wish it was real. I'd love to get an apology, even if it was in a letter after she died."

"Me too."

"You know, I really am not mad anymore. What's done is done. It'll all remain a mystery, but that's okay. I can live with it."

Kibby nodded. "Exactly. I feel the same way. I know. Let's just pretend that the dream was real and she did apologize. That would feel good."

"Okay, I'll drink to pretending. We accept your apology, Mother. Rest in peace." The sisters clinked their empty wineglasses together.

"And now I guess we better get off our duffs here and see to the few people left. I think this memorial has been a real success. I keep thinking Mother is going to show up at any time."

Roberta saw David sitting over by himself. She was glad to catch him alone. "How are you doing among all these newly found relatives? Are you exhausted?"

"Not at all. Everyone's being so kind and eager to have conversations with me. I guess the word is out that you have a son."

"Yes, and isn't it wonderful? I'm loving it that the secret is done. And I'm so glad they're being open to you. Kind of weird that Peter has been here for the whole thing, don't you think? He seems to consider himself part of the family."

David said, "Yeah, he's probably the epitome of a 'shirttail relative.' I hope it has been okay for him to be here so long."

"It's fine. I really haven't said a word to him today. I've done my part. I'm glad I had the opportunity to introduce you to him."

"Yeah. It was good that we did it."

"We've made a good start at making some history together, haven't we? Now let's go drink some beer or wine to salute the whole affair and to honor your grandmother."

—◆—

That evening after a family dinner at a local restaurant, Roberta and Kibby told their daughters they had a job for them. "This is a very important task. Someone has to do it; it's a dirty job, and you two, as junior members of NPR, have been chosen to do it."

Lisa groaned. "What now? Why can't you two do your own dirty jobs?"

Roberta looked sternly at the two younger women. "Because you're the chosen ones, that's why. We want you to take a Bud Light to the cemetery and pour it over your grandmother's grave. In fact, you better take two Bud Lights and pour one over your grandfather's grave as well. I'm sure he would appreciate it."

Wide eyed and with smiles on their faces, the girls replied, "Of course. We are honored to do that. It's the right thing to do. Just tell us where to go."

Epilogue: 2031

"AREN'T WE LUCKY TO HAVE such generous daughters to put up with us in our old, old age?" ninety-year-old Kibby said to her not very-young-either sister, Roberta, being careful to talk a little louder and slower than normal. Roberta had inherited their mother's hearing loss and didn't always remember to wear her hearing aids.

"I remember when we used to joke about how the girls were going to wheel us around to our No Penis Rendezvous when we got too old. Look at us! Where's the joke now? What a couple of old cooties."

Kibby frowned. "Speak for yourself, old lady. I can see that you've gotten old with your neck waddle, your tissue-paper skin, and your shuffle walk. I, however, am still quite young and vibrant."

"Ha, have you looked in the mirror lately, sister of mine? Did you forget that you're four years older than me? Quite frankly, you look it."

Kibby and Roberta laughed and then looked up to see Lisa and Ashley, who had walked onto the deck overlooking the Pacific Ocean, carrying trays loaded with huge margaritas, tortilla chips, guacamole, and salsa. The two girls had reached their own golden years at ages fifty-eight and sixty-five. Lisa was still as petite as ever, Ashley, a bit taller and plumper. Both had gray hair, not yet white like their mothers' hair. Both were nice-looking, older women who had inherited their grandmother Helen's genes of good skin and facial bone structure.

Lisa interrupted. "Okay, you two, quit your bickering. Pick up a drink, and let's have a toast to the matriarch of this No Penis Rendezvous."

The four women sat around the table, sipping margaritas and digging into the appetizers. Ashley was the first to raise her glass. "To my grandma Helen, the woman who inspired all of us to be strong and to strive to be and do whatever we wanted to be and do."

Lisa added, "She inspired us with her actions as much as she did with her words. She was an amazing woman and did so much in her life, most of it unusual for a woman of the times."

"She loved her margaritas and so placed us where we are today, continuing to have this NPR every three to five years and continuing to gulp down a few margaritas. Tomorrow it's on to Bud Light in the can in her honor," was Roberta's toast.

Kibby followed with, "To Helen…we know you're here with us in spirit." By this time, all four of them were tearing up. Since tears had never been Helen's way, she had to stop the sentimental jabber. "And now Roberta and I have taken her place in the old lady chair."

Ashley frowned at the sisters. "You two have to get off this old lady kick. After all, Lisa and I aren't spring chickens ourselves any more. If you're getting so old, we are too. Too bad there are no younger generation women to take care of us."

It suddenly came to Kibby's thoughts that this was probably going to be the very last NPR ever. She and Roberta wouldn't be able to travel much longer. In fact, this could be the last time she would ever see her sister again for the same reason. *Oh my, what a thought!* Kibby felt goose bumps move up her arms.

Later on that evening, the two cousins went for a walk on the beach to check out the sunset while Kibby and Roberta got down to a serious discussion. They were bundled up in blankets in outdoor recliners near a blazing firepit.

Roberta stared into the fire. "You know, I've been thinking lately."

"Uh-oh. Now we're in trouble."

"Oh, be quiet; this is serious. When I found my son, David, something released inside me. I felt free to be myself and to quit holding back so much. It didn't happen overnight, but after we connected, I was able to let loose more, to be silly if I wanted to, and to not feel everyone was judging me in some way, a kind of freeing of my spirit."

"I would agree with that. You did change. Maybe it did have to do with meeting him and finding a new you. But, you know, I changed after my kids were grown and gone too. I didn't feel like I had to be a certain way anymore and make everyone like me."

Kibby leaned forward. "I've always thought 'Late Bloomer' should be our family name. Mother was certainly a late bloomer. She dabbled in a few volunteer things when we were still at home, but it wasn't until later that she took off with her really big accomplishments. My career didn't take off until I was in my forties."

"Maybe you're right, Kibby. Look at the girls; Lisa certainly had a tough time of it until she was almost fifty. Ashley got an earlier start than all of us, probably because she didn't have a child until she was almost forty, but I see her spirit soaring as she's aged."

"I know what you mean."

"Anyway, my experiences, both good and bad, have made me what I am. I'm proud of who I've become, and you should be too. I'm certainly proud of who you are. We both must have done something right. We done good, don't ya think?"

"I know we done good. Look at those two lovely ladies walking up through the dune grass. We made them. We did that right."

"You better believe it. Aren't they gorgeous?"

—◊◊◊—

The next night, the two aging sisters found themselves in another serious conversation when they were again alone.

Roberta started out. "You know how we have talked in the past about all the women, including us, who found themselves with unplanned pregnancies? Did they question whether they had done the right thing, just as we did?."

"How would you answer that now?"

"I don't know. I recently read that the women who were advised to go away and give up their children, may not have been given the best advice. Professionals are saying that both birth mothers and adopted children have reported suffering lifelong emotional pain. In the past, it was assumed they were better off being separated. I know I suffered, as did other women I've talked to and read about through the years. David, growing up, wondered and struggled with why he was different from his family."

Kibby added her thoughts on the issue. "Think of all the controversy over abortions that still goes on and on with no real resolve in our society."

"That's true. And being saddled at twenty-one years of age with a newborn in this age of wonderful careers for twenty- and thirty-year-old women isn't always a great option either. Women are forced to be deprived of the joy of watching their children grow and develop on a day-to-day basis."

Kibby agreed. "Being raised by professionals is never as good as being raised by loving parents. I don't care how wonderful the daycare or the nanny is."

"I guess what we're saying is that time—I'm talking close to one hundred years of time—has not made the decision of what to do if you have an unplanned pregnancy any easier."

"So how do we help these women or couples make a decision? Instead of coaching an unwed mother on what's 'the right thing to do,' is the answer more in prevention of the unwanted or unplanned pregnancy?"

Roberta nodded. "It has to be. And it can't be anything as simple as a life skills class in public school. Or as simple as handing out birth control pills or condoms either. The education and prevention mea-sures have to begin at home and at a very young age."

"You're right. Both boys and girls must know very early on the consequences of having sex. Telling them the girl might get pregnant is not enough. They need to know having sex may have an impact on the rest of their lives, no matter how they choose to deal with a preg-nancy. It'll impact them emotionally, financially, socially and physi-cally. There's no going back when a baby enters your life."

"And how is that going to happen. How are parents going to get the skills to educate their children properly?" asked Roberta.

"Aw, ha, that is the big question."

"Right now, this old lady needs to go to bed. Helen's Bud Light is sending me off to la la land."

"Good night, Roberta Jo. I love you."

"Good night, Kibby Jane, you old lady. I love you as much."